LARRY DARTER

The Dedman Emergence

FEDORA
PRESS

First published by Fedora Press 2024

First edition

ISBN: 979-8-9876944-8-0

This book was professionally typeset on Reedsy.
Find out more at reedsy.com

In tribute to Robert Ludlum's memory.

emergence

noun

1. the process of coming into view or becoming exposed after being concealed.

2. the process of coming into being, or of becoming important or prominent.

—— Definition from Oxford Languages

Contents

Prologue

Emergence Genesis

On a moonless night in September 2011, a darkened U.S. Army Chinook helicopter swept low over the Tangi Valley, a strip of forbidding terrain in eastern Afghanistan teeming with Taliban and located just thirty-five miles south of the capital, Kabul. On missions like this one to insert an assault force, flying low, the pilots had to maneuver a machine weighing up to fifty thousand pounds over mountains, under cover of darkness, in swirling wind and dust, wearing night vision goggles. As was routine on such missions, two Apache attack helicopters provided cover and security for the Chinook. Circling above was also an AC-130 aircraft, a gunship that also provided surveillance.

Typical combat missions in Afghanistan left little margin for error, requiring Chinook pilots to land on tiny, makeshift sites on mountain slopes where any tree, bush or rock could hide an insurgent with a rocket-propelled grenade launcher. Despite the risk, operations like this took place with such frequency in Afghanistan they only made news when they produced a spectacular success, or when something went terribly wrong. On this night, something went terribly wrong.

The thirty-eight passengers inside the Chinook included two Afghan interpreters and an assault team of U.S. Army Rangers led by First Lieutenant Ethan Ross. Their objective was a compound on a mission to capture or kill a Taliban commander named Ahmad Noorzai, responsible for a series of attacks and ambushes against U.S. and Afghan forces in the Tangi Valley.

1

At the Chinook pilots' request, the AC-130 flashed an infrared spotlight, visible only through night vision goggles, to light up the landing zone. Nearby there were two hidden enemy fighters with rocket-propelled grenade launchers. They heard the helicopter coming, grabbed their RPGs, and fired in quick succession. They got lucky.

The first grenade missed the Chinook. The Taliban shot at the Chinooks all the time with RPGs. It was almost always a miss. But the second RPG struck the helicopter's tail rotor assembly. The Chinook plunged tail first. The pilot pushed hard on the cyclic stick to tilt the helicopter forward. As he did, he felt the craft leveling off. But it was too late. The Chinook smashed into the ground in a dry creek bed near Logar River, the force of the impact ripping off the pilot's night vision goggles. The front rotor shattered, and the back pylon sheared off. One engine flew off, and the other caught fire.

The crash killed everyone onboard the helicopter, except for Ethan Ross, the sole survivor. His commanding officer, Captain Tom Ramos, was among the first to arrive at the crash site. Despite the critical injuries to his spinal cord, Ramos and a medic stabilized Ross and then medevacked him to Bagram, where a C-17 airlifted Ross to Ramstein Air Base, Germany. Doctors at Landstuhl Regional Medical Center further stabilized him for transport back to the United States and then sent him on to Walter Reed Army Medical Center in Bethesda, Maryland. There surgeons performed three surgeries on his spine. Ross awoke a month later.

One of the first people Ross saw after awakening was a man wearing a white lab coat with a black plastic name tag identifying him as Dr. Gerald Wright. Wright told him because of the severity of his injuries, the Army would medically discharge him following his recovery. When Ross asked why the Army had sent a doctor instead of an admin type to tell him his military career was over, Wright smiled and said he wasn't a doctor, he was there to offer him a job. And that was when Ross first heard about Operation Hydra, a top-secret Central Intelligence Agency black ops program, although Wright didn't name the operation then and only explained the job he offered in the broadest possible terms. With his Army career ended, it didn't take Ross long to accept the job since it offered him the chance to get back in the fight.

Three months later, the doctors discharged him from Walter Reed with his medical separation from military service documents in hand. Ross on boarded with the Central Intelligence Agency. He underwent another medical procedure at Larsen Biointeractive, LLC, a private clinic in Virginia. Wright had assured him the procedure would mitigate his combat injuries and return him to full fitness for duty.

After another two months of intense physical rehabilitation and fitness training, Ross completed his basic training as an intelligence operative at Camp Peary, affectionately known as "The Farm," and was assigned to the Special Activities Center (SAC), a division of the Central Intelligence Agency's National Clandestine Service, responsible for covert action paramilitary operations. He received another nine months of training at Harvey Point, North Carolina, in such things as surveillance, countersurveillance, cryptography, paramilitary training, and other tradecraft.

The day Ross completed his advanced training, he met again with Gerald "Jerry" Wright. After officially welcoming Ross to Operation Hydra, Wright told him something that made Ross wonder what he had got himself into. Wright said, "You are no longer Ethan Ross, who died in a helicopter crash in Afghanistan. You are now Jacob Dedman."

Chapter 1

Istanbul, Turkey

The kill order, as always, had been straightforward—the target's name, description, location, and recent photo. The dossier had contained no justification for the kill order. They never did. That information was above the asset's pay grade. His job was following orders. Orders that came only from his handler, Jerry Wright, CIA Special Activities Center Coordinator and Chief of Operations in Europe for Operation Hydra. Besides, the target was a notorious terrorist leader. How much more justification for the planned extrajudicial execution did the asset need?

Yahya Sobeeh, a Hamas political bureau chief and the instigator of a series of coordinated terror attacks on Israeli civilians and military personnel in 2014, was a wanted man, the target of a Mossad kill order. Because of it, he had fled Gaza and operated from Doha, Qatar, since 2015. Qatar had sided with Hamas and endorsed its takeover of Gaza in 2007. It had provided political and financial assistance to the Islamist group in the years since, pumping an estimated $1.8 billion dollars into Hamas-run Gaza since 2007, while undermining the internationally recognized Palestinian Authority.

The Qatari government had been happy to allow Yahya Sobeeh to live a life of luxury in the complete safety of Doha until the Americans made it plain that they were unhappy with the Qatari government's decision to provide sanctuary to a notorious official of an organization on the United States terrorist list. While the Israelis were one thing, the Americans were something else entirely. The State of Qatar benefited from the country's

4

status as a major non-NATO ally of the United States and concluded allowing Sobeeh to remain in Qatar could complicate matters.

The Qatari prime minister summoned Sobeeh and apologetically invited him to depart the country. To soften the blow, the prime minister informed him that the Qatari Foreign Ministry had secured an agreement approved by the president of Turkey on Sobeeh's behalf. The Turkish government had agreed to welcome him and had pledged to protect him from Mossad. A few days later, Yahya Sobeeh reluctantly departed for Istanbul.

Loitering across the street from the Tarlabaşi Pazari market near Taksim Square, at the heart of Istanbul, Jacob Dedman sensed a problem, a threat to his operation and to himself, and it immediately occurred to him he was blown.

The American had years of training and experience that taught him to miss nothing and to question everything. While most people lived in a world of black and white, he inhabited a world in shades of gray and knew how to navigate his way. It had kept him alive so far, but he was uncertain he had recognized this evening's problem in time for his training and experience to save him.

It was a minor thing, but to Dedman it was unmistakable. The target's mannerisms were off. He would have to be a fool to believe he was as safe in Istanbul as he had once been in Qatar, and the asset didn't believe his target would have lived as long as he had in his line of work if he were a fool. He should have his head on a swivel. It should be second nature to him. The fact that the fifty-four-year-old terrorist leader moved through the market street stalls alone this cool Istanbul evening, idly looking over the fresh produce as if he hadn't a care in the world suggested to Dedman that this might be an attempt to lure him into a trap. Had the target made him? Dedman didn't believe he had made a mistake and given himself away. He didn't make mistakes. But he sensed trouble, and he trusted his instincts.

He didn't overreact in the face of danger. Instead, he strolled casually down the sidewalk, breaking contact, and then turned left into an alley, leaving Sobeeh and the crowded street market behind. If he survived the problem, he would regroup and seek another opportunity. The agency gave him the kill orders, but he chose the day, time and the strike point. Another day or two wouldn't matter. There was no deadline, only an expected result. He continued feigning casualness, but all his senses were on high alert. His mind raced, seeking a way out of his present predicament.

He only picked up his pace once he was out of sight of the market. This was a time for action, not reflection. But as he hurried through the darkness, he couldn't help but wonder what had gone wrong. How the hell did he get made? He was new to Istanbul. This wasn't his usual turf. But he felt supremely confident in his abilities to blend in with the crowd wherever he was. Yet, just as surely, he knew he was blown. No other explanation made sense. His objective now was to minimize the damage to the op and the danger to himself by getting clear of the area.

He was less than a hundred yards from the car that had been waiting for him in airport parking when he had arrived in Istanbul that morning, where he had left it near the target's apartment just down Makaracı Çıkmazı, on the far side of the heavily trafficked street. He visualized getting into the vehicle, pulling a U-turn, and getting back to his hotel in just minutes. The asset thought he was almost home free. He was not.

Four men, Turks by the look of them, probably National Intelligence Organization goons. They weren't cops. No, from their bearing and obvious confidence, the asset took them for Turkish state security. They had the look, the air of authority, and their eyes locked on him as they closed the distance. He saw no guns, but there would be guns. Dedman knew no one would approach him in this situation without a weapon.

The American could have drawn his own weapon, the 9-millimeter Beretta 92FS, inside his waistband at his back. But this wasn't that kind of op. He could go hands on if things went south, but he would not start a gunfight with Turkish spooks. It wasn't because he gave a shit about killing them, really. They were government thugs of a corrupt regime that was in bed with the Russians and Iranians. But officially, Turkey was still a NATO ally, even if in name only. He couldn't shoot them because the agency would burn him if he turned this into a bloodbath. The Beretta and the screw on silencer in his jacket pocket were intended for terminating the target and making it look like a street crime, not creating an international incident. They didn't just send him to kill. They sent him to be invisible.

The asset spoke little Turkish, so he spoke in unaccented Arabic, hoping to confuse them when he got close enough to the men, who were now blocking his path to the vehicle.

"Is there a problem, friends?"

One of the hard-eyed men stepped forward, his hands empty and down at his sides. When he got within striking distance, he threw a roundhouse punch. Dedman read it all the way, slipped the punch, and then drove a powerful left hook into the man's right kidney, dropping the Turk to the ground.

Two others advanced quickly from opposite directions. One man, as he moved forward, swung a steel expandable baton. The American sidestepped the blow, grabbed the shaft of the baton with his left hand, and yanking the guy wielding the baton off balance, drove the tip of the impact weapon into the solar plexus of the other man who had drawn a semi-automatic pistol. Dedman grabbed the man's gun hand at the wrist to control the weapon while violently wresting the baton from the other man's grip. Shifting his right hand from the gunman's wrist to the slide of the pistol, Dedman trapped the man's forearm between his own forearm and chest and violently shoved the barrel of the weapon downward, breaking the gunman's grip and gaining possession of the pistol. Almost simultaneously, he delivered a backhand strike with the baton to the side of the neck and the carotid artery of the man he had taken it from. Turning back to the disarmed gunman, Dedman struck him in the face with a backhand strike, using the handgun as an impact weapon.

Stunned from watching Dedman take out his three colleagues in mere seconds, the fourth man froze for an instant before reaching for his holstered pistol. He was too slow. Dropping the baton, the American pointed the liberated Heckler & Koch USP in a two-handed grip at the man's face and shook his head side to side slowly. Carefully, the man lifted both his empty hands above his shoulders to show his understanding of the situation.

In his periphery, Dedman saw the first assailant he had kidney punched, getting to his hands and knees. Without taking his attention off the fourth man, Dedman kicked the first man in the side of the head and the man collapsed on the ground, unconscious. Dedman, still pointing the firearm, circled the fourth man. Stepping up behind him, he struck him at the base of the skull with the pistol. The Turkish operative hit the ground like a bag of wet sand.

After dropping the magazine and clearing the chamber of the Heckler & Koch, Dedman pulled the slide back to line up the notch on the left side with the slide release lever, pushed the pin out, and pulled the slide forward to separate it from the receiver. He then dropped the disassembled pistol on the sidewalk before walking hurriedly to his car.

Knowing Turkish intelligence already had the license plate numbers and that Istanbul police would get them as soon as the four spooks woke up, he opened the trunk to retrieve his backpack, and then walked away from the car. A street over, he flagged a taxi and told the driver to take him to the Istanbul central bus terminal.

Chapter 2

Langley, Virginia

Jerry Wright reclined in his desk chair he had swiveled toward the flat screen television mounted on his office wall. He sat with his left elbow on the armrest, with two fingers of his left hand pressed against his bottom lip and his right leg resting on the edge of his desk. Wright was only half listening to the Cable-Satellite Public Affairs Network's live coverage of the Glover Committee, chaired by Senator James Glover (R-LA), while he mulled over his options.

After a traitorous asshole working as an NSA contract computer analyst had leaked classified intelligence information to the media from documents he had stolen and the deleterious impact of the media's handling of the sensitive data that shocked the American public, it spurred many of its representatives in Congress to demand an investigation into suspected "lawless" activities of the CIA, NSA, FBI, and other intel agencies. The month before, the Senate had voted, along party lines, 68 to 12 to form the U.S. Senate Select Committee to Study Governmental Operations Regarding Intelligence Activities, that was now called the Glover Committee, after its chair.

The media drew almost daily comparisons to the Church Committee of 1975. The only difference was it was the Democrats who had shoved a microscope up the ass of the intelligence community back then and this time it was the Republicans. Senate Minority Leader Dick Shoemaker (D-NY) had given an impassioned speech in opposition to forming the committee

9

during the debate, closing with an ominous warning to his fellow senators.

"Let me remind you, ladies and gentlemen of the Senate. By voting to form this committee, you will take on the intelligence community, and they have six ways from Sunday to get back at you."

Most of those on one side of the aisle had heeded the warning. Besides the twelve Democrat senators who voted against forming the committee, twenty others voted "present" to avoid taking sides. The Republican majority, who seemed unimpressed by Shoemaker's warning that dissing the intelligence community might result in retaliation against any politician foolish enough to take them on, easily passed the measure establishing the committee. If anything, maybe the remark had only strengthened their resolve. Today was the committee's first open hearing. They had called CIA Director Will Cooper as the first witness.

Wright paid little attention during the opening statements and introduction of the witness, but tuned back in to the hearing when Senator Glover asked Director Cooper the first question.

"Mr. Cooper, are you familiar with the provisions of Executive Order 12333?"

"I am familiar with the substance of it, Mr. Chairman, although I cannot quote it off the top of my head. It's a rather lengthy document."

"That won't be necessary, Mr. Cooper. To preclude any misunderstanding, I'll read the passage relevant to the questions I will ask you. Part 2, paragraph 2.11."

Senator Glover picked up a document, adjusted his reading glasses, and continued.

"No person employed by or acting on behalf of the United States Government shall engage in, or conspire to engage in, assassination."

Glover returned his gaze to Cooper.

"Is that your understanding of this provision of the referenced executive order, Director?"

Cooper shifted in his seat, cleared his throat, and then leaned toward the microphone in front of him.

"Yes, Mr. Chairman. That is my understanding."

"Mr. Cooper, to your knowledge, has any employee of the Central Intelligence Agency engaged in, or conspired to engage in assassination since the promulgation of this executive order, as amended?"

Cooper cleared his throat again and adjusted his tie.

"Mr. Chairman, and members of the committee. As I am certain you are already aware, the United States has carried out strikes against leaders of certain hostile terrorist organizations under the provisions of the Authorization for the Use of Military Force Act when approved by the president. Employees of the Central Intelligence Agency have taken part in some of these strikes in various degrees. Some, the ACLU and others, have characterized these strikes as assassinations. However, the government prosecutes these proportional strikes under the rule of law and the laws of warfare. I would not categorize these operations as assassinations."

"You're speaking of drone strikes, Mr. Cooper?"

"Yes, Mr. Chairman."

Glover nodded.

"At the moment, I am more interested in whether you have any knowledge of assassinations in the context of how most of us, most reasonable people, might define the term. To your knowledge, does the Central Intelligence Agency employ assassins?"

"Not to my knowledge, Mr. Chairman. Use of Central Intelligence Agency employees or resources in such a capacity would violate the provisions of the executive order you mentioned."

"Very well, Mr. Cooper. Let me ask you this. Are you familiar with a program designated as Operation Hydra?"

"Jesus Christ!" exclaimed Jerry Wright, slamming the palm of his right hand on his desk before swinging his leg off it and swiveling his chair to face the desk. Grabbing the phone, he punched in the extension for his assistant, Andrew Grossman. He had decided, or the senate had decided, for him. He had hoped to avoid it, but now it was necessary.

Andrew "Andy" Grossman picked up his phone and answered.

"Grossman."

"Andy, shut it down. All of it. Just like we discussed. Keep me updated on

11

the progress. Got it?"

"Copy, boss."

Wright hung up the phone just as his office door flew open and Herman Buckley, CIA section chief and Jerry Wright's superior, barged into the office unannounced. Buckley's face was red and his hair mussed. Closing the door, he leaned his back against it, glanced at the television, and then back at Wright.

"You heard it?" Buckley asked.

"I heard."

"This is a fucking catastrophe, the worst thing imaginable. Cooper has probable deniability. He will not go to federal prison. If it all comes out, we're both going to burn."

"I'm on it, Herman. I'm shutting it down and cleaning it up. Afterward, no one will find a shred of proof. I can explain it all away as a beta training program we never activated if it comes to that."

"Shutting it down? Explain it to me. I want to know what you're doing, Jerry."

"You sure you want to know? You've never wanted to know any of the details before."

"I've never been worried I would end up in federal prison for 40 years before. Explain it, Jerry. All of it."

"I'm shutting it down and sanitizing everything. It will be as if Hydra never existed except as a training beta on paper. I'm getting rid of everything, the clinic and the assets. By Monday morning at the latest, nothing will exist for anyone to find."

"Wait. Getting rid of the clinic and the assets? You don't mean..."

"That's exactly what I mean. It's the only way. You think we can risk someone finding them and just hope none of them opens their mouth?"

Buckley leaned his head back against the closed office door, closed his eyes, and ran a hand through his thick, gray hair.

"I don't know, Jerry," he said, opening his eyes and fixing his gaze on his subordinate. "The assets? Okay. I get it. We only have five left of the original nine, anyway. But the clinic? If you're suggesting murdering

American citizens on U.S. soil…"

"Herman, get a grip. We're going to put the assets down. It's the only way. We have no other options. We will preserve the science and after this blows over, we can start over with a new generation of assets."

Wright paused, two fingers touching his mouth, when he continued.

"I'm only shutting down the clinic. I called Larsen and told him to close the facility, to layoff his staff, and to get all the equipment out of the building. After the dust settles from the hearings, he will set up somewhere new, and we'll start again."

"That sounds a hell of a lot better than killing a bunch of civilians. But how can we be sure Larsen and his staff won't talk if the committee uncovers something?"

"They won't talk. I had to read Larsen in on the full program. But each of his staff members knows only about their own discrete roles. And I'm not worried about Larsen talking out of school. You think he would risk a 20-year prison stretch for revealing classified information? A senate committee has no power to shield him from that. He can't cut a deal."

Buckley nodded, but then recognition dawned in his eyes.

"My God, Jerry! You've already started without even consulting me."

"It had to be done. Wet teams have already terminated the assets in Madrid, Paris, Rome, and Athens. None of the teams knew who they were or why. They were simply told we sanctioned them to eliminate enemies of the United States."

"That's only four. What about Berlin?"

"He was already en route to Istanbul on a live mission. But he won't get the chance to complete it. I passed the word to a Turkish National Intelligence contact that we have a rogue asset on the way who took an Israeli contract on someone the Turkish government has given sanctuary. The Turks will take him into custody and hold him for us, or eliminate him if necessary. I told you. I'm cleaning it up."

Buckley shook his head.

"I hope you are, Jerry. I sincerely hope you are. And understand this. If we're lucky enough to keep this from blowing up in our faces, destroy the files, all of it. This stops now. We aren't starting another program even if this all blows over. It ends here."

"Let's try to be adults here. Okay, Herman? Hydra has been the most successful off book rendition and lethal direct-action program in the agency's history. You know that as well as I do, and you know why. No red tape. No more painstaking work getting bad guys in our sights only to watch them escape while we wait for a bunch of pearl clutching bureaucrats to make a decision and give us the approval to act. Of course, we're starting over."

"We don't even know what the senate committee has, Jerry!"

"They can't have anything except the program name that probably came from some white paper when it was in the planning stages. They have no proof the program ever went active. All that information resides on a dedicated server at the off-site facility. Once I've shut down the program and tied everything off, they won't find a scintilla of evidence that Hydra ever existed as anything more than a beta training program that never went live."

Buckley gaped at Wright like he was a madman. He was supposed to be in charge, but slowly Buckley had realized the truth. Wright was running everything and always had. Wright had only used him to get Hydra financed and up and running. He hadn't been in charge since the day he had allowed Wright to persuade him to go active with a black program no one else in the agency or anyone else in the government even knew existed. Buckley had no means of stopping Wright now without implicating himself. And no other human instinct was stronger than self-preservation.

Chapter 3

Exfil

Dedman tried to relax as he slouched in a seat with a window designated as an emergency exit near the rear of the 45-foot motor coach bus bound for Alexandroupoli, Greece. But he knew he wouldn't truly relax until he was across the border and out of Turkey. Given his present circumstances, Dedman would have preferred to avoid all public transportation, but believed the Turkish authorities would focus more on air, rail, and the ferry system. Getting across the Turkish border crossing by car was also a no-go. The bus had seemed the best of many poor options.

Things hadn't always gone according to plan on his previous missions, but Dedman had never found it necessary to abort one until now. But knowing Turkish intelligence and probably every Turkish law enforcement agency, including the Turkish National Police manning the border crossings, probably had his name, description, and photo, Dedman felt he had no choice but to abort. He had no interest in seeing the inside of a Turkish prison. He hadn't signed up for that shit, or whatever else the Turkish spooks who had accosted him back in Istanbul might have had in mind for him.

The protocol, if a mission got compromised, was to phone in an SOS to the agency to request an emergency exfil. However, that hadn't been an option either. Dedman didn't feel comfortable doing that because he didn't know who had compromised him and the mission. He was only damn sure it hadn't been him. Besides his handler, only one other person on the planet could have known he had been on a live mission in Istanbul. It seemed likely one of them had betrayed him to Turkish intelligence. There was no other rational explanation. And Dedman was determined to find out who.

About five hours after leaving Istanbul, Dedman caught his first glimpse of the Kipoi Turkish border crossing. While he felt relief Turkish authorities hadn't stopped the bus en route, he now faced the sticky problem of getting out of Turkey and into Greece. Just before the motor coach came to a stop in one of the commercial vehicle lanes behind a line of buses and semi-trailer trucks, Dedman settled on a plan. Maybe not a great plan, but the best he could come up with. Picking up his backpack, he headed for the small restroom at the back of the motor coach.

After closing and locking the door, Dedman yanked handfuls of dry paper towels out of the dispenser on the wall. He wadded them into a ball and stuffed them inside the refuse bin. He added a roll of toilet tissue. Then he removed two small bottles of alcohol-based hand sanitizer from his backpack. Holding the bin flap open, he emptied the hand sanitizer on the pile of paper. Taking out a disposable lighter, he set alight the paper in the bin and then exited the restroom and strode back to his seat without making it obvious he was in a hurry. The bus stopped just as he sat down and peered nonchalantly out his window. Moments later, a fire alarm inside the restroom meant to discourage smoking sounded.

Dedman turned his head along with all the other passengers to look toward the rear of the bus when the alarm sounded and he saw smoke was already billowing. A woman screamed. Looking toward the front, Dedman saw the driver had left his seat. When he saw the smoke, he quickly opened the front and side door of the bus and grabbed a microphone from the dash. He spoke in Turkish, but Dedman assumed the driver was telling his passengers to exit the bus. The smoke grew denser, and soon the passengers were jostling and shoving their way toward the exit doors. Dedman stood and calmly unlatched his emergency exit window and pushed it open. After dropping his backpack out the window, he clambered over the window frame, grasped the frame for a second to steady himself, and then dropped to the asphalt roadway. Scooping up his backpack, he headed across two lanes of traffic between the stopped vehicles and into a car park. Winding his way through the parked cars, he slipped the backpack straps onto his shoulders and made for the rear of an administration building.

Arriving at a back corner, he spotted a drain pipe. After testing to make sure the drain pipe held securely to the building, he quickly climbed up it and onto the metal roof of the one-story structure. On his hands and knees, Dedman crawled across the roof to the adjacent high roof of the metal awning over the border crossing booths below. He pulled himself up and onto the awning and then low crawled to the forward edge. Looking back at the motor coach, he saw smoke boiling out the open doors of the bus, which was surrounded by passengers and the Turkish authorities. It seemed he had created an adequate distraction.

Less than two minutes later, a semi-trailer truck appeared beneath him, headed toward the Greek aide of the border. Dedman quickly got up and stepped off the awning. Landing on the top of the trailer, he flattened himself atop the truck on his stomach. A short time later, after crossing a bridge, the truck slowed and stopped at the crossing on the Greek side of the border. Dedman felt concealed adequately from the view of anyone at ground level.

As the truck inched toward the awning ahead, he knew it would be a tight fit. The builders probably hadn't allowed from the additional height of a body atop a truck trailer. Dedman turned his head so that his cheek was against the top of the trailer and hoped for the best. His body cleared the overhang with only scant inches to spare. The truck idled beneath the awning for several minutes until finally Dedman heard the air brakes releasing and the rumble of the truck's diesel engine as his new ride rolled on into Greece.

For the sake of convenience, he hoped the truck would at least pass through Alexandroupoli, since he doubted he had been lucky enough to choose at random a truck bound for his intended destination. If the driver turned off short of Alexandroupoli, he would have to get off at his first opportunity and look for alternative transportation. Then a problem developed. As the truck picked up speed on the motorway, the wind coming across the top of the trailer pushed Dedman's prone exposed body toward the rear. He started sliding.

Chapter 4

Greece

Dedman tried to dig the toes of his shoes in to stop his rearward slide, but it only slowed him down a little. Reaching into the pocket of his pants, he pulled out a folding tactical knife. Flicking the blade open, he drove it into the thin aluminum top of the trailer and then twisted it sideways. Gripping the handle of the knife with both hands, the embedded blade finally jammed against a support beam and arrested his slide. Relieved for the moment, Dedman just hoped he could hang for about another forty kilometers.

Glancing at his wristwatch periodically and by mentally calculating the time, distance, and approximate speed equation, he could keep a rough estimate of the distance traveled. His arms ached, but Dedman knew if he lost his grip that he would probably become road kill. He gritted his teeth and fought through the growing discomfort.

After the truck had traveled what Dedman estimated was around 30 kilometers, his hopes of at least passing through Alexandroupoli grew. He just hoped the truck stopped or slowed substantially sometime within the next fifteen minutes so he could jump off. Ten minutes later, he felt the truck slowing. Looking ahead, he saw what looked like a truck stop or petrol station ahead. The driver downshifted, and the truck veered to the right onto the exit ramp. The driver steered the rig into the driveway, parked up alongside several other semi-trailer trucks, and shut down the engine. Dedman heard the cab door open and then slam shut. A few moments later, he saw the back of the driver as the man walked towards the sprawling building.

Dedman pulled his knife free of the trailer covering, folded the blade, and then stuck the knife back into his pocket. Raising up onto his hands and knees, he looked around. He saw no one off to the right of the truck and crawled that way. Looking down, he saw the distance to the parking lot below was about the equivalent of a fall from a two-story building. No sweat. He threw his legs over the side and sat on the edge for a moment.

Pushing off with his hands, Dedman plummeted toward the concrete below. Just like he had learned back at jump school at Fort Benning, Dedman performed a parachute landing fall. With his chin and elbows tucked tight against his chest, his fists pressed to his forehead so that his forearms protected his face, and with his knees slightly bent, Dedman hit the pavement on the balls of his feet and then he threw his body sideways to distribute the landing shock sequentially. First the side of his calf, then the side of his thigh, then his buttock, and finally the side of his back hit the ground.

Getting to his feet, Dedman make a quick assessment of his body and found he had broken nothing. Dusting himself off, he walked around the back of the trailer and then headed for the building complex. His first stop was a restroom.

After emptying his bladder, he stood at a sink and washed his face and hands, stalling until two other men finished their business and left him alone. Then he grabbed some paper towels and dried his hands. Quickly, he pulled the Beretta out of his waistband, dropped the magazine and cleared it, and then wrapped the weapon and magazine in the paper towels. He dumped the firearm in a refuse bin on his way out of the restroom. He had already dumped the silencer before boarding the bus, along with his cell phone and SAT phone, to prevent anyone from using GPS to track him after he left Istanbul.

Dedman walked into one of the two restaurants and bought a sandwich and a bottle of water. He sat down and ate, feeling much better about his circumstances. Alexandroupoli, along with Dimokritos International Airport, was close by and there he intended to buy a ticket on a flight to Athens. He felt confident his problems in Turkey hadn't followed him to

Greece. While they were NATO allies, anyone who knew much about the region also knew about the longstanding bad blood between Turkey and Greece. Dedman felt he could safely continue his trip home to Berlin by air.

Inside the restaurant, he overheard a British couple at a table next to his discussing the sites they planned to visit when they arrived in Alexandroupoli. Dedman struck up a conversation with them and learned they were retired and traveling the area in a camper van. They told him they had stopped for petrol and were on their way to Alexandroupoli to see the sites. After they had talked for several more minutes, he told the couple he also was bound for Alexandroupoli and would be happy to pay them for a lift into the city. Both assured him no payment was necessary since they were going there anyway and were happy to give a nice Yank a lift.

The British couple dropped him in the center of the city after they had said their goodbyes. Dedman grabbed a taxi to the airport. Before entering, he dumped the tactical knife, the only weapon he had kept, in a refuse bin, knowing he wouldn't get through security with it. Then he went to the ticket counter. Dedman saw there was an Aegean Airlines flight departing for Athens in forty-five minutes. He booked a seat on the flight and a seat on a Lufthansa flight departing Athens for Berlin an hour after his expected arrival there. He paid cash for both flights and collected his boarding pass for the Aegean flight. After passing through security, he walked to the gate and waited for his flight.

Once he boarded the Aegean Airlines Airbus A320, Dedman relaxed, believing he was finally home free. Once he was back home in Berlin in a few hours, he could sort out how his op got compromised.

First, he intended to go see Kara Jansen, the Operation Hydra safe house field operative in Berlin who coordinated logistical support and operations and monitored the mental health of the Hydra European operatives. Jansen was the only other person in a position to know about his job in Istanbul.

Dedman didn't know Jansen well. He had only met her twice, in a manner of speaking, when she had handed off equipment or documents he needed for missions using brush passes. Besides that, he only communicated with her through secure text messaging.

Jansen hadn't been involved in the Istanbul op. Dedman had received the mission directly from Langley and they had provided the direct logistical support. But Jansen was still in a position where she could have known about the job. If she satisfied him she hadn't compromised him, Dedman would then go higher up the food chain.

Safely out of Turkey and on his way to Athens, Dedman felt comfortable and confident he would be back in Berlin in a few hours. But he was unaware of the trouble awaiting him in Athens.

Chapter 5

Manassas, Virginia

Four men wearing blue hard hats and blue coveralls with the name of the local natural gas utility printed on them exited the stairwell door on the first floor at Larsen Biointeractive, LLC, a private medical research facility. Passing through the front lobby on the way to the front exit, one of the utility company employees looked over at two muscular young men with military haircuts wearing navy windbreakers with SECURITY emblazoned on the front. The jackets concealed the Heckler & Koch automatic weapons hanging from slings over their shoulders. The utility company employee held up his right hand with four fingers extended. Both security officers nodded and followed the utility workers out the front the door. The workers quickly stowed their tool boxes and got in a large work truck while the security officers got in a sedan. Both vehicles left the parking lot and sped away.

* * *

CIA Headquarters, Langley

Jerry Wright sat at his desk watching a live CNN report on the flat screen television. The news anchor switched to a reporter named Holly Danforth on the scene of a disaster in Manassas, Virginia. There was a two-story building behind the reporter, fully engulfed in flames and many emergency vehicles, including the fire trucks whose crews were directing their fire hoses on the structure to bring the blaze under control. The anchor asked the reporter what she could tell the audience about the scene in the background.

"Thanks, Jay. What our viewers are seeing behind me is a major structure fire involving a private medical research facility here in Manassas, Virginia. The alarm, according to a fire department spokesperson I talked with, came in less than an hour ago. They also told me when the first fire department units arrived at the scene, the structure was already fully involved."

"Any word about how the fire started, Holly?"

"Obviously, it will be some time before fire investigators can begin their investigation. Right now, they are struggling to contain the blaze and bring the fire under control. But according to the person I spoke with, they believe a natural gas explosion is at fault for the fire."

"Any suspicion terrorism might be involved? Unfortunately, these days, that is always a concern that comes to mind."

"At least at the present time, while they haven't ruled it out, the fire department has no evidence this was a terrorist attack. They seem to believe it is more likely that this is only a tragic accident resulting from a natural gas leak inside the building."

"Any word on casualties, Holly?"

"It's believed some thirty people, doctors, medical researchers, and support staff work at this private research facility. While we have no firm numbers yet from authorities, given it's the middle of a normal workday, the fire department fears the worst. It's believed everyone inside the building at the time of the blast perished."

"What a tragedy, Holly."

"Yes, it is, Jay. It's just a horrific afternoon here in Manassas."

"That was Holly Danforth reporting from Manassas, Virginia, at the scene of a truly tragic disaster. And now, in other news…"

Wright picked up the remote and turned off the television. He regretted the loss of life. Larsen and his staff had done some very important work, but operational security had demanded swift and decisive action. And now that Larsen Biointeractive had ceased to exist, Hydra was almost completely shut down and only Wright could now access the Hydra research files stored on the off-site dedicated server.

Deep in thought, Wright started when his phone rang. He picked up.

"Wright."

"Boss, your Turkish contact is on the line. He says it's urgent."

"Put him through, Andy."

When the call transferred, Wright spoke first.

"Murat, my friend. I trust you have good news for me."

"I have news, but it isn't good."

Wright sat up straight in his chair.

"Let me hear it."

"We picked up your asset outside his target's apartment, and he followed the target to a neighborhood market. Our people stayed back to entice your asset to strike. Apparently, he sensed something was wrong and aborted his operation. We followed, but were out of position and soon lost your asset in the streets."

"He escaped?"

"Not immediately. We had already located the car you described near the apartment of the man we are protecting. I had a team on the car and they confronted your asset when he returned to the vehicle."

"What happened?"

"Long story short, your asset put four of my men in the hospital. It took him only seconds. Then he abandoned the vehicle and disappeared."

"Don't tell me he fired on your people."

"No, not at all. Your asset, he was the weapon. I assume he believed shooting my men would have been far too time consuming. I've spoken to two of my people who regained consciousness. Both told me they had seen nothing like this man."

"No one has spotted the asset since?"

"No. Of course, we have the airport, trains, and ferries covered. We have alerted the national police at all border crossings and we have local police at the central Istanbul bus station looking for leads. I'm not confident they will find anything. The average total traffic per day there represents about fifteen thousand buses and over a half million passengers. You show up, show identification and pay the fare and they give you a printed ticket. It's low tech with many bus companies. The police have the asset's photo, but what are the chances anyone will remember one face out of a half million?"

"How long since your people lost contact with him?"

"Six hours, perhaps a little longer."

"He's probably crossed the border by now. The asset has received extensive SERE training. He probably avoided public transportation altogether."

"My apologies that we could not be of more help."

"No, not a problem, Murat. As I told you, he is no ordinary asset. Your people aren't at fault. We lost control of our asset and I appreciate your efforts on our behalf. I'm just thankful he didn't kill anyone."

"Thank you, Jerry. Yes, it could have gone worse. We will continue surveillance at the airport, trains, ferries, and border crossings for a while longer. But as you said, he is probably out of Turkey by now. In Greece, perhaps."

"Yes, Greece would be his logical destination. I can't imagine him entering Russia or Syria. Anyway, thank you for the help, Murat. Call me when we can return the favor."

The two men said goodbye and disconnected.

"Damn it, Dedman!" Wright exclaimed, hanging up the phone. "Why couldn't you die for your country like a good soldier?"

Chapter 6

Wright strode out of his office and into the operations center.

"People, listen up. We have a priority one national security threat situation."

Everyone in the room turned to look at Wright. He pointed at Grossman.

"Andy, give me Dedman's profile," Wright said, then pointing to a large plasma screen at the front of the room.

Grossman nodded and typed on his keyboard. A moment later, Dedman's photo and profile information filled the screen.

"Our target is Jacob Dedman, a special operations officer who has gone off the reservation. He aborted a live mission in Istanbul without authorization or explanation. He attacked and put four Turkish intelligence officers in the hospital for unknown reasons. Dedman is now on the run. Best guess is he has crossed the Turkish border and is somewhere in Greece. We need to find him immediately."

Wright looked back at Grossman.

"Andy, I want a flag on his passport."

Grossman nodded again and began typing on his keyboard.

Turning back to the analysts, Wright continued. "I want flight manifests for all departures from whatever airport in Greece is closest to the Turkish border, starting with the first flights out this morning. Then keep working the later departures for today."

A young woman in the group of an intelligence analysts raised her hand tentatively. Wright pointed at her.

"What?"

"Do we have an idea about how he got out of Turkey, sir? Mode of transportation?"

"Turkish intelligence says he didn't fly, take a train, or a ferry. Best guess is he traveled by bus or car."

"Thank you, sir," the woman said. "That means he probably crossed into Greece at the Kipoi Turkish border crossing. The closest airport is at Alexandroupoli, Dimokritos International Airport. Even though they consider it an international airport, I traveled through there recently on vacation and most of the outbound flights from there are domestic flights to Athens for people connecting to international flights."

"That's useful information," Wright said. "Let's focus on the manifests for departures from Alexandroupoli to Athens first. Also, we believe Berlin may be Dedman's final destination. I also want manifests for all Athens to Berlin departures. See Andy Grossman for your specific assignments, and he will sort you out. All right, let's get to it."

Herman Buckley walked into the room from a corridor and gaped when he saw Dedman's profile on the plasma screen.

"What's going on, Jerry?" Buckley asked.

Wright jerked his head toward his office. "Let's talk in my office, Herman." Looking back at the room, he said, "We need to find this man, people. I need your best efforts on this one."

Buckley followed Wright into his office. Wright closed the door and then walked over to his desk, sat on the edge, and looked at Buckley.

"Why was Dedman's profile up on the screen, Jerry? What's going on?"

"The plan for Dedman didn't work out. When Turkish intelligence tried to take him into custody, he took out four of their officers and escaped. No sighting in Turkey for five or six hours, so Dedman probably made it out of Turkey into Greece by now. We need to find him."

Buckley stood unblinking for a moment, trying to process what Wright had just told him. His eyes widened in alarm.

"You said you had everything in control, Jerry! It doesn't sound like it to me."

"It's only a minor setback, Herman. I thought the Turks could handle it, but they didn't take Dedman seriously enough. They only sent a four-man team. Dedman took them out and got away."

"You mean to say a U.S. Central Intelligence Agency asset just shot it out with and killed four intelligence officers of one of our allies and NATO partners?"

"No, Herman. Dedman did not kill them. There was no shootout. He only incapacitated them when they tried to take him into custody. It's an embarrassment for the Turks and they aren't squawking about it. There was no international incident, no blow back on the agency."

There was a knock at the office door, and then it opened. Grossman stood in the doorway.

"We just got a hit on the passport. Dedman is on the manifest of a flight from Alexandroupoli to Athens. He lands in less than an hour."

Wright nodded. "Call the chief of station in Athens with a heads up. Tell him to get someone ready to head to the airport."

Grossman nodded, turned, and shut the door.

Wright turned back to Buckley. "See, we found him."

"Fine, then let's talk about something else. What I came to see you about."

Wright crossed his arms and eyed Buckley.

"Shoot."

"That explosion and fire in Manassas this afternoon. Was that us?"

"You asking me a direct question, Herman? You really want me to answer it? Look, I don't have time for this. I'm going to Athens to put Dedman in a body bag, and then this will be over and we will be clean."

"You're not going anywhere, Jerry. I've lost confidence in you. This has spun out of control. It's getting uglier by the second. My God, I heard it on the news. You just blew up twenty-nine civilians at that research facility. I'm shutting this down. We need a fresh perspective on this problem. I'm bringing in some people from upstairs."

"I would rethink that, Herman. I'm one step away from cleaning this up by terminating Dedman. Now you want to staff a committee and do what? Talk Dedman to death?"

"I'm not asking, Jerry. I'm telling you. Your methods are unsound."

29

"You don't have the stones for this, Herman. People like you come down here with a wink and nod and I send guys out and get things done. The guys upstairs get what they want and you're clean. The bunch of you stay wrapped in deniability. When something goes wrong, guys like me take the fall. Well, you know what? Not this time. You are in the shit right along with me. If I go down, you can be damn sure you're going down with me. Or you can stay out of my way and let me finish this and we will both be in the clear."

Buckley said nothing. He just shook his head. Wright snapped. He brushed past Buckley, yanked his office door open, and shouted at Grossman.

"Andy, get me a plane. We're going to Athens."

Turning back, Wright grabbed a briefcase off his desk, and his sport jacket and a dark gray trench coat from the coat stand beside the door.

"I've got a plane to catch, Herman. I've got to put a bag over Dedman. We trained the assets to be ghosts. If we don't get Dedman in Athens, we may never find him again."

Wright turned and went out the door without waiting for an answer. Then he and Grossman disappeared down the corridor.

Chapter 7

Athens, Greece

Jacob Dedman stood in a line at the passport control point inside the terminal at Athens International Airport Eleftherios Venizelos. Citizens of European Economic Community (EEC) countries did not have to go through airport passport control. Citizens of non-EEC countries, such as the United States did, and Dedman was traveling on a U.S. passport.

Virtually all the passengers on the Aegean Airlines flight had been Greek or EEC citizens. The process moved along quickly and smoothly. Dedman made his way to the counter and handed his passport over to the Greek official with a friendly smile to be glanced at and scanned. Dedman had done this at least hundreds if not a thousand times before. His CIA provided passport was so solid that he allowed his mind to wander, contemplating his last leg in the journey back to Berlin. There, he intended to get answers about what had happened to him in Turkey.

The Hellenic Police officer looked at the passport, then looked at Dedman to compare his face to the photo. Then he ran it through the scanner. Looking at his screen, the officer did a double take. He slowly held up a finger, signaling Dedman to wait just a moment. Then he reached for the phone beside his computer, and Dedman knew he had a problem.

In an instant, two uniformed officers appeared at the American's shoulder. They were young and fit and armed.

"Mr. Dedman," one said in English with a Greek accent, "please come with us for a moment."

"Why?" Dedman asked, in the character of a concerned tourist.

It wasn't completely an act. He was concerned. Obviously, someone had flagged his passport.

"Just come along, please, and we will get this straightened out."

Dedman accompanied the officers with the straps of his backpack in his hand. Neither officer had touched him, but they moved close beside him, making it clear they were ready if he tried something foolish.

Two more uniformed and armed police officers stood in the corridor with radios in their hands. One asked Dedman for his backpack. He handed it over and the five of them continued down the corridor.

Anger built inside Dedman. Someone had burned him in Istanbul and now had flagged his passport to make sure the Greek authorities would detain him on his arrival in Athens. His situation seemed to grow darker by the hour. He considered taking out the four officers and taking a weapon from one of them. But then what? Was he prepared to shoot his way out of the airport? He knew he wasn't, so he kept walking, trying to affect the manner of a confused and offended tourist.

They took him into a small interview room, patted him down, and relieved him of his wallet and keys. He had no other property on his person since he had already discarded everything but his wallet and keys before arriving in Athens.

One officer told him to have a seat, pointing to a plastic chair beside a desk, and told him there was a slight problem with his passport. The officer then left him alone in the room. When the door closed behind them, Dedman heard the distinctive click telling him the heavy steel door locked automatically when closed. It required a key to open it from the inside. Obviously, the police officers didn't know who they had detained because Dedman figured if they did, he would be in leg irons with his hands handcuffed to a belly chain.

* * *

Two hours out of Dulles International over the Atlantic, Wright and Grossman sat across from each other on the Gulfstream CIA business jet. Grossman's phone buzzed inside his jacket pocket. He took it out and answered. Grossman nodded to himself as he listened and then spoke into the phone. He retrieved a pad and pen from his shirt pocket and wrote something on the pad and then disconnected the call.

"The police at Athens International Airport have detained Dedman and the intelligence officer they sent from the embassy just arrived at the airport. They said he should be with Dedman in about five and gave me his phone number."

Wright nodded. "Give him a few minutes to get inside and then dial the number and hand me the phone."

The door to the interview room opened, rousing him from his thoughts. That hadn't taken his watch, so he glanced down and saw he had been inside the room for over two hours.

The same police officer who had taken it from him entered, holding his backpack, followed by a young man in a navy pinstripe suit carrying a manila folder in his hand. Dedman knew a CIA intelligence officer when he saw one and this one looked like he hadn't been on the job for over three years, tops. The police officer placed the backpack on the table, along with a plastic bag containing the wallet and keys they had taken from him.

The American intelligence officer eyed Dedman for several moments to appear intimidating, but failing. After glancing at the man, Dedman returned his gaze to the imaginary spot on the wall he had stared at for the past two hours, making no effort to hide his pissed off look.

"What brings you to Athens, Mr. Dedman?"

Dedman didn't look up at the CIA officer and said nothing.

"Where are you coming from?"

Dedman said nothing.

"I don't know what you've done, but I know who you are."

I doubt that. Dedman thought it. But he didn't say it. If the guy knew anything about him besides the name on his flagged passport, two armed men wouldn't be standing within three feet of him so casually when he was

33

not in handcuffs. He had seen the bulge of the man's suit coat at his waistline on the left side. Probably a cross draw rig.

The intelligence officer sighed and then sat down on the front edge of the desk. Twisting at the waist, he held his right hand in front of Dedman's nose and snapped his fingers several times.

"Hello. Anyone home? Listen, Dedman. I've got questions and you will give me answers. One way or another."

Then his phone buzzed inside his pocket. The CIA officer stood up, taking out the phone. He took a step to Dedman's left and turned his back to him while he took the call. Dedman glanced at the Greek cop to his right and saw he looked bored.

"Edwards," the CIA officer said into the phone.

"Officer Edwards, this is Special Activities Division Coordinator and Chief of Operations Gerald Wright from Langley. Do you have a man named Jacob Dedman in custody?"

"Yes, sir, I do," Edwards said, glancing over his left shoulder at Dedman. "I'm standing right beside him."

"Tell me, officer, is Dedman in handcuffs?"

"No, sir."

"How long have you been with the agency, Officer Edwards?"

"Almost two years, sir."

"Okay, if you want to make your anniversary and then get to year three, I need you to listen to me carefully."

"Yes, sir."

"Jacob Dedman is a tier one special operations officer credited with fourteen kills. He could snap your neck and sever your spinal cord in under two seconds. Besides firearms and knives, he is an expert in every martial art you've ever heard of and some you haven't. Until you get him in handcuffs, I want you to put him on the floor prone and hold him at gunpoint. As soon as I hang up, I will call and get a team on the way to you and they will take it from there. Keep Dedman at gunpoint until they arrive. Am I clear?"

"Crystal, sir."

Dedman heard the change in the CIA officer's tone. He sounded frightened.

"Good. I will call you back with an ETA for the team as soon as I get it, officer."

"Yes, sir."

Dedman glanced at the Greek cop and then focused on the CIA officer, who slowly transferred the phone from his right hand to his left hand. Then Dedman saw the tell. The officer, with his back still turned to Dedman, used the fingers of his right hand to unbutton his coat. That was a major tactical blunder. Dedman was already on his feet as the intelligence officer drew his weapon and whirled right toward Dedman.

Dedman grabbed the slide of the SIG Sauer P228 to control the muzzle and then delivered an explosive left hook that struck the officer just below his right ear, fracturing and dislocating his jaw. Dedman ripped the pistol from his grip as the officer fell to the floor on his left side.

Rotating away from the man on the floor to the Greek police officer, who was trying to draw his pistol, Dedman backhanded the cop with the SIG Sauer, striking him in the right temple. Before the cop had hit the floor, Dedman had the pistol in a two-hand grip, scanning back and forth between the cop and the CIA officer. Satisfied both men were unconscious, he shoved the pistol inside his waistband at the back, unzipped his backpack, and tossed the bag with the wallet and keys inside. Then he picked up the CIA officer's phone where it had fallen from the man's hand and tossed it inside the backpack.

Checking the man's suit coat pockets, Dedman found his passport the police had seized and a set of car keys and fob. He tossed the passport into the backpack, zipped it, and put it on his back. The cop didn't have a police radio, but Dedman found a cell phone inside his uniform shirt pocket and the key to the interview room tucked inside the cop's belt behind the buckle. Dedman was ready to roll if the corridor was clear. He inserted the key in the door lock, opened it, and stuck his head out far enough to quick peek in both directions. The corridor was empty and there was a door at the end of it to his left with a lighted exit sign above it.

Dedman stepped out into the corridor and let the door lock behind him. He hurried to the exit. Glancing inside an open door on his right on the way and saw it was an empty break room. He paused for a moment when he saw a refuse bin just inside the open door. Dedman dropped the cop's cell phone and the key into the bin and then yanked the SIG Sauer out of his waistband and tossed it into the bin. He hoped to escape, but he still would not shoot his way out of the airport, so he didn't need a firearm. And if they caught him on the way out, having a weapon on him would probably get him shot.

Dedman breathed a sigh of relief when no alarm sounded when he opened the exit door. Outside, he found a car park filled with civilian cars. He assumed it was an employee parking lot. He started pressing the button on the key fob as he walked around the vehicles and it rewarded him with flashing lights and a double chirp from a gray sedan. Dedman opened the door, tossed his backpack on the front passenger seat, and got it. He inserted the key, started the car, and backed out of the parking space. He navigated through the airport, found the exit, and turned onto a service road. Minutes later, he took an on ramp onto a motorway and sped away.

Chapter 8

Dedman stopped at a petrol station on the Olympia Odos A8 motorway after leaving the northwestern outskirts of Athens. He retrieved the phone he had taken from the CIA officer at the airport and turned it back on. When it powered up, he saw many missed calls from the same number. He clicked on the most recent call and put the phone to his ear.

* * *

After calling the number for Officer Edwards again and again and getting only the voicemail greeting, Wright tossed the phone back to Grossman in frustration.

"I'm sure Dedman took Edwards out and escaped somehow. We will just have to wait for an update until the team gets there. Call the Athens station back and have them call the police at the airport to see if they can find out what the hell happened."

Grossman nodded and punched a number into his phone. When he connected to the Athens Central Intelligence Agency station, he told the individual on the other end of the call that their officer at the airport was not answering his phone. Then Grossman asked them to find out what the Hellenic Police at the airport knew about the situation there and ended the call.

"It's done," Grossman said.

"Great," Wright growled. "This is just great."

Grossman's phone buzzed in his hand. He looked at the screen.

"Finally, it's Edwards calling back." He handed the phone to Wright.

Wright answered and put the phone to his ear.

"Edwards, what the hell…"

The individual on the other end of the call interrupted. "This isn't Edwards. Last time I saw him, he was taking a nap."

"Dedman?"

"What are you trying to do to me?"

"What am I trying to do? What the hell are you talking about? What are we into now, Jacob? And what happened with the mission, soldier? What in the name of God have you been doing?"

"Someone burned me in Istanbul. Someone flagged my passport. What did I do? What did you do and why are you doing this?"

"What?" Wright said, feigning surprise. "We didn't know you were in trouble. We didn't know because you didn't check in. You aborted the mission without a word and disappeared. Listen, Jacob, I can't fix it if I don't know what the problem is. Tell me where you are and we'll pick you up."

"I don't think so. I think you intend to kill me, and I want to know why."

Wright fished his cell phone out of his pocket and tossed it to Grossman. He hit the mute button on the phone he was holding. "Call Athens. Find out where he is."

"On it," Grossman said, calling the Athens CIA station.

Wright clicked the mute off and resumed the conversation.

"Of course. We have to try. You left the reservation. What was I supposed to think? You're a malfunctioning multi-million-dollar weapon, soldier. We can't have that. But we didn't know you were in trouble. Now we know and it's time for you to come in so I can fix this. Listen…"

"No, you listen, Wright. I don't trust you anymore, and I don't want to work for you anymore. I quit."

"That's not a decision you can make, soldier. I thought we were on the same side. You're U.S. government property. If you don't come in now, we will not stop until we're satisfied."

"I'm on my own side now. Don't try to find me. If I get even a whiff that you're on my tail, I will bring the fight to your doorstep so fast and so hard you won't know what hit you. Ethan Ross is dead and now Jacob Dedman is dead. I'm gone."

* * *

Dedman turned off the phone, snapped it in half and tossed the pieces out of the car window. The CIA would know where he had called from, but he would be long gone before they could get anyone to the petrol station. Dedman also figured they probably knew he had stolen the car from the airport by now and had reported it to the Greek police. He needed a new ride. He got out of the car with his backpack, leaving the keys in the ignition. Using a coin as a screwdriver, he removed both the front and back license plates and walked away.

Walking along the side of the petrol station where he had parked to stay out of the view of the cameras he had seen at the front of the building, he chose a parked vehicle. Quickly, using the coin again, he switched out the license plates from the CIA pool car for the ones on the car he had chosen. Then, with the new plates concealed inside his backpack, he went looking for a car to steal.

* * *

Wright and Grossman exchanged phones. Wright leaned his head back against the seat headrest and ran his hand over his face.

"They said the phone was on the outskirts of Athens off the Olympia Odos A8. But before we finished talking, they told me the phone had gone dark. He either pulled the battery or destroyed it. Also, they said the pool car the officer that they sent to the airport had driven there was missing from the

39

airport. Along with the officer's sidearm."

"Fantastic," Wright said with sarcasm. "It just keeps getting better. That Edwards must be a hell of an intelligence officer. He supplied Dedman with a phone, a ride, and armed him. I wonder if he loaned Dedman some cash for travel expenses while he was at it?"

Grossman assumed the question was rhetorical.

"Call Langley. I want a standing kill order issued on Jacob Dedman with an advisory, armed and dangerous."

Grossman nodded and went back to his phone.

Chapter 9

Dedman found a car he liked. He had squatted to switch out the license plates when headlights lit him up. He dropped the license plate back into his backpack and stood up. The source of the headlights, a dark green Fiat Panda parked up in the space next to the car Dedman had intended to steal. He continued to stand at the back of the car, pretending he was about to open the trunk. An attractive young brunette with shoulder length hair got out of the Fiat. She looked at him, smiled, and gave a small wave.

"Yassou," she said in accented Greek.

Smiling, Dedman nodded. "Hello." Then he went back to pretending he was messing with the trunk of the car, but while watching the young woman as she walked away. She entered the fast-food restaurant attached to the petrol station. Dedman glanced at the back of the Fiat and saw it had an Albanian license plate. Quickly, a new plan formed in his head. Maybe he wouldn't need to steal a car after all.

After taking two thousand euros from his backpack, he folded the money and stuffed it into his pocket. Then, after zipping the backpack, he hefted it and walked toward the restaurant. Through the glass, he watched the brunette order at the counter, pay, and then carry a plastic tray to a table and sit down. Dedman entered the restaurant and went to the counter. He ordered a chicken gyro and coffee. After paying, he picked up his tray and walked to the table the brunette sat at. She looked up at him.

"Hello again," Dedman said with a friendly smile.

"Uh… hey," the woman said in accented English.

"Would you mind if I sat with you? I hate eating alone."

"I was only being polite before. I wasn't trying to pick you up."

"Oh, I know. I didn't think that at all. I would just enjoy talking with someone while I'm eating. But if you're uncomfortable with it, no problem. I'll get another table."

Dedman turned away.

"No, wait. It's okay. Please sit. I can practice my English."

"Thank you," Dedman said, putting his tray down and sitting across from the woman. "I'm Jake."

"Drita."

"Hello Drita. Pleased to meet you. Lovely name. Albanian isn't it."

"Yes, I'm from Tirana. American, right?"

"Yep, I am."

They both ate a few bites of their food.

"Are you on holiday here in Greece, Jake?"

"Not really. I had some business here."

"Then back to America?"

"No, I live in Germany at the moment, actually. I have a job in Berlin."

"How exciting. What do you do?"

"I'm in waste management."

"I see."

"How about you?"

"What?"

"Are you here on holiday?"

Oh. I was just visiting friends in Athens for a few days and I'm on the way back home."

"To Tirana?"

"Yes."

"Mind if I ask you something, Drita?"

"I suppose not, although if it's too personal, I may not answer," Drita said with a grin.

"Oh, nothing like that."

"In that case, yes. Ask your question."

"By coincidence, I'm going to Tirana as well. Well, near there. The rental my company got me is out there in the car park and won't start. Any chance I could get a ride to Tirana with you? I'm happy to pay."

"I don't think so," Drita said, her smile wilting. "We don't know each other. I'm sure you understand my position."

"Oh, sure, I get it. You're an attractive woman traveling alone. I know you must be careful of strangers. But I could really use the ride and I'm willing to pay you two thousand euros."

"Two thousand euros? Is this some sort of scam? You could fly to Tirana for about three hundred, or take the bus for less than one hundred."

"No scam," Dedman said, pulling the two thousand euros out of his pocket and putting the money on the table in front of the woman. He smiled again. "Simple. You drive and I pay. I won't be any trouble at all. And by the time we got to Tirana, I'm sure we would be great friends."

Drita picked up the folded stack of euros and counted the money.

"Wow! Two thousand euros."

"So, how about that ride?"

Drita looked at the money in her hand and then back at Dedman with a wistful smile.

"Two thousand euros is a lot, but... I don't think so. I don't know you, Jake. I'm sorry."

"No problem. I have trust issues too. I'll find another ride. Can I have my money back?"

Drita looked at the money in her hand again.

"You must admit, it's weird. You're offering to pay almost seven times the cost of a plane ticket for a long car ride."

"Sure, I understand," Dedman said, holding out his hand for the money.

"Are you in some kind of trouble?"

Dedman smiled brightly. "Nope. No trouble. I'm just trying to solve a problem. Trying to find a ride to Tirana. You seemed like a nice person who I might enjoy talking with on the way and thought I'd ask. But it isn't a problem. I'll just take my money back and find another ride."

Drita stared at the money again, glanced at Dedman, and then picked up her small purse. She opened the flap and put the money inside."

"Do you have identification, Jake?"

"Yes, a passport."

Drita held out her hand.

Dedman took his passport out of his backpack and handed it over.

"Jacob Dedman?"

"Yep, that's me. But everyone calls me Jake."

Drita nodded. She picked up her phone and snapped a photo of the passport identification information page before handing it back. "Okay, Jake, we have a deal. I'll give you a ride to Tirana."

"I'd appreciate it."

"Just don't get any ideas. I'm not looking for romance. Nothing like that. I'm only offering a ride."

"That's all I'm looking for, Drita."

They finished their food without speaking further and then left the restaurant together. They got in the Fiat and a minute later were back on the Olympia Odos A8, heading for the border of Greece with Albania.

Chapter 10

Berlin Safe House

Kara Jansen, Operation Hydra Berlin safe house field operative, sat at her desk looking out the window at Wilmersdorfer Straße in the Charlottenburg-Wilmersdorf District of the Berlin western city centre. The safe house occupied the top floor above a travel agency in an older, nondescript, two-story building. It could not have appeared more innocuous. The only signage out front belonged to the travel agency, a legitimate business, leading passersby to assume the travel concern occupied the entire building. The first-floor entrance to the safe house was a door opening off the alley behind the building.

Besides her role as caretaker of the safe house, Kara Jansen also coordinated logistical operations, monitored the mental health of the Hydra European operatives, shuttled them one by one back to the United States to a private clinic in Virginia when their semi-annual medical evaluations came due, and a few other things. At least she used to until things got weird.

When Kara first began her current posting in Berlin, the program had nine operatives, called assets. During her first two years, the number had declined to five. No one at Langley had ever told her what had happened to the other four. But she had worked for the Central Intelligence Agency long enough that she could make a pretty good guess. All she knew about the assets was they frequently performed missions assigned by her boss, Gerald Wright. Kara knew little about the missions. She accepted that information was above her clearance level and everything in the agency was always on a need-to-know basis, regardless of what a person's clearance level was.

One of Kara's key responsibilities was keeping track of the assets, knowing their locations anywhere in the world. She did this by tracking them electronically. Unfortunately, science and industry hadn't quite managed to design and produce a workable implantable beacon like those often imagined by fiction writers who wrote spy novels. Miniaturization technology wasn't that advanced yet. But each asset had an electronic tether that allowed Kara to keep track of them.

The tether or leash was a beacon chip inside the phones issued to the assets by the agency and which the agency mandated they keep charged and on their person, or within reach at all times. Kara didn't know what the exact consequences for violations of the agency directive were. But she knew failing to acknowledge an official communication immediately, much less missing one, was an unpardonable sin for the assets that would bring swift, dire repercussions.

The tracking devices installed inside the phones, along with the software on her computer and the corresponding app on her phone, allowed Kara to pull up a world map at any time of the day or night. On the map she would see small icons with a numeral inside that marked the location of every asset, or more specifically, the location of the asset's phone. As long as the phones had power, whether switched on or off or even if in airplane mode, the beacons were active and the icons were present.

Protocol required Kara to report it immediately to her contact at Langley if an asset's icon disappeared. She had done that four times during her first thirteen months in Berlin. Knowing each asset had been engaged in a mission when the icons went dark, Kara suspected that each time it had happened, a flesh and blood operative had also ceased to exist.

Kara hadn't had to contact Langley about a missing icon for over eleven months. That was until two days ago. First, four of the icons disappeared on the same day within minutes of each other. Only a single icon had remained, the one belonging to Hydra-6, the Berlin asset. That's when things really got weird.

When she had reported to Langley, she had expected to detect something at least akin to anxiousness in the voice of her contact, but he had seemed devoid of any emotion. It had seemed as if he had almost expected the report or had already known about the missing assets. That was a far different response from what she had gotten before when reporting the disappearance of single icons. This time, when reporting four had disappeared almost simultaneously, she had expected a much stronger response and none had come. In a disinterested tone, the contact had simply said they would look into it.

A day later, the last icon, which had been hovering over Istanbul, Turkey, also went dark. Again, when she reported it to Langley, the response from her contact had been underwhelming. And what had Berlin been doing in Istanbul, anyway? That wasn't his area of operation. Langley hadn't tasked Kara to provide the Berlin asset any logistical support if the asset had received a job in Istanbul, and that too was strange. The disappearance of all the five remaining assets was weird enough, but there had been other strange occurrences.

Kara stayed abreast of the news back home and routinely she visited the CNN, U.S. version, website. She was aware of the senate hearings that had convened after an NSA contract computer nerd had leaked a lot of highly classified information to the news media. She had been drinking coffee when she watched a clip of the first day of the hearings and had spit coffee all over her desk and computer keyboard when the chairman of the committee had asked CIA Director Cooper about Operation Hydra. The security classification, even on the program name, was far higher than top secret. And then the next day she saw something even more troubling on the CNN website.

It was a news report about a massive explosion at a private genetic engineering research facility in Manassas, Virginia, which, according to the report, had killed all twenty-nine of the facility's staff members. Kara knew little about what went on at the clinic, but she knew very well that she received an email from that facility whenever a semi-annual medical evaluation came due for an asset. Clearly, that facility had a connection to the CIA and to Operation Hydra.

Kara was a technical operative, not an intelligence officer, but her time with the CIA had honed her intuitive nature and she couldn't help feeling all the weirdness connected somehow. The senate hearings, which could have sweeping effects for the entire intelligence community, the disappearance of all five remaining Hydra assets in less than two days' time, and the explosion in Manassas. She didn't know enough to understand what was happening exactly, but the recent events had unsettled her.

Deep in thought, Kara flinched when the phone rang. It was the dedicated line she used to communicate with her contact in Langley. She punched a button on the phone and picked up the receiver.

"Hello?"

"Who is this?"

Kara recognized the voice. "This is Kara Jansen."

"Code in," the caller said.

"Romeo, x-ray, seven, tango, four, echo."

"Authenticated. Hold one."

Another male voice came on the line. "Kara, this is Gerald Wright."

"Code in, please," Kara said.

"Alpha, uniform, seven, whiskey, kilo, niner."

"Authenticated."

"Kara, have you heard from Dedman?"

"No, sir."

"No reason you should have. Just wanted to make sure."

"All I know is what his locator showed before it went dark."

"Okay, listen. I'll arrive in Berlin tomorrow from Athens and will stop by your location. Tomorrow, I want you to shut it all down and pack everything. So, wear casual clothing. You know the drill. Arrange for a commercial mover and ship everything to the storage facility."

"I'll try to get a mover set up, but might not get one on such short notice."

"Do the best you can. You can knock off for today. Then get started bright and early tomorrow morning."

"Yes, sir."

"I will see you tomorrow, probably by 1300 hours."

"Yes, sir."

The line went dead and Kara replaced the receiver. She had hoped the agency would send replacement assets, but evidently, her job in Berlin had ended. Kara wondered if that meant she was going back to Langley for reassignment. She felt disappointment at the thought because she enjoyed living in Berlin.

Chapter 11

Athens CIA Station

Wright had already learned that Dedman had escaped custody and disappeared before the plane landed in Athens. But with the asset's passport flagged, Wright knew air travel wasn't an option for him. So instead of refueling and flying to Berlin immediately, Wright decided to overnight in Athens and fly to Berlin the following day.

He still felt confident Dedman would return to Berlin. The man had been on a mission and it seemed certain Dedman would have to return to Berlin to get the resources he needed before dropping off the grid. Cash, if nothing else. All Dedman would have had was the money advanced to him for expenses while he was executing the Istanbul job.

Wright had called back to Langley and ordered a six-person team of targeting officers and analysts to Berlin to find and fix Dedman when he arrived in Berlin, so a team could terminate him. Grossman had also been on the phone with Langley since they had landed coordinating with the operation center team to locate Dedman. Grossman hung up the phone and looked at Wright.

"They got something," Grossman said, working at a computer terminal.

"What?"

"The police in Greece found the stolen agency car abandoned at a petrol station outside Athens on the Olympia Odos A8. We got the name of the company who monitors the security cameras there. An analyst hacked their system and found some recordings."

Grossman opened the video Langley had just sent him. He and Wright gazed at the screen.

"What are we looking at?" Wright said.

"This first one is a view from a camera inside a fast-food restaurant at one end of the petrol station pointed towards the front doors."

A couple, a man and a woman, crossed in front of the cameras on their way to the exit. It was an oblique shot, but Wright knew what he was looking at.

"Jesus Christ, it's him. It's really him. Even with from just a profile, I'm sure that's Dedman. But who the hell is that with him?"

"They're still working on it, but we don't know yet. Here is the other video."

This time, as they watched, a small green car drove into view.

"This is from another camera at the front of the petrol station."

As the car entered the frame, a man in the passenger seat turned his head and looked toward the station. Wright smiled.

"That's a confirmed identification. That's Jacob Dedman in that car."

They watched as the car drove across the parking lot near the pumps. The turn indicator flashed, and the car turned right out of the lot onto the service road in front of the petrol station and disappeared.

"Back up. Can you read the plate?"

Grossman rewound the video and stopped it. Then he enlarged the image. Thanks to the light above the license plate, the plate number was easily readable.

"Langley already has this. It's an Albanian registration and they are trying to run it down now."

"Albania. What the hell is he going to Albania for?"

Grossman rubbed his chin while looking at the still image, then offered his opinion.

"He could just be getting out of Greece to look for a place to lie low where the local authorities aren't looking for him until he thinks the heat is off. But my best guess is if he makes it into Albania, he will head for the coast and try to get a boat to Italy. Public transportation in Albania sucks. No trains or buses he can catch direct to Germany. Just micro buses mostly.

He would have to keep changing buses and it would take him a week just to get out of Albania to somewhere with some decent infrastructure. It's a popular choice for migrants who want to get into Europe to claim asylum. And he's on a favored smuggling route. The migrants get into Turkey, cross into Greece and then find a smuggler to get them into Albania. There they connect with another smuggler to take them to the coast and across to Italy by boat. Once they are there, it solves most of their problems with the lack of proper travel documents. In Italy, they are in an ECC country and stand a much better chance of making it to their destination of choice. And even if they get caught, they can just claim asylum."

"So, he found some woman who is going to drive him to Albania? How the hell does he know anyone in Albania? He's never worked there."

"Maybe he just picked her up at the petrol station if she was a local passing through. Or maybe he already knew her, called, and she came and picked him up."

"I want to know everything there is to know about that woman."

"They're working on it back at Langley. We should have a name as soon as they get into the Albanian automobile registration system. We're here for the night. I'm confident they will get the information for us before we leave tomorrow."

"Good work, Andy. I think you're right about the boat and Italy. But we need to identify the woman before we send a team to intercept. One entire border of the country is on the water. No way we can cover the entire coastline. We need to know where she lives to narrow it down."

"They're working on it, boss."

"Well, tell them to work faster. Tell them to find another gear."

Chapter 12

Northern Greece

Drita looked over at her sleeping passenger, his head pressed against the window, thinking she had probably never done something so foolish. She had allowed a complete stranger in the car and agreed to drive him to Tirana. Yes, she needed the money he had paid her. And she admitted she found him attractive. But she was taking an enormous risk. Somehow, sitting so close within the confines of the compact car, he suddenly looked intimidating.

Jake was fit and had a military style haircut. Perhaps he was in the American military. He had the look of a soldier. Her passenger even reminded her of Aleksei, a Russian guy she had a brief fling with during a beach holiday in Ksamil. After they had slept together the first time, she learned he was a soldier on a seventy-two-hour R&R pass with a few colleagues before they returned to Russia from a tour in Syria.

What she knew for sure was Jake was no waste management executive. Why had he lied? What else had he lied about? Was he a criminal fugitive? The smart thing would be to stop before the border and tell him to get out of the car. But then, she would feel obligated to return his money. And she was broke and needed the money. She had spent her meager savings on the trip to Athens for petrol, food, and a night in a cheap hotel.

Perhaps she could not condemn Jake for lying. She had lied also when she told him she had been in Athens visiting friends. She had gone to Athens to audition as a backup vocalist for a mildly successful pop band. Drita thought she had performed well. But the band manager had not offered her the job. He said he would be in touch when he decided. Drita wasn't hopeful she would ever hear from him. He had not seemed impressed by her talent. It was only a stupid dream. She wanted to leave Albania permanently, for somewhere she could have a real future. A future as a famous singer and money to live a decent life. Maybe she had some raw talent, but she had received no musical training. Who was she kidding?

Jacob Dedman woke up, but he didn't move or open his eyes. They hadn't stopped since leaving the petrol station. Cracking one eye open, he glanced down at his watch and saw he had slept for almost three hours. It was the first sleep he'd had since Turkey. They couldn't be more than an hour from the Kakavia border crossing and he needed a plan. He couldn't just flash his useless passport and ride across the border with Drita. Thanks to the dust up at the airport, he knew he had more problems than a flagged passport. The Greek police at every border crossing would have his name and description.

He would have to come clean with Drita and hope he could persuade her to cross the border alone and then wait on the Albanian side for him while he found another way to cross and then rejoin her. He could make something up, lie to her again. But even though truth telling wasn't exactly a healthy option in his profession, he was leaning toward telling Drita the truth. At least as much of it as he could.

He knew he would probably lose his ride if he did that. But he didn't want to straight up lie to her again. No matter what she said afterward, after crossing the border alone, she could just keep driving. She already had his money. But if he waited until they were close to the border, at least he had a chance to cross over and could come up with another plan for transportation the rest of the way to Durrës. There, he hoped to pay someone for passage across the Adriatic to Italy.

Drita could tell when a man found her attractive. When Jake had asked her to give him a ride, she had been sure he was only angling for a chance to get in her pants. That's why she felt so foolish for agreeing to give him the ride. But he had tried nothing. Before falling asleep, he had been a perfect gentleman. No, she didn't think he was a bad man who might harm her and probably no criminal. But she felt certain he was in some sort of trouble with the authorities in Greece. There seemed no other reason someone would pay two thousand euros for a ride to Albania when he could have flown for far less. Jake lifted his head, stretched, and then he glanced at her and smiled.

"Good morning. I guess I drifted off. I can't believe I slept."

"Good morning, even though it is now the middle of the night. You seemed tired. Did you sleep well?"

"Yes, I feel fresh as a daisy now," Dedman said with a chuckle. "How about you? Are you tired? I could drive for a while if you want."

"No, I'm okay."

"If you change your mind, just tell me."

"Okay… you're from Berlin, huh?"

"Yes, I live there now."

"Do you have someone waiting for you there?"

"Well, I have my colleagues at work."

"No, I meant a wife, kids, a girlfriend."

"Oh… nope. No wife, no girlfriend. No kids. At least none I know of." Dedman chuckled again.

Drita looked over and grinned. "You're not gay?"

Dedman flashed a grin of his own. "Nope. Absolutely not. Not gay."

"You ever think maybe you will want a family?"

"I've thought about it. I don't know."

Neither spoke again for several minutes. Then, suddenly, Drita looked at Dedman again and said, "Who pays two thousand euros for a ride to Tirana? That's just crazy. I think you are in some sort of trouble. And I don't believe for one minute you are some Berlin executive in waste management. And I doubt you drive the truck that collects the rubbish bins. You look to me like a soldier, perhaps."

"Know a lot of soldiers, do you?"

"I knew one, and you remind me of him. You're quite fit and you have the haircut."

Dedman laughed. "Well, I was a soldier once, but not anymore."

"I see. So, what are you now? I mean, really. No more lies."

"I don't want to lie to you anymore, Drita. For your own good, I can't tell you everything. But I'll tell you as much of the truth as I can if you really want to hear it."

"Yes, I want to hear it."

"Okay. I can't tell you anything about my work, but the people I work for flagged my passport. When I was returning to Berlin from a job, the national police at the airport in Athens detained me because of the flag. I didn't want the people I work for to pick me up at the airport until I can find out why they have done a couple of things to make my life difficult. So, I assaulted a national police officer at the airport while escaping from custody. That's why I can't take a plane and needed an alternative means of transportation."

Drita looked at Dedman wide eyed. "You're talking about your government, right? I mean, who else could flag a passport and have you detained?"

"I can't talk about it, Drita. For your own good. It could put you in danger, which is the last thing I'd want."

"Okay, but it sounds like your passport is no good. How do you expect to get across the border into Albania? The national police will arrest you if you show them your passport, right? It's no good and probably they will arrest you anyway for what you say happened at the airport."

"Yep, that is about the size of it. And, no, I have no plans to try to just ride across the border with you."

"Why are you going to Tirana?"

"Actually, I want to go to Durrës. I planned to ask you to let me out before Tirana."

"Why Durrës?"

"I need to find passage across the Adriatic to Italy, and then maybe I'll get back to Berlin."

Drita slowed, pulled to the shoulder, and stopped the car. She switched on the dome light and looked at Dedman.

"I guess this is where I get out?"

"Not yet. Tell me, Jake, are you a criminal? Please don't lie to me."

56

"Technically, yes. I assaulted a national police officer and escaped custody. But otherwise, no, I'm not a criminal. Circumstances forced me to do something I wasn't happy about doing because I had to escape. Not to be dramatic, but I think the people I work for want to kill me and I don't know why because I've done nothing wrong."

Drita stared a moment longer at her passenger, then she switched off the dome light and sat back in her seat, staring straight ahead. She took several deep breaths before speaking.

"That is one insane story, but I admit, I think you told me the truth just now."

"I lied before, but I'm not lying now. I swear what I've told you is the truth. As much of the truth as I can tell you without getting you involved and putting you in danger."

Drita said nothing for several minutes.

"Look, if you want me to get out, I understand," Dedman said. "I'm not your problem."

"If you get out, I will feel obligated to return your money. Honestly, I need the money. I spent all the money I had, which wasn't much, on my trip to Athens. I'm broke."

"It's okay. You can keep the money. But if you could see your way clear to do it, I'd appreciate it if you could get me a little closer to the border before you ask me to get out."

"I don't need your trouble, Jake. I have more than enough troubles of my own."

"Sure. I understand. No problem."

Dedman reached for the door handle and opened the passenger door. The dome light came on. He put his right foot out and grabbed his backpack from the foot well. Looking at Drita, he said, "It was nice meeting you, Drita. Thank you for the ride and drive safely."

As he moved to get out, Drita grabbed his arm. "No, don't get out. Close the door so we can get going."

"You sure?"

"Yes, sit down and close the door, please."

Dedman dropped his backpack, pulled his foot back inside the car, and closed the door.

"Migrant smuggling is a big thing now, here in northern Greece and in Albania. I don't approve of it, but I know people who smuggle migrants for money. I can't blame them, really. People are poor and there is not so much work in Albania. People get desperate and sometimes good people do bad things to survive."

"Yep, it's the same all over."

"Since I know some people involved in people smuggling, I sometimes hear things."

"What things?"

"About twenty kilometers ahead, there is a road off this motorway that goes east and then turns north again. It leads to a border crossing that they don't man at night, although there may be a locked gate. I've heard the migrant smugglers use the crossing. If we can cross there, we could then return to the motorway on the Albanian side."

"Great. Let's do it."

"Okay. I hope I don't regret this," Drita said. Then she laughed, put the car in gear, and pulled back onto the motorway.

Chapter 13

Athens

Wright was inside his hotel room, had showered, and was about to retire for the night when his phone rang. He picked it up from the bedside table and answered.

"Wright."

"Boss, we got the car registration information," Grossman said. "But it's no help. The name on the car registration isn't a female name. The registration says it belongs to some guy named Besnik Tafa with an address in Tirana."

"Damn, she must have borrowed it from someone."

"The only option I see is contacting the owner to get the name of the individual driving around in his green Fiat Panda. How do you want to handle it?"

"Let's do this first instead of scrambling a team to send to Tirana. Let's try the locals first. Call the duty officer at the Tirana station. Tell them to give the local cops some story and get them to contact the vehicle owner. Tell them we need the woman's name, her address if he has it, and when he expects to get his car back."

"On it."

"We hear anything back from the Air Force yet?"

"Not yet. The request is still making its way through the channels."

"Okay, after you coordinate with the Tirana station, get some sleep. I want to make an early start in the morning."

"Yes, sir."

Wright ended the call, shut off the lights, and climbed into bed.

* * *

Greek-Albanian Border

Drita and Dedman had exited the motorway and followed a secondary road east that had alternated between gravel and poorly maintained asphalt for almost sixteen kilometers until the road curved northward. After the turn north, thick forests bounded the road on both sides. At just after four o'clock in the morning, they arrived at the Greece side of the border and the obstacle. They found no border check point, no police, and no locked gate. Instead of a crossing, they found a fence stretching across the road as far as the eye could see until disappearing into the darkness in both directions.

When Drita and Dedman got out of the car to examine the fence by the headlights of the Fiat, they saw a crumbling concrete foundation where a structure had once stood beside the road and steel posts sunk into the ground on either side of the road which Dedman assumed had once supported a crossing gate of some kind.

"Guess things have changed since you heard of this place," Dedman said, examining the twelve-foot fence. He estimated how much work it would require to force an opening through it.

"Yes, I heard there was only a gate here the authorities locked overnight."

"I guess the Greek government erected the fence to slow down the migrants and dismantled the crossing altogether."

"What now?"

"It could be much worse," Dedman said. "The fencing the Greek government is erecting on the border with Turkey to stop the refugees and asylum seekers is far more robust. Here it's only stacked concertina wire. You have any tools in the car?"

"I don't know," Drita said, glancing back at the Fiat. "This isn't even my car. I borrowed it from a friend for my trip to Athens."

"Pop the trunk and let's see. Otherwise, we will have to wait until daylight and drive to the closest town with a hardware store. Then we'll have to find a place to hang out until it gets dark again before we can come back here."

Drita walked back to the car, leaned in through the open door, and lifted the trunk release lever. Dedman walked to the back of the Fiat and opened the trunk, causing a bright interior light to come on. He spied a black, hard plastic tool box. Dedman pulled it closer, flipped the latch, and opened the box. He smiled when he saw a pair of heavy-duty wire cutters with red, rubberized grips. He grabbed the wire cutters and a small flashlight from the tool box. Noticing a multi-tool, he grabbed it too and shoved it inside his pocket.

"This will take a while," Dedman said to Drita as he passed her on the way back to the fence. "Turn off the car and try to get some sleep. I'll wake you when I've finished."

"Okay," Drita said. She got in the Fiat, killed the engine, and then switched off the headlights, plunging the area back into darkness.

At the fence, Dedman switched on the small headlight and held it clamped between his teeth while he went to work with the wire cutters. He had chosen a section off the roadway where the two steel posts were far enough apart to allow the Fiat to squeeze through. He knew he only needed to start at ground level and then cut the first eight or nine rolls of concertina to accommodate the height of the compact economy car.

It took about an hour for Dedman to cut and pull the wire aside to form an opening the car could pass through. Since he had no gloves, he had accumulated many nicks and minor cuts from the razor-sharp barbs on the wire and knew he would have blisters from working the cutters to sever the thick, stubborn steel wire. Once satisfied he had created a large enough gap for the car to pass through, he returned to the car and found Drita sleeping soundly, slumped behind the steering wheel. With a gentle shake of her shoulder, he woke her. Drita sat up and rubbed her eyes.

"All done?"

"Yes, I think I cut a large enough opening." He pointed the beam of the small flashlight to show her where he had cut the wires. "I will walk over to the other side and direct you while you drive through so you don't scrape the side of the car on a post or the wire."

"Okay."

Drita started the Fiat and Dedman walked through the fence and positioned himself in the center of the gap about ten feet from the fence on the Albanian side, illuminated by the car headlights. She eased ahead, steering right or left as Dedman directed her with his hands. She passed through the fence without scraping the posts to either side, although Dedman heard the wire scraping a little along the top of the car as Drita drove through the gap. When she pulled to a stop on the Albanian side, Dedman got in after taking the wire cutters out of his hip pocket. He stowed the cutters and the flashlight in the glove box and Drita drove north.

After less than a kilometer, the headlights illuminated a large white building to the left of the roadway.

"That must be the Albanian border check point," Dedman said.

"What should we do?"

"It looks abandoned. There are no lights."

"Perhaps they closed it when the Greeks erected the fence."

"Probably so. No need for a border check point on a road with no traffic."

Drita had slowed while approaching the check point but didn't stop and soon they passed by the building which showed no signs of occupancy. Sheets of wood covered the door at the center of the building and the windows facing the road.

"Well, that was easy," Dedman said as they left the abandoned check point behind.

"Yes, simple."

"Do you know this road?"

"Not well. But I believe it continues northwest for a while, passing through several small towns, and then bends back to the southwest before intersecting with the motorway running north from the Kakavia border crossing we avoided."

"Okay, cool."

"I'm so sleepy now," Drita said. "I think it was a mistake to nap back there.

It only made me more tired."

"Pull over. I can drive for a while and you can sleep."

"Yes, thanks. I'm afraid I'll fall asleep at the wheel."

Chapter 14

Southern Albania

Drita pulled onto the shoulder and stopped. Dedman got out, and they switched seats. Then he put the car in gear and drove back onto the road and continued following it northwest. In minutes, he could tell from the rhythm of her breathing that Drita had fallen asleep. He drove on through the night.

They passed through three small towns and then, as Drita had predicted, the road bent southward. They left the forests and Dedman saw the first hints of dawn. Once they passed through another village, about thirty minutes later, they entered another. The sky grew lighter, but it was not yet daylight when they passed out of that town. On the right, Dedman noticed a white car with no lights parked on the shoulder. As he passed by it, the headlights came on. The car pulled onto the roadway and then followed at speed.

Damn, a cop. Dedman checked the speedometer and saw he was not exceeding the posted speed limit. He had been careful about that. *What is up with this cop?* The car was rapidly overtaking the Fiat. Dedman reached over and shook Drita awake.

"What is it?"

"We're about to get pulled over by a cop. And no, I wasn't speeding."

Drita, immediately wide awake, glanced over her shoulder at the approaching headlights in alarm.

"Policia Rrugore, the road police, needs no excuse to stop you for a chat.

They probably assume we are up to no good driving at this hour and want to know why we're on the road."

"Well, that is going to suck for them. Listen, Drita, I can't risk interacting with law enforcement right now."

"What do you mean?"

The white sedan had overtaken them, and if they had any remaining doubts about it being a police vehicle, the bright blue flashing lights that came on settled it.

"I mean, I'm about to do something you probably won't enjoy watching," Dedman said, as he slowed the Fiat, pulled to the shoulder, and stopped.

"What are you going to do?" Drita asked, her voice betraying that she was even more alarmed.

Dedman didn't respond. Instead, he put his hand on the door handle and unlatched it. Two minutes later, he watched in the side mirror as a male dressed in tall black boots, a blue uniform, a yellow-green traffic high-vis safety vest, and ball cap approached. Checking the other mirrors, it relieved him to see the cop was alone. Dedman unbuckled his seat belt.

The cop stopped at the window which Dedman had already lowered and said something in Albanian. Dedman smiled up at the officer and shrugged his shoulders.

"Sorry, dude, I didn't catch that. Do you speak English?"

The cop said something else, but not in English.

"He asked for your identification," Drita said helpfully. "Your license."

The cop seemed pleased someone in the Fiat understood Albanian and waited patiently.

"Sure thing, dude, one second," Dedman said, raising his hips slightly and pretending to reach for his wallet.

Instead of getting his wallet, in a flash, he turned his body toward the door, put both hands on the closed, but unlatched door, and pushing off with his lower body, slammed the door open into the officer, putting all his weight behind it. The cop flew backwards, falling.

Springing out of the car, Dedman landed atop the surprised officer at almost the same instant the cop hit the roadway on his back. His fists were a blur. A quick right cross, left hook combo put the cop to sleep. Dedman felt along the officer's belt until he found the handcuffs. Then he rolled the man onto his stomach and handcuffed his wrists behind his back. He yanked the semi-automatic from the cop's holster and threw it across the road into the weeds.

"You killed a police officer!" Drita shrieked.

Dedman looked up to see Drita had got out of the car and was standing over him.

"I didn't kill him. I don't kill innocent cops. He's just sleeping. He'll be fine when he wakes up. More or less."

Getting to his feet, Dedman grabbed two handfuls of the traffic vest and dragged the unconscious police officer back to his car. After opening the rear door, he lifted the man into the backseat. Then he jogged to the other side, opened the rear passenger door, and pulled the officer the rest of the way inside, turning him onto his side with his back against the seat back. He reached in, folded the cop's legs, and pulled the door at his feet closed. Then Dedman crawled out and closed the rear passenger door.

Jogging around the front of the police vehicle, Dedman got behind the steering wheel. He found the switch and killed the overhead lights. Then he put the car in gear and eased it further off the shoulder and down the embankment, into a shallow depression running beside the road. He continued easing the car forward until it was behind some thick, overgrown bushes and concealed from view of anyone passing by on the road. He switched off the engine and pulled the keys from the ignition. Then he ripped the microphone cord out of the police radio, got out, and closed the door. Dedman tossed the microphone and then the car keys further into the weeds and then jogged up the incline to the Fiat. Drita was leaning against the car with her arms crossed over her chest, shaking.

"Who are you? I can't believe you just assaulted a police officer like that!"

"Listen, Drita, it's okay. You can wait here for the police. But I have to go. I'm sorry, but I need the car for a while longer. You wait here. When they call on the radio to check his welfare and he doesn't answer, they will send more cops here. Tell them I kidnapped you in Greece and forced you to drive me across the border. Tell them I knocked out their buddy, put you out of the car, and drove off in it. Stick to the story and you won't get into any trouble. You will be fine."

Drita kept her arms folded tightly over her chest, shaking. Dedman thought she might be in shock.

"I can get away, but I have to go. I have to go now!"

Drita said nothing, but she dropped her arms at her side, turned and walked around the back of the Fiat. She got in the passenger seat and shut the door.

Shit! He got behind the wheel and started the car. "Last chance, Drita. You should wait here for the cops."

Drita said nothing.

"Look, I can get us out of here, but we have to go right now."

Drita fastened her seat belt and stared straight ahead.

"Okay, then," Dedman said, putting the car in gear and mashing the accelerator. With spinning tires, the Fiat fishtailed out onto the roadway and they were gone.

Chapter 15

Wright and Grossman were back in the air on the Gulfstream bound for Berlin working their phones. Grossman was on the line with the operations center back in Langley and Wright was on the phone with Air Force Lieutenant Colonel Bradley Richards, commander of the 317th Reconnaissance Squadron RPV/RPA at Aviano Air Base in northern Italy. The commander confirmed the Air Force had approved the CIA support request and a MQ-9 Reaper had already taken off that would be in Albanian airspace in less than thirty minutes. Richards wanted the specific mission requirements.

"As stated in the UAV support request, colonel, we're after a foreign actor who escaped from us in Greece and we believe is driving north into Albania on the SH97 motorway in a dark green Fiat Panda." Wright looked down at his notes and then read off the license plate numbers. "We don't have a current location and need your UAV to recon SH97 from the southern border with Greece north."

"We have a sighting," Grossman said to Wright.

"Colonel, can you hold one? We might have more information coming in for you."

Grossman continued. "Langley says an Albanian police officer stopped the Fiat outside the town of Mahala. After radioing his location and the registration and vehicle description, they lost contact with the officer. They located him injured and handcuffed in the back of his police vehicle about forty-five minutes ago. According to the officer, the Fiat was traveling west on a secondary road towards SH97."

"They must have avoided the motorway border crossing and found another way across east of it into Albania," Wright said. "Now they are going west to rejoin the motorway to continue north. Where does the secondary road intersect SH97?"

Grossman pulled up a map on his laptop. "A little north of Vagalat."

"Colonel," Wright said into the phone. "We just got an intel update. The vehicle we're looking for is probably somewhere north of the town of Vagalat on SH97. That's the new start point."

The Air Force colonel acknowledged, said someone would be in touch if they located the vehicle, and ended the call.

Before leaving the hotel in Athens, Wright had phoned a colleague in SAC back at Langley to ask if the ground branch had a team deployed anywhere in Europe. He learned there was a team coming off a mission for the Tirana station, returning to the U.S. as soon as doctors released a hospitalized team member. His contact had told him the team was still under the operational control of the Tirana chief of station.

Wright had then called the Tirana chief of station to request the loan of the ground branch team for a grab mission north of Vagalat. He had given the station chief a different phony cover story than the one he had given the Air Force. The chief agreed to provide the mission support, but had advised Wright the team had only four operational paramilitary officers. Wright assured him a four-man team was plenty for what he needed.

Wright told the man they had a rogue intelligence officer traveling north through Albania from Greece by car to meet with adversarial foreign intelligence officers somewhere near Tirana. Wright also revealed he had requested UAV support from the U.S. Air Force in Italy and when he got it, he needed the team to take down the target as soon as the UAV got on top of him. The chief of station agreed to put the ground branch team on alert to assist when needed.

"All we need now is actionable intel from the UAV and I'll call for the ground branch team I've coordinated," Wright said to Grossman. "Anything else from our people at Langley?"

"Yes, we got the woman's name, Drita Nikolli, twenty-eight-year-old

69

Albanian national. The Albanian state police contacted the vehicle owner. She lives somewhere in Tirana, but he told the cops he didn't know her address. She moves around a lot. The guy said they've been friends since university and he loaned her his car because she needed to go to Athens. He is expecting her to return the car sometime today."

"Now we're getting somewhere. I want to know everything about her. We need her passport information, identification, what she does for a living, everything. I want to know what she's going to do next before she does."

"They are working it, boss."

"I don't believe Dedman abducted her. Whoever she is, I think she is willingly providing him transportation. Regardless of how they intersected, it's obvious she consented to help him. Otherwise, when he assaulted that cop, she would have separated from him. She must know he's running."

"Maybe he just has a way with women. You know, getting them on his side."

"I think there's more to it than that," Wright said. "But we'll see when we find out more about her. And we *will* find out more about her. Stay on Langley."

* * *

Berlin

Kara Jansen drove along Wilmersdorfer Straße two blocks from the safe house thinking about what she had learned from her internet search the previous evening. She felt even less at ease than she had the afternoon before after seeing the news report about the clinic in Manassas, Virginia, getting destroyed by a natural gas explosion.

Kara had searched the archives of various European news agency websites looking for reports of unidentified males killed the day the locator beacons representing the Hydra assets in Athens, Rome, Paris, and Madrid had gone dark. And she found what she was looking for.

Authorities in all four cities had discovered male victims with no identification. Three had died in various types of accidents and one by suicide, according to the local authorities. Both the date and the times included in the media reports coincided closely with when the beacon icons disappeared from Kara's computer screen. The young woman had been with the CIA long enough that she didn't believe in coincidences of that magnitude.

The explosion at the clinic that had killed the entire staff and the four unidentified bodies convinced Kara that Wright or someone was shutting down Hydra. Someone was tying off loose ends because the senate committee was probing U.S. intelligence activities and Operation Hydra had got compromised.

Jansen had also researched Turkish media outlets for the day Berlin's locator beacon had disappeared. But she found nothing that fit. Either the Turkish authorities hadn't found his body yet or Berlin was still alive and had destroyed his phone. Whichever the case, it wasn't the welfare of the Berlin asset that concerned her. She was worried about *her* welfare.

Jansen knew a lot about Operation Hydra too, even if she didn't know the specifics about the asset's missions. If someone really was terminating everyone associated with the program, chances were she might be on the kill list.

Pulling into a parking space at the curb on a side street in the block occupied by the safe house, Kara felt deeply conflicted. Should she go into work and start shutting down the safe house and start packing up as Wright had ordered her? Or should you run while she had the chance?

Lacking confidence in her knowledge about how to run and stay off the grid, she worried if she ran and they wanted her, then they would probably catch her before she got out of Germany, let alone Europe, and back to the United States. With a sigh, she got out of the car and locked it. Then she hurried across the wet street in the early morning drizzle, heading towards the alley and the building's rear entrance.

Chapter 16

With Dedman still behind the wheel of the little Fiat, he and Drita arrived at the junction SH97. He saw a sign showing there was a village nearby. Dedman turned the car onto the motorway, but heading south instead of north. Dedman felt relief they had not encountered an Albanian state police roadblock at the junction he had half expected. He assumed they hadn't yet located their missing road police officer. Drita stared stoically straight ahead out the windshield. She hadn't spoken a word since they had left the officer and his car out of sight off the secondary road they had just left. She hadn't even seemed to notice they were going away from Tirana, not toward it. Dedman tested her mood before telling her something she probably wouldn't take well.

"You've been quiet for a while," he said. "Sorry you didn't stay behind and wait for the police?"

"It wasn't an option."

"What do you mean? I didn't force you to come with me."

"I told you. This isn't my car. It belongs to a friend and I'm responsible for it. Did you think I would just let you steal it and leave me behind?"

"I hate to break it to you, but we're getting rid of this car when we get to Vagalat and finding alternative transportation."

"What? Why?"

"Because the cop back there would have radioed the license plate numbers to his dispatcher when he stopped us. It is a standard procedure. If we keep driving it, it's only a matter of time before the police find us and stop us again."

"I have to return this car to my friend."

"Okay, then I'll get out at Vagalat and find another ride. You can turn around and continue on towards Tirana. And when you get stopped, just tell the cops what I told you to say before. Some guy kidnapped you from a petrol station outside Athens and made you drive him into Albania. You will be fine. They will let you go, eventually. You have broken no laws."

"I helped smuggle a fugitive into Albania by bypassing the border checkpoint. I think that's probably a crime."

"Just say you were under duress. They can't prove you weren't."

"I'm not sure what it's like in America, but in Albania, the police don't worry about proof. They do whatever they want."

"Look, Drita. We need to split up. I can't run with you. I can't protect you. The longer we're together, the deeper you're getting into something dangerous you don't understand. The people looking for me might just start shooting if they catch up to us and they won't worry about collateral damage."

"So... just like that, you plan to leave me all alone after I've helped you?"

"It isn't like that. I just don't want you getting hurt because of me."

"You have already involved me, okay? You want to leave the car in Vagalat? Fine. Just don't leave me all alone."

They had entered the town. Instead of continuing the conversation, Dedman began looking for a place to ditch the Fiat. He looked left and right down each side street they passed. Spotting a possibility, he slowed, made a U-turn, and headed back to the last intersection and then turned right.

In the middle of the block on the side street, he slowed and inspected the closed petrol station that had caught his eye. Someone had removed the pumps that had once stood out front and boarded up the entrance doors and front windows. There was an attached garage bay on one side of the building with a sagging, rusting, partially open overhead door. Dedman pulled the Fiat into the lot and stopped outside the garage.

Getting out, he walked up to the door, grabbed the bottom edge, and lifted. The metal rollers in the rusted door tracks squeaked and squealed in protest, but he got the door raised high enough to accommodate the small Fiat. He got back in the car, put it in gear, and rolled it slowly forward into the garage bay.

Dedman switched off the engine. "The car should be safe in here for a while. You can call your friend and tell him where to find it. He can get someone to give him a lift here from Tirana and pick up his car."

"Oh, right. That will thrill him. I'll tell him I have a new American friend who enjoys beating policemen, so we had to abandon his car to avoid arrest."

Dedman laughed. "Well, maybe work on a better story before you call him. Now, get your stuff out of the back. We can't come back to this car."

"Okay."

Dedman pulled the keys from ignition and they both got out. While Drita retrieved her small suitcase from the back of the car, Dedman hid the car keys atop the left rear tire inside the fender and then put his backpack on his back.

"What now?" Drita asked.

"We'll get something to eat and then I'll get us a room. We'll lie low until dark and get some sleep. Then I'll find us some transportation out of here."

Drita nodded, and the pair walked back towards the main road they had turned off from. A few blocks north, they found a small restaurant, went inside, and ordered breakfast. It was the first meal either had eaten since leaving the petrol station outside Athens. When Dedman asked, the server directed them to a hotel in town, the only hotel. They walked over and Dedman rented a room on the second floor of the small establishment.

They found the room small but clean and it had a private bathroom. There was a double bed, a small closet, and a table with two cheap plastic and metal chairs. Drita put her suitcase on the table and sat down on the bed. Dedman tossed his backpack on the floor of the closet. He walked over and looked inside the bathroom, noting there was a window over the tub. It was small but large enough to climb out of if they needed an alternate exit.

"It isn't the honeymoon suite exactly," Drita smirked.

"No, but we will only be here for the day. You take the bed. I'll grab a pillow and sleep here on the floor."

"Mind if I take a shower?" she asked.

"Sure, go ahead. I'll shower when you've finished."

Drita opened her suitcase, took some things out, and then went into the bathroom and closed the door. Dedman heard the shower running. He closed the curtains on the window in front and then pulled one chair to the door and jammed the back rest beneath the doorknob. Then he sat down on the other chair.

About ten minutes later, Drita came out of the bathroom wearing sweatpants and a blue T-shirt, running a comb through her wet, dark brown hair.

"All yours."

"Thanks," Dedman said, getting to his feet. The Dopp kit he had left Berlin with was back in his Istanbul hotel room unless they had thrown it out already. There were no extra clothes in his backpack or anything else he needed. He went straight into the bathroom, knowing he would wear the same clothes and underwear when he came out after showering and the same stubble on his face. One hot shower later, he exited the bathroom wearing his pants but carrying his shirt in his hand, and found Drita sitting on the edge of the bed now wearing the T-shirt and panties.

"We're both adults," she said with an impish grin. "We can share the bed."

"I'm all good with the floor," Dedman said, bending and reaching out to snag a pillow.

When the American straightened with a pillow in hand, Drita stood up in front of him, grabbed the pillow and tossed it back on the bed. Then she stepped closer and put her hands on Dedman's hips, looking up at him, her face so close to his he felt her warm breath. Neither spoke. Then, tentatively, Drita pressed her lips to his, surprising him. When he didn't respond, she pulled away for a moment, giving him a questioning look, and then leaned in and kissed him again. This time, he kissed her back, putting his arms around her. Dedman felt her fingers unfastening and unzipping his pants. Once they dropped around his ankles, she pulled away, grabbed the hem of her T-shirt and pulled it off over her head, revealing she wore no bra. He kissed her again, and she put her hands to the sides of his face, pulling him even

75

closer. They stood together, kissing and touching. Then, still intertwined, they sank down on the bed together. For now, at least, they were both safe. Whatever danger for them the evening might hold, it seemed far away.

Chapter 17

An hour out of Berlin, Wright's phone rang. He answered and after Lieutenant Colonel Bradley Richards identified himself, the Air Force officer gave Wright the news he had hoped for.

"We located the vehicle."

"Where?"

"Vagalat."

"Is it still traveling north on SH97?"

Richards had even better news. "No, it's stationary. Just as the aircraft arrived on station, the RPA pilot banked to follow the motorway north and the camera picked up the target vehicle entering Vagalat from the north. The pilot maintained a holding pattern and the sensor operator observed the vehicle enter a garage on a side street off the motorway."

"Any sign of the occupants?"

"Yes, a male and a female exited the garage. They returned on foot to the road they came in on, walked north several blocks, and entered a building. The sensor operator zoomed in and identified it as a restaurant from the external signage. Less than an hour later, they exited the restaurant, walked to the city center and entered a tan stucco two-story building we've identified as a hotel. They took an exterior stairway up and entered a room on the second floor. We're still loitering over the area and no one has exited the room."

"Excellent work, colonel. How long can you maintain surveillance on the hotel?"

"We can loiter over the target for another sixteen hours before recalling the RPA."

"We shouldn't need the UAV that much longer. I'll get a team started from Tirana to take down the target, and it shouldn't take more than a few more hours. Please call me if the situation changes. Unless I hear from you first, I'll call you as soon as the team is on site."

The Air Force officer acknowledged and then ended the call.

"We've found and fixed them," Wright said to Grossman. "Now we just have to lay hands on them."

Grossman looked at his boss expectantly, eager to hear the entire story, but Wright was already placing a call to the embassy in Tirana to coordinate an assault on the hotel in Vagalat. Once the station chief in Tirana came on the line, the man said he would get the four-man ground branch paramilitary operations officers en route to Vagalat.

The station chief told Wright he had no air assets available and the team would have to drive and it might take them four or five hours to arrive. Wright told him he believed the team would arrive in plenty of time because he felt confident the target was lying low in a hotel room, possibly until dark. Only after ending the call with the station chief did Wright bring Grossman up to speed.

"The UAV observed the car enter Vagalat and then park inside a garage, and the Air Force tracked them to a hotel near the town center. Dedman is probably using it as a bolthole until nightfall. The Tirana station chief is dispatching the ground branch team to Vagalat and we should have a bag over Dedman and the woman long before dark."

"What are the rules of engagement for the team?"

"The station chief wouldn't authorize lethal force for the team except in self-protection. Unless Dedman engages them, they have a grab mission. I'll sort that out after they get him and turn him over to us."

* * *

A half hour after Wright had hung up with the Tirana station chief, the pilot of the Gulf Stream banked over the airport, lined up with the runway, and touched down at Berlin Schönefeld Airport. The aircraft rolled to a stop on the tarmac and as Wright and Grossman descended the steps, a black U.S. government Suburban stopped near the aircraft.

Two CIA officers got out and loaded their luggage in the back of the vehicle as Wright and Grossman settled themselves in the back passenger seat. Once the two Berlin officers got in, the front seat passenger turned to Wright and asked him where he wanted to go. Wright told him to drop them at the Grand Westin Berlin so they could check in and then he and Grossman would walk to the embassy to see the chief of station. Thirty minutes later, the Suburban delivered them to the front entrance of the hotel.

* * *

While Wright and Grossman were walking to the front desk to check in to their hotel, Carter Johnson, the CIA Special Activities Division/Special Operations Group Echo Team leader and his three paramilitary operators were loading their gear in a black GM Defense Heavy-Duty Sport Utility Vehicle in Tirana.

At a glance, the vehicle looked like a commercial-off-the-shelf Suburban, but it was a purpose-built, armored vehicle to support missions requiring protected mobility. The manufacturer designed and produced the vehicle for unique U.S. government security missions with a unique body-on-frame chassis and suspension designed to support increased performance requirements, higher payload capacity and greater ground vehicle weight over commercial-grade SUVs.

After stowing their gear, Adam Jones got behind the wheel as Johnson climbed in the front passenger seat. Martin Garcia and Lincoln Rollins climbed in the back passenger seat and the vehicle rolled out of the embassy compound onto the street. At full strength, Echo Team was a six-man unit. But one of Johnson's guys was in a hospital battling a staph infection after suffering a gunshot wound during the team's previous op. The other, his assistant team leader, had returned stateside on emergency leave.

Johnson wasn't concerned about catching an op while two of his men were down. The primary tango was only some sad sack CIA field officer who had pissed someone off royally upstairs at Langley and the secondary some Albanian civilian female. Four of some of the world's most highly trained commandos was probably overkill for this simple grab mission, anyway.

Johnson glanced at his Luminox wristwatch and estimated they would hit the target area in Vagalat about three hours before nautical twilight, which would give his team plenty of time if the intel he had received on the tango was accurate. He felt confident that within an hour after the team hit Vagalat, he and his boys would have snatched the Dedman dude and the civilian Albanian chick out of their hotel room, and stuffed them into the vehicle in flex cuffs for the trip back north to Tirana.

At thirty-five, Johnson was young to be running his own ground branch team. But he had proven himself in the teams as a SEAL before leaving the U.S. Navy for the CIA, as well as during his time as a CIA paramilitary officer and assistant team leader before his promotion. He reclined his seat, pulled his black ball cap down over his sunglasses and tried to catch a little sleep during the long drive.

Chapter 18

Dedman woke up well before dusk. The room was darker now than when they had arrived, but light coming through the fabric of the closed curtains revealed the sun hadn't yet set. He turned his head, waiting for his eyes to adjust to the dim lighting and expecting to see the outline of Drita's sleeping form. But she was gone. Dedman turned his head in the opposite direction towards the bathroom. The door stood open, and it was dark inside.

"Drita?" he called out. There was no answer, and he sensed he was alone in the room. Dedman sprang out of bed and switched on the lamp beside the bed. Then, looking towards the front door, he saw the chair he had jammed beneath the doorknob was off to the side of the door.

Shit! Dedman silently chastised himself. He had intended that neither of them left the room until after dark and had planned to warn Drita against leaving the room. But after the love making it had slipped his mind. His gaze shifted to the table. Her open suitcase still lay on top, but her purse was gone. She hadn't done a runner then, but had just gone out somewhere.

Dedman found his clothes on the floor and quickly dressed. He had to go out and find his traveling companion and get her back in the hotel room.

* * *

Drita walked back to the hotel from the restaurant where they had eaten breakfast with the takeaway order. She thought they should eat something before leaving the hotel when it got dark. Since she didn't know what

Dedman had planned for the evening, she thought she should go out for food. Whoever he worked for was looking for him, not her, so she thought it safer to go alone.

As she turned the corner and walked past the building next to the hotel, she stopped dead in her tracks. Four large men wearing casual clothes and holding pistols moved stealthily toward the exterior stairway while looking up towards the door of the hotel room Dedman had rented. They looked like either law enforcement or military. Somehow, someone had found them.

When one man glanced in her direction and she knew he was looking right at her, Drita dropped the bags containing the takeaway food.

"JAKE! RUN!"

After shouting the warning, Drita wheeled to the right and ran north through the gap between the hotel and the adjacent building she had just passed. Before she made it to the alley behind the hotel, she already heard footsteps pounding after her. Drita turned left, running west down the alley behind the hotel and then, after passing the building, she veered right and ran north up an intersecting alley. She knew the footsteps behind her were getting closer.

* * *

Sitting on the bed, Dedman had just finished tying his Merrell hiking shoes when he heard Drita scream the warning. He bolted to the front window, pulled the edge of the curtain back slightly, and peered out. Two guys holding handguns and wearing civilian clothes, sunglasses, and ball caps stood at the ground floor landing of the stairway. They were looking east and one guy had a finger to the earpiece in his ear and his mouth was moving. Dedman knew the man was in comms with someone other than the guy standing right next to him and he also knew a ground branch team when he saw one.

Dedman jammed the chair back under the doorknob and relocked the deadbolt. Then he scampered into the bathroom, stepped in the tub, and opened the window with frosted glass to look for the paramilitary operators he expected were securing the back of the hotel. But what he saw was worse than he had expected. Drita ran west through the alley beneath the window and then turned and ran north up an intersecting one. Just as she disappeared from view, two guys dressed like those in the front of the hotel turned and ran north up the alley in hot pursuit.

Dedman ran to the closet and grabbed his backpack off the floor. He started back for the bathroom, but with a groan, turned and hurried over to the table. Opening the backpack, he shoved two handfuls of Drita's things into it before closing the pack. Then he ran back to the bathroom, shut the door, and locked it.

With his butt against the tile wall, he put his feet on the edge of the tub, ducked his head and used his legs to push his upper body out the window until he was sitting on the windowsill. He pulled the backpack outside and around his body and shrugged into the straps. Then he reached up, grabbed the top of the exterior window frame and pulled himself up to a standing position with his feet on the windowsill.

Taking a breath, he bent his knees and then jumped vertically and grabbed hold of the gutter at the edge of the roof. He pulled himself up and then scrambled over the gutter onto the tile roof. Just as he gained the roof, he heard splintering wood followed a couple of seconds later by the explosion of a flash-bang grenade detonating inside the hotel room he had just vacated.

Getting to his feet, Dedman sprinted west along the roof until he was just short of the alley entrance where he last saw Drita and her pursuers. He jogged to the peak of the roof and down the south side. Then he turned and sprinted back up to the peak and down the other side. Just as he reached the edge, he launched himself into the air, windmilling his arms to maintain his balance.

Dedman sailed across the narrow alley behind the hotel and then landed atop the roof of the one-story building north of the hotel. When he hit the roof, Dedman tucked into a shoulder roll, landed on his feet, and continued sprinting north along the roof. Scanning the alley to his left, when he reached the end of the roof, he again launched himself and sailed across the gap onto the roof of another one-story building. Just before he reached the edge of that roof, he skidded to a stop.

In the alley below, he saw the two guys struggling with Drita, who wasn't going quietly. She tried to scream, but it wasn't loud because she was probably out of breath from the sprint. One guy had Drita in a headlock and pressed against the cinder block wall of a building, trying to keep her from kicking him in the shins. The second operator had dropped his pack and knelt on a knee beside it, in the middle of the alley. Dedman leapt from the roof and dropped like a heat-seeking missile.

Chapter 19

Just as the kneeling operator pulled a pair of flex cuffs from the pack, Dedman crash landed on his upper back after an eight-foot drop tilting the man's upper body forward. With hands on both of his shoulders, one to either side of his neck, Dedman used his momentum to slam the operator face down onto the hard-packed dirt and there was a sickening thud when the man face planted.

Turning as he regained his feet, Dedman saw the second operator still holding onto Drita with his left hand. But he shoved her away while drawing his sidearm from his thigh holster with his right. Dedman shot out his left leg in a side kick, connecting with the man's gun hand. Without waiting to see the result, he shifted his feet, raised his right knee, pivoted, and delivered a violent round house snap kick. His right foot struck the man in the left jaw and he went down hard. Dedman bent over and scooped the SIG Sauer P320 the operator had lost his grip on after the side kick and as the man pushed up off the ground onto his hand and knees, Dedman backhanded the side of his head with the pistol. The operator collapsed on the ground and stopped moving.

After glancing left and right, looking for the other two operators, Dedman tucked the weapon into his waistband. He snatched the radio off the unconscious operator and switched it off.

"Lift the dumpster cover," he said to Drita, who was staring at him in disbelief. "Now, Drita, now!"

Finally comprehending what Dedman wanted, Drita hurried to lift the plastic cover at one end of the dumpster. It flew up and back until it struck the wall. Then she stepped back. Dedman tossed the radio into the dumpster, then he lifted the operator from the ground and tossed him in after it. He stripped the radio from the other unconscious operator, pulled the earpiece loose, turned the volume up to the max, and then threw the radio up and over the building to the west as hard as he could. He grabbed the unconscious man by the back of the collar and pulled him over to the dumpster. Then he picked him up and tipped him over the side into the dumpster on top of his partner. Dedman reached out, grabbed the side of the cover and pulled it closed.

Returning to the operator's pack out in the alley, he picked up the flex cuffs and dropped them back into the pack and then hefted it by a shoulder strap. He spun Drita around and put the pack on her back. Noticing a folding tactical knife clipped to the pack, Dedman pocketed it and then guided Drita around the side of the dumpster and pushed her into the gap between the back of the dumpster and the cinder block wall. Then he dropped to his knees and scooted backwards into the gap next to her, facing outward with the pistol in his hands.

Dedman and Drita had barely concealed themselves behind the dumpster when he heard approaching running footsteps. He knew professional special operators would stop and check behind the dumpster when searching an alley, but he bet they would run right past the hide, believing their guys were somewhere up ahead with at least one of their targets. And that's exactly what they did.

The sound of the footsteps faded quickly toward the north. Dedman squeezed out from behind the dumpster, got to his feet, and reached in to grab Drita by the arm. He pulled her out, helped her stand, and then, holding her by the upper arm, pulled her along as he broke into a jog back south.

"Where are we going?" Drita asked between labored breaths once they got back to the east-west alley behind the hotel.

"Away from here," Dedman said as he then pulled her east towards a main road in the center of the town. When they arrived at the road, they left the alley and turned back north again. Dedman slowed to a walk. They continued moving with a purpose, but not so fast that they would arouse suspicion from any passersby. Three blocks north of the hotel, Dedman spied exactly what they needed and headed for it.

Chapter 20

Six blocks north of the alley behind the hotel, Carter Johnson, call sign Echo one, called a halt. Adam Jones stopped beside his team leader, his head on a swivel.

"They should have caught that bitch by now," Johnson growled. He spoke into the microphone attached to his earpiece. "Echo one to Echo three, sitrep." When he got no response, he spoke again. "Echo one to Echo six. Do you copy?"

Jones cocked his head while his team leader kept trying to raise Garcia and Rollins, sure he had heard something in the distance. He took several steps away from Johnson and then he knew he heard something. He could hear a radio to the southwest.

"Carter, I can hear your transmissions on a radio southwest of our position."

"You sure?"

"Yeah, I'm positive."

"Let's split up. You go back south the way we came. I'll go a block west and then move parallel to you. We'll take turns broadcasting and zero in on that radio."

Jones nodded, and the two men broke into a run. Johnson transmitted, "Echo three, Echo six, sitrep." Then Jones repeated the transmission using his call sign, Echo four. Each time the other transmitted on the radio, they both knew they were getting closer. Finally, they converged on the radio lying in the dirt where it rested against a building wall.

"This isn't good," Johnson said, picking up the radio. "We have to find our guys. We'll go back to that north-south alley behind the hotel and start searching north from there."

The two operators ran south to the alley behind the hotel, turned north and then slowed to make a careful search. About three blocks north, they saw Garcia hanging half in and half out of a dumpster that Johnson recalled passing earlier. Garcia lifted his head and looked at them when he heard them running toward him. Johnson and Jones grabbed him by his arms and pulled him out of the dumpster. He immediately sank to a knee and put a hand against the dumpster to steady himself. He shook his head, still trying to clear the cobwebs from the pistol whipping he had suffered.

"Where's Rollins?" Johnson asked.

"Inside the dumpster," Garcia replied. "He's fucked up, dude. He's still unconscious."

Jones grabbed the edge of the dumpster and vaulted inside. He took his teammate under the arms and lifted him up and over the edge of the dumpster, where Johnson grabbed his arms. Jones climbed out of the dumpster and helped his team leader pull Rollins out. They laid him on his back on the ground beside the dumpster. His face was bloody and his nose was broken, but he was breathing. On his knees beside Rollins, Jones pulled a medical kit from his pack and administered first aid.

Johnson looked over at Garcia, who still looked dazed. "What the fuck happened?"

Garcia lifted his head. "We had the Albanian chick. I was controlling her and Rollins was getting flex cuffs from his pack. Then some dude came out of nowhere, like he dropped from the sky. He face-planted Rollins and before I could get my weapon up, he kicked it out of my hand. Then, while I tried to untangle myself from the woman, I think he kicked me in the head. When I tried to get up, he cold cocked me with something, maybe my own weapon. I've never seen anything like it, dude. He was fast, and he had skills. Did you guys get Dedman or was that him that jumped us?"

Johnson shook his head. "The hotel room was a dry hole. It looked like he went out the bathroom window while we were breaching the front door. It was probably Dedman you tangled with."

"Tangled with? That asshole kicked our asses in ten seconds flat and I doubt he even broke a sweat. If it was Dedman, he was no ordinary field officer. He's just like us. Maybe better than us."

Johnson felt his anger rising. Evidently, there was a lot the chief of station back in Tirana hadn't told him before sending his team after Dedman. If he had known Dedman was dangerous, he would never have split the team and allowed Garcia and Rollins to chase the squirter. Johnson intended to kick someone's ass when they got back to Tirana.

* * *

Leaving Drita concealed in a dark doorway, Dedman walked over to the blue Yamaha XSR700 parked in front of a business. He had ridden one before and knew it had neither a keyless ignition lock nor an alarm. After checking around and finding no one looking at him, Dedman put his hands on the handlebar grips, swept the kickstand up with a foot, and then walked the bike in a half circle and then straight back down the street to where he had left Drita.

After telling her to act as a lookout, Dedman took out the folding knife he had liberated from the paramilitary operator, yanked the ignition wires out and stripped them with the knife blade. After hot-wiring the motorcycle, Dedman climbed on, shifted his pack from front to back, and told Drita to climb on. He pulled the helmet off the handlebars and handed it back to her.

"Put that on. You ever ride?"

"No."

"Well, just put your arms around my waist and hang on. You go where I go, lean when I lean and you'll be fine."

Dedman rode southwest until they reached the road where they had left the Fiat at the closed down petrol station. There he turned right, opened up the throttle, and they roared west to SH8, a coastal motorway. As Dedman slowed to make the turn north, Drita asked where they were going.

Dedman shouted over his shoulder. "We've got to find the nearest port and transportation across to Italy."

"Okay, that's Vlorë," Drita shouted back over the wind and roar of the engine. "There's a ferry to Bari there." Dedman opened up the throttle again, and they sped north.

* * *

Johnson had sent Jones for the vehicle where they had parked a block west of the hotel. When he got back with it, Johnson and Jones loaded Rollins into the back. He had regained consciousness and was in a lot of pain.

Jones helped Garcia into a back seat while Johnson called in a report to Tirana. Johnson was still seething, but controlled his anger since he intended to have it out with the chief of station face to face, not on the phone. But the chief expressed such dismay and outrage of his own when Johnson told him they had suffered two casualties, both of whom needed hospital immediate care that Johnson wondered if someone had also duped the chief of station. Maybe he hadn't intentionally withheld vital intel about the target's capabilities. Maybe Johnson owed the ass kicking to someone else.

The chief of station immediately aborted the op, recalled the team to Tirana, and told Johnson to make getting his men the medical care they needed his priority. Bloodied but not broken, Echo Team headed back to Tirana. He didn't know how his team felt about it, but Carter Johnson hoped they got another shot at Dedman and next time, if there was a next time, they would be ready.

Chapter 21

Embassy of the United States Berlin

Wright and Grossman entered the embassy through the main entrance, showed their credentials, and passed through the security checks. An attractive young blonde in a business suit wearing identification on a blue lanyard around her neck stepped forward to greet them. She shook their hands and introduced herself as Heather.

"The assistant chief of station is waiting for you in the fifth-floor conference room," she said, leading the men to an elevator. They all stepped inside, and the elevator rose to the fifth floor. When they got off, Wright and Grossman followed Heather down the corridor until she stopped outside a closed door. After knocking lightly, she opened the door and nodded to the men to enter. Once they passed through the door, Heather pulled it closed behind them.

Carlton Harrison, the assistant chief of station, sat alone at the oak conference table with his back to the windows. He stood as Wright and Grossman entered. Wright and Harrison had joined the agency the same year and had attended training at The Farm together. Wright hadn't seen the man more than a dozen times since, but thought they were on friendly terms.

"Hello, Carlton, it's been a while," Wright said, extending his hand across the table. The men shook. Turning to Grossman, Wright said, "This is Andy Grossman, my assistant." Harrison and Grossman said hello and shook hands, and then Harrison invited them to sit. He sat back down, and Wright and Grossman took the two chairs across from him.

Harrison pointed to a silver coffee carafe and matching silver tray loaded with pastries on the table and invited his visitors to help themselves. Grossman got up and filled two porcelain cups with coffee, passing one to his boss before selecting a pastry. Wright looked at his assistant with annoyance, then turned to Harrison and got down to business.

"Are you able to provide the support I requested?"

Harrison took a sip of his coffee and then set the cup back on the saucer. "I spoke with the chief of station after you called me," he said. "He is curious why you aren't using a ground branch team."

"We don't want to risk an incident in Berlin. The optics would be awkward. You know how it can go when you use door kickers and shooters. This isn't that kind of situation and my boss wants to keep it low profile. This situation calls for finesse, not a team of knuckle dragging paramilitary officers with automatic weapons. I have a team of analysts arriving this afternoon, so we have that covered. We will find him. I only need a team to grab the target."

"The people we have are security officers. They are competent with firearms, but definitely not door kickers or shooters, Jerry."

"That's fine, Clark. It's a rendition, not an assassination."

Harrison nodded and sipped more coffee. "What can you tell me about the issue you're here to resolve?"

"Not much. You know that. It involves a code-worded program. All I'm at liberty to say is we've got an asset off the reservation. We sent him to Istanbul on a mission. The mission failed, and he didn't check in. We established contact with him and asked him nicely to come in, but he refused. So, we've got to go another route."

"Why is he in Berlin?"

"He isn't at the moment, but we know he is en route to Berlin. Last seen in Albania. He should arrive within the next twenty-four hours."

"Why Berlin?"

"We believe there is something here he wants to retrieve before going off the grid, and this is our best chance to apprehend him sooner rather than later."

Harrison nodded again. After draining his coffee cup, he placed it back on the saucer and then fixed his gaze on Wright. "The chief of station authorized four men to support you and for only seventy-two hours."

Wright shook his head. "He's got to be reasonable, Carlton. I need six officers, minimum, with no time restriction."

Carlton raised his hands palms up in a gesture of helplessness. "That's the offer, Jerry. We go back a long time. I'd do more if I could, but it isn't my call. The chief of station said to tell you, take it or leave it."

"What is his problem? This is a serious situation, Carlton."

"The problem isn't my boss, it's the ambassador. The man is no friend of the CIA and has the president's ear. He has already put so many restrictions on us since the unfortunate leaks and the senate hearings started, we can barely do our jobs as it is. If this situation of yours goes sideways and the German government gets wind of it, the ambassador is going to be looking for scalps."

Wright sighed. "Okay, I'll take it. Four men and seventy-two hours, beginning tomorrow morning. Hopefully, my people can run down our asset's location by then and we can make it work."

* * *

CIA Headquarters, Langley

Herman Buckley stopped outside the glass door of the office suite belonging to his superior, Chief of Special Operations Group Maxwell Newton. He dug the roll of antacids out of his pocket and popped two more tablets in his mouth. As he chewed them, he straightened his tie and wiped the sweat from his brow with a handkerchief. Then he pushed through the door and entered the outer office. Newton's secretary, Ava Simmons, looked up from her computer screen and gave him a tight smile.

"Good afternoon, Mr. Buckley."

"Hello Ava."

Simmons stood and stepped out from behind her desk. "The chief is waiting for you. I'll need your phone before you go in."

Buckley nodded. He reached inside his jacket, pulled out his cell phone, and placed it in Newton's outstretched hand.

"Thank you," she said, walking to the door of the inner office and opening it. She nodded, and Buckley walked through. The door closed behind him. Newton put down the document he had been reading on top of a stack of papers in the center of his desk. He took off his reading glasses and motioned to a chair in front of the desk.

"Have a seat, Herman."

Buckley nodded and sat down, waiting nervously to learn why his boss had summoned him. He knew the secretary had taken his phone to ensure Buckley didn't record what they discussed during the meeting. And he knew that wasn't a good sign.

Newton tapped an index finger on the pile of documents on his desk. "I've been reviewing your black budgets, Herman. Tell me about this operation you're devoting just over fifty-eight percent of your budgets to. I want to know about Hydra."

Buckley's mouth felt like it was full of cotton as he tried frantically to decide how to respond. "It's a beta program, a training project."

"A beta program—a training project," Newton repeated, not bothering to hide his disbelief. He leaned back in his chair, continuing to fix Buckley with his gaze. "How is it I've heard nothing about Hydra before, Herman?"

"Well, sir, it was only a beta program. Gerald Wright brought it to me. It looked promising at the beginning. But it hasn't been as cost effective as we had hoped. And it's all but shut down now."

"Beta infers it was never operational."

"That's correct, sir."

Newton leaned forward, placing his palms on his desk, his eyes smoldering.

"Let's cut the bullshit, Herman. As I'm sure you know, Senator Glover and his committee are raking Director Cooper over the coals. Glover asked him about Operation Hydra specifically. Since then, some of our friends on

Capitol Hill tell us that Glover believes Hydra is an off books blacker than black CIA assassination program. An assassination program that has been active for the past several years."

Buckley looked down at his hands in his lap, willing them to stop shaking but failing. Without meeting Newton's gaze, he said quietly, "Hydra is such a program. Gerald Wright went live with it without consulting me. I didn't learn about it until he had terminated a half dozen targets." Then Buckley looked at Newton. "Sir, you know how reliant they forced us to become on Reapers and Hellfire missiles to take out bad actors. And all the red tape, all the hoops we must jump through to even use that option. It isn't always an appropriate or effective option. Hydra filled the gap."

"Herman, have you taken leave of your senses? What in God's name were you thinking? And let me tell you, throwing your subordinate under the bus will not save you anymore than me throwing you under the bus would save me. If this gets out, you and Wright may have brought this entire agency down."

"I'm not throwing anyone under the bus. Wright is my subordinate and I accept my share of responsibility. My oversight wasn't as robust as it should have been, But Wright has shut down the program. He is cleaning it up and swears it will be clean."

"The director wants to know if there is even a single shred of proof the Glover Committee might unearth to prove Hydra was an active, unsanctioned assassination program."

"There shouldn't be. Not when Wright finishes cleaning it all up."

"What do you mean shouldn't be?"

Buckley took a deep breath. "Wright has pulled the plug on Hydra and terminated everyone associated with the program with enough knowledge to damage the agency. That includes all the deniable assets. He began with nine. Four died over the years during missions, leaving only five. Four of those are now deceased. But Wright's plan to put an end to the fifth asset failed. He's in Europe now to rectify that."

Newton reclined back in his chair, open-mouthed. "You're saying we have a CIA-trained industrial strength killer off the reservation and running free around Europe?"

"A deniable asset," Buckley said hastily. "No one can connect him with the agency. And Wright assures me he will resolve the situation in another twenty-four to forty-eight hours. It's just proven more difficult than he expected."

"What do you think will happen, Herman, if this deniable asset goes to the media or the senate and tells them what he knows? Let me enlighten you. Wright, you, probably me, and maybe even the deputy director, will go to federal prison. You better make damn sure Wright resolves the situation."

"He will. He's in Berlin on the hunt as we speak. We stay in close contact and I expect to hear any day now..."

Newton held up a hand, shaking his head. "When you leave this office, I want you to pack your things and get on a plane to Berlin. You get over there and you stay on Wright until that asset is in a body bag."

"Yes, sir," Buckley said glumly.

"Where are the program files? Shredded by now, I hope."

"Nothing is committed to paper. All the files are on an off-site dedicated server. Only Wright has access."

"That's just great, Herman. If it all blows up, Wright could use those files as his get out of jail free card. Where do you think that leaves us? Do you know where the site is?"

"I can find out. I've never wanted to have any connection with the files."

"Good, lord," Newton said, wiping his face with his hand. He glared back at Buckley. "Go to Berlin. Get that asset in a body bag and take care of Wright. He's as much a threat to us as the asset."

"Wright? You mean..."

"You heard what I said, Herman. Now get out of my office. You've got a plane to catch."

Buckley nodded and stood up. He turned and headed for the door. As he reached for the doorknob, Newton spoke again.

"And, Herman?"

"Yes?" Buckley said, turning back to look at his boss.

"This meeting never took place and our conversation never happened."

"Understood." Buckley said, his shoulders sagging. He opened the door and walked out.

Chapter 22

When Wright and Grossman left the embassy, they took a taxi to the Berlin safe house. Wright used a key card to unlock the ground floor door at the back of the building, the private entry to the safe house. Then the men climbed the spiral staircase to the second floor. Wright knocked on the door. After a few moments, Kara Jansen opened it. He knew she had watched them on the security monitor from the moment they entered the downstairs door.

"You're early," Kara said, stepping back so the men could enter.

"Yeah, the plane made good time from Athens and the meeting at the embassy was shorter than expected. How much do you have left to do?"

"I packed everything except the electronics, and I've been shredding documents for the last two hours. The movers won't be here until tomorrow morning. It was the best I could do on such short notice."

"That's fine," Wright said. "We're holding off on that. We may be here for a couple more days. It depends on Dedman. Has he called you?"

"No, haven't heard from him. What's going on?"

"I'm not getting into that," Wright said, walking out of the front room Kara used as the operations center into the room behind it and then the kitchen area, and back again.

"Looks good," Wright said, more to himself than anyone else. "Andy, you and Kara move the table from the kitchen in here. It will give the team a place to set up when they get here. All the wiring for their computers is in here."

"What team?" Kara asked.

"Analysts from Langley. They are arriving this afternoon."

"To help find Dedman?"

"Enough with the questions, Kara. Anything you need to know, I will tell you. Everything is need to know and you don't need to know. You know the drill."

"Sure, got it," she said and turned to follow Grossman into the kitchen. Wright saw the semi-automatic pistol stuck in her waistband at the back.

"Why are you armed, Kara?" he asked.

Jansen turned back. "It's from the field box. You told me to shut down and pack up. I thought there might be a threat, so I got the weapon from the field box as soon as I got here this morning."

"Okay, well, why don't you give that to me now that we're here?"

"Yes, sir," Jansen said, pulling the pistol from her waistband and handing it butt first to her boss. "There's one in the chamber."

"Got it," Wright said, shoving the SIG Pro SP2009 into his waistband on his left side.

Jansen turned and went to the kitchen to help Grossman with the table, feeling a hell of a lot more ill at ease now that Wright had arrived and disarmed her.

* * *

A few minutes past four in the afternoon, someone pressed the buzzer at the downstairs entrance to the safe house. Kara looked at the monitor for the security camera above the door and saw a male and three females with luggage at the door. Wright looked over her shoulder from behind.

"That's our team from Langley," he said.

Kara reached over and flipped a toggle switch next to the desk, and the male opened the door when the lock released. Then he and the women trooped through the door and ascended the stairway. A minute later, they arrived at the upstairs door. Wright crossed the room, unlocked the door, and opened it. The four new arrivals entered, and Wright closed the door behind them.

"This is the operations center," Wright told them. "Set up there at the table." He pointed to Jansen. "This is Kara, the caretaker. If you have questions about power outlets or internet connections, Kara will sort you out. Once you're set up, get to work. We have seventy-two hours to find the asset and put him in a body bag."

Grossman walked into the room from the kitchen to join the group, holding a mug of coffee. Wright continued giving instructions.

"Everyone works until eight this evening. Then I want you to break down into teams of two. I want two people working rotating four-hour watches throughout the night while the rest of you get some rest. There are two bedrooms at the back of the house you can use. Andy here and Kara are folded in, so that gives us the three teams. Questions?"

Even though Wright had rebuffed all of her questions, Jansen spoke up. "What makes you so sure Dedman is coming back here to Berlin?" To her surprise, Wright answered her question.

"He was on a live mission with maybe one change of clothes and the equipment he needed for a one- or two-day op. Everything he owns is here in Berlin and he must come back here to get money, if nothing else, before he goes off the grid. Whatever he has left of the money we advanced for the mission expenses won't last long."

Wright slapped his hands together. "Let's get with it, people. The clocks ticking. We've flagged Dedman's passport so he can't fly. Trains and buses are dangerous for him, but possibilities. He's resourceful and he will find a way to get here tomorrow or the day after. Meanwhile, let's do everything we can to get a lead on him and the woman he is traveling with."

Wright turned to Kara. "I have something for you to do." Opening his briefcase, Wright took out some documents, paper clipped together, and handed them to her. Looking at them, she saw a photocopy of a photo of Dedman with all his information below it. Flipping to the second page, she saw a similar document with the image of a young woman with brown hair and her personal information. Then Wright handed her a flash drive.

"The originals are on the flash drive," he said. "Put together a one-page flyer with the photos and information for both targets on it with the usual boilerplate that the U.S. government wants them for questioning and add our contact information here. Then put it out to all federal, state, and local law enforcement agencies from Rome to Berlin. Maybe we will get lucky and one of those agencies will find Dedman and the woman before they even get to Berlin."

Jansen nodded, sat down in front of her computer, and inserted the thumb drive. Then she went to work.

Wright went back to the back office, sat behind the desk, and threw his legs up on it. He intended to stay at the safe house until eight to make sure everything was running smoothly. Then he would go back to his hotel to get some sleep. Wright thought about calling Buckley with an update, but decided against it. He would call him the following morning when maybe he would have something worth reporting to his supervisor. He was just glad Buckley was back at Langley and not here looking over his shoulder and getting in the way. Wright felt confident he would have this all cleaned up in another day or two.

Chapter 23

When they arrived in Vlorë, Dedman abandoned the motorcycle and they set off on foot. Using Drita as an interpreter, he got directions from a local to a second-hand clothing shop. At the shop, he found what he was looking for. Dedman purchased a pair of denim work pants, a heavy canvas shirt, a pullover cable-knit sweater, and a black watch cap.

Having lost her suitcase and most of her things back in Vagalat, Drita also picked out some clothing to make do until she got something she actually wanted. Dedman paid the clerk, and after leaving the shop, they began searching for a restaurant. Along the way, they came across a tourist information center and Drita picked up a map of the city and a ferry brochure with schedules inside. Finding an appealing restaurant, they went in and got a table. After perusing the menus, they ordered.

Drita sipped wine and studied the ferry schedules while they waited for the food they ordered. Dedman studied the map to determine how to find the commercial port area.

"Hey, there is an overnight ferry crossing to Bari that departs at eleven this evening.," Drita said. "If we take that one, we won't need to get a hotel tonight."

Dedman looked up from the map. "That's perfect. But for you, not us."

"What do you mean? You're not going? You're abandoning me?"

"No, I'm not abandoning you. I know how ferries work. They will require a passport on this end to board and a passport check point and customs in Italy. They flagged my passport. I can't take the ferry. But you can. I'll find another way across and we'll meet in Bari."

Drita looked at him without speaking for a moment. "Is this how you intend to get rid of me? I'd rather stay here than make the crossing to Italy only for you to never show up."

"You have no obligation to continue with me," Dedman said. "But if you want to stay together, you'll have to trust me. I'm not looking to abandon you. I will find you in Bari if you take the ferry. You have a solid passport, so that is the easiest way for you. I'll have to do something more difficult to get into Italy."

"Like what? How will you make the crossing?"

"After I put you on the ferry, I'll go to the commercial port and find a freighter. I'm sure there are plenty of ships that carry cargo back and forth between here and Bari. When I find one, I'll stowaway on board. I've done it before."

"But what happens if that works and you get to Italy without a valid passport?"

"I'll think of something. I bought the clothing so I'll blend in. Customs at commercial points of entry aren't usually as intense as those where tourists arrive. I'll look like every other merchant seaman, and I'm confident I'll find a way to slip through."

"How will we find each other in Bari?" Drita asked, feeling a little less suspicious that Jake was trying to dump her.

"After we finish eating, we'll find a place where I can buy a burner. I'll put your number in it and call you as soon as I get to Bari."

"Okay, if it's the only way."

"It's the best way. I would have a hard time getting us both on a ship without getting detected. And a ferry cabin will be much more comfortable for you than hiding in a cargo hold."

Drita still didn't like them separating, but what Jake said made sense. "Why must we go all the way to Berlin? Couldn't we simply disappear here? It seems that would be much simpler."

"I have to go to Berlin. I've already told the people I worked for that I quit and told them to stop looking for me. You saw how that worked out. I'm going to end this and I have to go to Berlin to do it."

"Yes, yes, fine. If we must go to Berlin, then we must. I get it."

* * *

After finishing their meal, Drita and Dedman went in search of a shop that sold phones. With a little over two hours before the ferry sailed, they had plenty of time.

It actually took them less than fifteen minutes to find a shop. Dedman purchased two prepaid phones. When he used burners, he never used the same one for long before tossing it and getting another.

A few minutes later, he bought them cups of coffee. They walked to the ferry terminal, and he purchased a ticket for Drita. Then they found a place with a bench near the terminal to wait until time for Drita to board. Dedman saved Drita's number on one burner and she saved the burner's number on her phone.

"What should I do when I arrive in Bari? Book a hotel?"

"If you don't hear from me within a couple of hours after you arrive, book something near the Bari Centrale train station. I may not find a ship sailing earlier than tomorrow morning and may not arrive until hours after you. I would have to be extremely lucky to find something sailing tonight. If I'm delayed longer than early tomorrow morning, I'll call you when I know you've arrived."

Dedman reached into his pack and pulled out another five hundred euros and offered the money to Drita. "Here some cash for expenses."

"I have money, remember?"

"Yes, I know, but we'll spend mine first."

"Thank you," Drita said, accepting the money and stuffing it inside her purse. But she felt more anxious that she might never see Jake again. Was that why he insisted she save her money? Before she put her thoughts into words, he spoke again.

"I've got some of your stuff from your suitcase in my backpack that I grabbed on the way out of the hotel back in Vagalat. Look inside your backpack and see what's in it. I'll take anything useful and we can throw away everything else to give you more room for your stuff."

"Okay," Drita said, opening the backpack Dedman had taken from one man who had grabbed her in the alley hours earlier.

Drita pulled out two flex cuffs, a roll of black duct tape, earphones for a cell phone, a small flashlight, three protein bars, and two plastic water bottles. Reaching in again, she withdrew a dark gray plastic covered cylinder and saw it had a lens at each end. "What's this?" she asked.

"Put the small lens to your eye and look through it," Dedman said.

When she put the cylinder to her eye, she saw a magnified view of the boats along the pier. "Oh, cool."

"It's a monocular. Sort of like one half of a pair of binoculars for viewing distant objects with one eye. We're definitely keeping that."

Drita handed the monocular to Dedman and rummaged inside the pack again. "I think that's it. Oh wait, what's this?"

Drita pulled a folded document from the pack. When she unfolded it, she gasped. It was a photocopy of two photos side by side, a photo of Jake and a photo of her. She scanned the print beneath her photo. There she saw her complete name, date of birth, complete physical description, address in Tirana, passport number, and her Albanian driver's license number. She knew the photo was an enlargement of the photo from her license.

"They had my picture! Why? Why did they have my picture?"

Dedman took the document from her. He put a hand on her arm. "Calm down, Drita. I'm sorry they violated your privacy. But please, calm down. We don't need to attract attention."

"Calm down?" she shrieked. "How did they get my picture?"

Dedman tightened his grip on her arm and told her to calm down again. This time more forcefully.

"You're hurting me, Jake."

"I'm sorry," he said, removing his hand. "But you have to calm down. People are looking at us. That's not what we want."

Drita took several deep breaths. "Okay, okay. But I don't understand how they got my picture."

"They probably found you through the car. I told you that the cop would have recorded the license plate number. These people chasing me can get the photo and information of anyone in the world if they want it bad enough."

"It wasn't even my car. My name wasn't on the registration."

"They either went to your friend and got your name or had the state police do it."

"Oh, my God. I forgot all about the car. I need to call my friend and tell him where it is."

"No, don't worry about it. I'm sure the people I worked for tipped off the state police and they probably have the car by now. The police should get it back to him. Anyway, now that they know who you are, you can't call him. From now on, no friends, nothing familiar."

"This is crazy. You said the people you worked for want to kill you. Now they know everything about me. Will they kill me too?"

"No, nothing like that. They wanted to know about you because they thought it might help them find me. They have no reason to hurt you."

"But you said they have no reason to kill you, yet you're sure they will if they catch you."

"They probably think they have a good reason to kill me. Something has gone wrong that I just don't know about. I know things. Things they wouldn't want me telling anyone. I don't know why they believe I would tell anyone what I know, but they must believe I'm a threat to them. It's the only thing that makes sense."

"What do you know that threatens them, Jake?"

"I can't tell you that. I can't tell you for lots of reasons, but the biggest reason is I would put you in danger if I told you."

"This sucks, Jake. I'm really frightened now, and I don't want to go on the ferry alone. I'm not sure I even can."

"You can, Drita and you must. You will be much safer on the ferry alone than you would be here with me. And I can't cross over to Italy with you. We have to stick to the plan. You will only be in Italy alone for a few hours and then I'll be there to protect you."

"But I'm so scared, Jake."

"I know," Dedman said, putting his arm around her. She leaned her head on his shoulder. "I'm so sorry I involved you in this. We should have said goodbye as soon as we crossed the border from Greece. You would be back in Tirana by now."

Drita raised her head, looked up at him, and put a hand on his face. "But I didn't want to say goodbye then, and I don't want to say goodbye now. I'm going with you to Berlin so you can end this."

"Okay, but you have to do what I say, Drita. Take the ferry."

Drita sighed. "Yes, yes. Okay, I will take the ferry. And I won't lose it again. I'll remain calm."

"Thank you."

Drita pressed her lips to his, and they held each other tightly.

Chapter 24

Dedman put Drita on the ferry at ten thirty, the moment the crew opened up passenger boarding. He knew she was scared and reluctant to go it alone, but she had calmed down a little by the time he left her. He felt pressed for time and needed intel to find a suitable ride to Italy.

Ducking into a public restroom, he changed into the clothes he had bought at the second-hand store and tossed the clothes he had been wearing in a trash bin on his way out. Then he headed for the commercial shipping port, looking for bars close by when he arrived.

Bars next to a commercial port were goldmines of good intel for someone looking to hitch a clandestine ride on a freighter. Soon he found what he was looking for, a run-down place filled with a lot of drunk merchant sailors.

The American found a place at the crowded bar, ordered a beer, and kept his ears open. He didn't understand more than a few words spoken in Albanian, but after several minutes he tuned into some men down the bar speaking Italian, one language Dedman spoke very well.

As soon as a barstool opened up next to the Italians, he picked up his beer, moved down the bar, and took the vacant stool. He sipped his beer and listened. In under ten minutes, he learned everything he wanted to know. The sailors were from a ship called the *Barbana*, set to sail for Bari at midnight. He had finally caught a break. He would leave for Italy only an hour behind Drita. And if the *Barbana* got underway on time, they would probably both get to Bari within one or two hours of each other. He got off the stool and walked out of the bar, heading for the docks.

* * *

Once Dedman found the *Barbana*, he took out the monocular he had retrieved from the confiscated backpack. He saw no lookouts posted, although there was a sailor standing at the top of the accommodation ladder to check anyone boarding the vessel. Staying in the shadows, Dedman walked back down the cement pier until he reached the stern of the ship. He looked up and down the pier and saw no one and felt confident the man on the deck amidships at the ladder didn't have an unobstructed view of the stern.

Dedman strode across the pier to an aft mooring line. With his pack on his back, he leaped up and out, grabbing the hawser above the circular, galvanized iron rat guard someone had put on the mooring line after the ship docked. Dedman threw his legs up and wrapped his feet around the thick rope. Then, hanging beneath it, he climbed the rope hand over hand until he reached the hawse hole where the mooring line passed out. There, he maneuvered himself on top of the line and reached up and grabbed the rail with one hand. Carefully, he pulled himself up until he was standing on the rope with both hands on the rail and then vaulted over, landing on the deck. Quickly, he crossed an open area at the stern and pressed against the steel superstructure beside an open hatch. Peeking around the edge of the hatch, he looked down a long, dimly lit passageway and saw no one.

Entering through the hatch, Dedman quickly, but silently, walked up the passageway until he came to a ladder. He climbed down cautiously.

After descending a second ladder, he found himself in a cargo hold containing large wooden crates and palletized stacks of shrink-wrapped boxes. With no internal lighting illuminated, the deeper he worked into the hold among the cargo, the darker it became. He got the small flashlight out of his pack, switched it on, and began looking for a good hide where a crew member wouldn't stumble on him if anyone came down to the hold.

Soon he found it, a large wooden crate that reached almost to the top of the hold. Using smaller crates stacked around it, he scrambled up until he could get his hands on the top edge of the large crate. Then he pulled himself up on top. He had to move on his hands and knees because of the limited space between the crate and the top of the hold. It made a perfect hide. As long as he stayed near the center of the massive crate, even someone standing on the deck below wouldn't have a sight line to him from any direction.

Dedman lay down on his back, putting the pack beneath his head. His accommodations were short on comfort, but Dedman had slept in worse places. Much worse. He was tired and wanted to sleep, but was determined to stay awake until the ship left the harbor at midnight. Raising on an elbow, he pulled a protein bar and a bottle of water out of the pack. After swigging some water from the bottle, he lay back down and munched on the protein bar. Estimating an eight-hour crossing, Dedman knew he wouldn't have to raid the galley in the middle of the night as he had done on past longer voyages as a stowaway. The protein bars and water he had in the pack would be sufficient.

A while later, Dedman looked at the luminous face of his TAG Heuer Link chronograph when he heard one prolonged blast from the ship's horn. The *Barbana* was getting underway on time at midnight. Dedman relaxed and closed his eyes. He knew once underway; besides the bridge watch, the rest of the crew would be in their bunks sleeping and that's exactly what he planned to do. In about eight hours, he should complete another step towards Berlin.

Chapter 25

Eighteen minutes past midnight, almost ten hours after departing Dulles, Herman Buckley descended the stairs from the CIA corporate jet that had just landed at Berlin Schönefeld Airport. Reaching the tarmac, he headed for the terminal, where he flashed his U.S. government diplomatic credentials and passed unchallenged through German customs and immigration.

Minutes later he exited the terminal, walked to the taxi stand out front, and hired a cab to drive him to the Grand Westin Berlin where he had reserved a suite. Buckley had only dozed fitfully during the flight and he needed several hours of solid sleep to prepare for what lay ahead of him. It had been twenty years since he had been in the field as a case officer and carrying out Maxwell Newton's order would require him to do something he hadn't done in a long time. He wasn't looking forward to it, but he knew carrying it out successfully was his only chance to save himself and he was determined to see it through.

* * *

Underway Aegean Sea

Dedman woke up and listened. He heard nothing but the dull thrum of the ship's engines decks below him. Looking at the luminous dial of his watch, he saw it was almost seven a.m. and knew he had got a little over six hours of deep sleep. He reached into the pack and grabbed another protein bar and the other full bottle of water. Dedman knew the ship should only be about an hour from the port at Bari, and he needed to find a new hide. Crewmen would probably enter the hold soon to prepare the cargo for unloading.

After making quick work of his breakfast, he returned the water bottle and wrapper to the pack, zipped it closed, and put it on his back. Then he crawled to the edge of the crate, his eyes straining in the darkness to pick up any movement. Seeing and hearing nothing, he climbed back down to the deck and made his way swiftly to the ladder he had descended to the hold. He regained the passageway he followed into the ship from the stern and made his way to the hatch leading out to the stern, finding it closed. He lifted the handle to release the dogs securing the hatch and pushed open the watertight door. It was still dark outside. He stepped out the hatch, closed the door, and turned, almost running into the sailor standing there looking at him.

"Who are you?" the sailor demanded in Italian.

"Lorenzo," Dedman, recovering from the surprise, answered in flawless Italian without having to think about it.

"I've never seen you before," the man challenged, clearly suspicious.

"I'm new on the ship," Dedman said.

"I don't think so. I run the crew and we have no one new on this ship."

Uh oh, Dedman thought.

"Let's go see the captain and see what he wants to do with you, Lorenzo. Looks like we have a stowaway on board."

"Sorry," Dedman replied. "That idea doesn't work for me."

The seaman, a wiry-looking but muscular man about Dedman's height, reached to his waist, pulled something out of a leather holster, and then flicked open the wicked-looking knife.

"But I insist, Señor. Unless you wish to get cut."

Dedman still had the SIG Sauer pistol in his waistband at his back and really wanted to shoot this idiot through the eye who had been dumb enough to bring a knife to a gunfight. But he didn't, knowing the report of the firearm would bring the entire crew down on him. Instead, he sidestepped and backed up a few feet, waiting for the sailor to make his move. And when the man realized Dedman had no intention of going anywhere with him, the sailor lunged, the blade in his right hand.

Dedman saw immediately the man knew how to handle a knife, which didn't surprise him. Knife fights in real life weren't like those movies portrayed. The man didn't slash at Dedman, but drove the knife straight towards Dedman's belly with an upward thrust. The American juked left just enough to avoid the blade and blocked the thrust with his left wrist, striking the sailor's wrist behind the knife, but still felt the blade slash through the side of his sweater. Immediately, Dedman grabbed the wrist behind the knife with both hands. He took a step forward and head butted the man in the face, breaking his nose.

As the man's head snapped back, Dedman drove the sole of his foot into the inside of the man's right knee and heard the pop of tearing ligaments. The man's right leg bent at an unnatural angle. While taking out the knee, Dedman simultaneously shifted his left hand to the man's right upper arm and then turned the sailor's wrist with his right hand to lock the outstretched arm at the elbow. Lifting his right knee, Dedman slammed the arm at the elbow against his knee, breaking the arm at the elbow joint.

The knife dropped from the seaman's hand and clattered onto the steel deck. Just as the man screamed in agony, Dedman released the fractured arm and drove his right forearm into the man's jaw, knocking him unconscious. The merchantman sagged and Dedman dropped to a knee, letting the man fall onto his shoulders.

Lifting the unconscious sailor in a fireman's carry, Dedman strode to the rail and dropped the man over the side into the sea. The body disappeared for several moments and then popped to the surface in the ship's wake about thirty yards aft of the stern. Quickly, Dedman searched for the man's knife and when he found it, he tossed it overboard after its owner.

Shit. Dedman had never had to kill anyone on any of the ships he had stowed away on in the past. But this had just been pure bad luck. *You should have left me alone.* It hadn't bothered him to kill the man while he was doing his best to gut him with the knife. He had killed before and it had never bothered him. Yet this was different. He had only killed those he felt were deserving of extrajudicial execution. People who were threats to the national security of his country. At least that's what they told him when giving him the missions and the targets.

Swiftly, he moved to a ladder and climbed it to the main deck, looking for another hide before the sun broke above the horizon. He tried to put the killing out of his mind, but bitterly acknowledged something. Something he only now admitted for the first time. He was tired of the killing and he just didn't want to do it anymore.

Chapter 26

Drita Nikolli walked off the ferry at seven-fourteen a.m., passed through customs and immigration without incident, and then into the streets of Bari, Italy. The ferry cabin had been comfortable enough, but she had hardly slept. As much as she wanted to believe Jake would join her here, she had a strong premonition she had seen the last of the American. She felt it so strongly that she had almost bought a ticket for the ferry loading to return to Vlorë. But she hadn't because she wasn't ready to give up all hope. Not yet. She longed for him to come back to her.

Stupid, she chided herself. *Stupid*. Yes, there was the lovemaking she had initiated, but she couldn't believe she had already developed such powerful feelings for a man she didn't even really know. What she knew should have unsettled her. She sensed Jake was dangerous. But he attracted her in a way no man ever had.

Yes, the American was a dangerous man. That was obvious. Hadn't she seen it with her own eyes? First, with the Albanian road policeman. The man hadn't had a chance against Jake. And he had been equally brutal and violent when rescuing her from the two Americans. But with her, he had been so gentle. She knew he was unlike any man she had ever known.

What unsettled Drita was the predictable insecurities that came with believing you cared about someone deeply while also knowing they probably didn't care for you nearly as much. It frightened her to think putting her on the ferry alone had only been a ruse he had used to separate himself from her. Drita acknowledged how desperately she hoped it wasn't true. With a sigh, she entered a clothing store. Even if Jake didn't come for her, she might as well do some shopping, so she had at least something to show for her trip to Bari.

* * *

Once again, luck smiled on Dedman when the ship docked. After a crane had lifted and set the accommodation ladder in place, a man standing on the docks holding a clipboard had scurried up it and immediately engaged the two deckhands in conversation. Dedman had concealed himself next to some machinery on the deck near the landing of the accommodation ladder. He worked out from the conversation the man was in charge of the stevedores on the docks and was organizing the unloading of the ship's cargo.

Caught up in discussion, none of the three noticed as Dedman passed behind them and then descended the metal ladder to the pier. He walked briskly past the dockworkers, who paid him no attention. Why would they? They looked at his clothing and saw what they expected to see. An ordinary merchant sailor.

Dedman bypassed the queue at the customs and immigration checkpoint. He walked along the eight-foot chain-link fence, securing the commercial dock area until he found stacks of crates next to the fence. Squeezing through a narrow channel between the stacks, he made his way to the fence. There, he found a sufficient space between the stacked crates and fence so he could scale it. He climbed the fence at one of the steel posts, grabbed the bar at the top, and pulled himself up until his waist was level with it. Then he threw his legs sideways over the wire spikes at the top, let go, and dropped onto the grass on the other side, relaxing his legs to absorb the fall and ending up in a crouch with his palms on the ground.

Dedman stood and hurried away from the fence, crossed a street, and ducked into an alley. He assumed a security camera somewhere had caught him going over the fence. After dropping the pack for a moment, he took off the watch cap, pulled the sweater off over his head, and tossed them both into a trash bin. He removed his burner phone and earphones from the pack and then put it back on his back. Walking out of the alley, heading for a park a block away, he switched on the phone and put the earpiece in. Then he pressed the button where he had stored the phone number. She answered on the second ring.

"*Alo?*"

"It's me. I'm here. Where are you?"

"Jake? You're here?" It surprised Dedman hearing the obvious relief she communicated with only a few words.

"Yes, where are you?" He had also heard a catch in her voice, like she was about to cry. "Are you okay, Drita? What's wrong?"

"I'm fine. It's just that… I didn't think you would come."

"Why wouldn't I? I told you I'd meet you here."

"I know… but… it doesn't matter. I'm just so glad you're here."

"We're wasting time. Tell me where you are."

"I was just looking for a hotel. You said if I didn't hear from you in two hours…"

"Near the train station?"

"Yes, I can see it from here."

"Great. Go to the station entrance and wait for me. I'll be there as soon as I can."

"Okay, Jake. Hurry, please."

"I'm on the way. See you soon."

Dedman ended the call. He crossed the street to a stand offering tours. He picked up a city map and located the central train station.

"*Posso aiutare?*" a young woman attendant asked.

Dedman looked up at her when she asked if he needed help. He replied, speaking Italian.

"I want to go to the central train station."

"*Bari Centrale?*"

"Yes. I see it here on this map. Can you show me where we are so I can get there from here?"

"Oh yes, simple." She moved beside him and placed an index finger on the map.

"Here we are."

"Thank you," Dedman said, folding the map and offering it to her.

"No, please. Keep it. The maps are free."

Dedman thanked her again and then turned and walked away, scanning right and left for transportation. The train station was over four kilometers away and he didn't have time for a long walk.

A man on a scooter pulled into a parking area ahead of him. Dedman changed direction to intercept him as he got off the scooter and dropped the key into his jacket pocket. Dedman sped up and as the man stepped onto the sidewalk, Dedman bumped into him purposely.

"*Mi scusi*," Dedman said, his hand closing around the scooter key he had lifted from the man's jacket pocket. The man looked at him, nodded, and walked away. As soon as he disappeared into the crowd, Dedman climbed on the scooter, inserted the key and started it. Then he motored out onto the street, heading for the train station.

Chapter 27

Dedman dumped the scooter a block from the train station. Walking there, he passed a tourist souvenir shop with racks of merchandise out front on the sidewalk. Without breaking stride, he snatched a blue souvenir ball cap off a rack and held it against his thigh on the street side. Then he grabbed a colorful scarf from the next rack and stuffed it into his pocket. He jerked the price tag off the hat, rounded the bill, and put it on his head, pulled down low to conceal his eyes.

Nearing the station, he spotted Drita in the crowd, searching for him, looking first in one direction and then in the other. Dedman stopped. He removed the cap. Putting his thumb and index finger to his mouth, he whistled and then waved the cap when Drita looked toward him. She smiled and then ran toward him.

To his surprise, Drita threw her arms around him and hugged him. Then she kissed him and hugged him again. Dedman felt wetness on his cheek. He put his hands on her upper arms and took a half step back.

"You're crying. Why are you crying?"

"Happy tears," she said with a crooked grin. "I thought… you put me on the ferry to leave me."

"Why would I do that? You're the only friend I have."

Drita looked at him with an expression that looked part irritation and part joy.

"Friends? If you had told me that before putting me on that ferry, maybe I wouldn't have worried so much." Then she smiled.

"Okay, anyway, we need to get a train to Rome. Here, I got this for you."

120

Dedman pulled the scarf from his pocket and handed it to her. She took it.

"For my hair, right?"

"Yes, we have to be careful of the cameras inside the station."

"Okay," Drita said, tying the scarf on to cover her hair.

"The people chasing me will probably access the cameras. They will look for us together. So, we need to split up inside the station. Once we find a train, I want you to go to the platform and wait where the front of the train stops. I'll get the tickets and when I get to the platform, I will stand at the opposite end. Get on and go to the second-class car and find a seat. When I get on, I'll come and find you."

"So, at least we will sit together on the train?"

Dedman smiled. "Yes, no cameras on the train, just inside the station."

"Okay, anything else?"

"Yes, in the station, look down always, when you walk, when you stand. That, plus the scarf, should make it hard for the cameras to catch your face."

"Got it."

"Is that a new outfit?"

Drita smiled. "Yes, I went shopping when I got off the ferry. Do you like it?"

"I love it. A camera probably caught you when you got off the ferry. Now you look completely different. It will help with the cameras at the station."

"Oh, I see."

"One more thing," Dedman said, removing and opening his backpack.

"What?"

"Let me see your phone."

"Okay," Drita said with a confused expression. She took her phone out of her bag and handed it to him.

Dedman pulled the SIM card and dropped it. Then he snapped the phone in half and dropped it into the gutter.

"What are you doing?" Drita asked in alarm. "You just destroyed my phone!"

"Now that they know who you are, they will access your phone records,"

Dedman said. "They know you're here and could use your phone to track us." He handed her the other burner from his pack. "You can use this one for now. I already saved my number in it."

"This phone is shit. Do you know what I paid for the phone you just destroyed?"

"I'll replace it when we get to Berlin. And they won't have your number for a while. Hopefully, before they do, this will all be over."

"Okay, Jake. I understand."

"Good. Go inside the station and look up at the train schedules for a moment and then walk toward the platforms. I will do the same a distance away from you. After I choose the train, I will call you with the train information and platform number. And I'll buy the tickets from a kiosk."

Drita nodded. "Go now?"

"Yes. I'll see you on the train."

Drita leaned in and kissed him. "See you." Then she headed into the station.

Chapter 28

Berlin, Germany

Wright stood at the bathroom sink in his hotel room shaving, brooding about the lack of resources making the job of tracking Dedman down harder than it had to be. But getting more resources would mean going to Buckley and then Buckley would have to go to his boss who might have to go to his boss.

The higher this went up the CIA food chain, the more questions that would get asked. Wright wanted no part of that when all he needed was to get rid of Dedman, to make all his problems go away. No, he would just have to soldier on with the limited resources he had and hope Dedman came to him here in Berlin. Then he would decide what to do about Kara Jansen. It had occurred to him she was also a loose end.

After shaving, Wright dressed in a crisp, clean white dress shirt and a charcoal suit with fine maroon pinstripes. He stuck the SIG Sauer pistol he had taken from Jansen inside his waistband on the front left, covered by his suit coat. After running a comb through his dark brown hair, he grabbed his briefcase and key card, left his room, and took the elevator down to the lobby. He got off the elevator and strode toward the front entrance, where he would get a taxi back to the safe house.

It was his first full day in Berlin. The makeshift team of security officers would arrive at the safe house in the next hour and the seventy-hour clock would start ticking. He hoped Dedman would arrive in Berlin today, but he felt sure it wouldn't be any sooner than tomorrow. As he approached the front doors, he caught sight of a heavy-set man sitting in a chair in the lobby with an open newspaper. He could just make out the man's disheveled gray hair above the top of the newspaper.

The newspaper came down and Wright did a double take. It was Herman Buckley, staring at him, right here in Berlin. Buckley stood and stepped into Wright's path.

"I was just about to call you," Wright said. "What are you doing here?"

"Newton sent me to oversee the operation."

Wright knew Maxwell Newton. Chief of Special Operations Group and Buckley's immediate supervisor.

"You went to Newton with this? I thought we agreed we wouldn't do that, Herman."

"I didn't go to Newton. He called me into his office and asked some very pointed questions. Then he told me to get over here and to take charge of the operation."

"I'd re-think that, Herman. You're not really cut out for what needs to be done, and I've already got everything under control. I told you I'm cleaning it up and it will be clean. Having Newton involved is only going to complicate things."

"Be that as it may, I am going to do what I'm told, Jerry. And so are you. How do things stand at present?"

Wright sighed. "We located Dedman in Albania. I borrowed a ground branch team that was in Tirana coming off another mission and sent them to the hotel Dedman and the woman were staying in."

"Tell me they got them."

"Wish I could, Herman. But I can't. The team let them get away after Dedman put two of them in the hospital."

"My God. Can this get any worse?"

"Look, Herman, I know he is coming here to Berlin and if the local cops don't get him en route, then we will when he gets here. This will all be over within the next forty-eight hours."

"I'm here to make sure it is, Jerry."

"So, now, when we're finally making progress, you want to take over the operation?"

"You run the operation, Jerry. I'm just here to provide oversight."

"Whatever you think is best, Herman. I'm on my way to the safe house. I've set up the operations center there and have the team there I brought over from Langley."

"Let's get over there then, find Dedman, and finish this."

The two men walked to the front doors, went out, and Wright hailed a taxi.

* * *

Kara Jansen looked up at the clock on the wall for at least the tenth time in under five minutes, willing eight o'clock to arrive and the end of her four to eight a.m. watch. Then she looked back at her commuter screen, awaiting responses from each of the three mobile phone carriers in Albania. After the Tirana station had cut through the Albanian government red tape, she had submitted requests to all three companies for the phone records of a customer named Drita Nikolli. With no way of knowing which carrier the woman used, Kara had sent the same request to all three.

Jansen wanted to be out of the safe house and on her way to her apartment before Gerald Wright arrived more than she wanted those phone records. He hadn't told her specifically not to leave the safe house, but she suspected he would keep her here if he arrived before she could leave.

Kara wanted to shower before getting the four hours of rest due her, and then to change clothes before returning to the safe house. Assuming she returned. The more time she spent around Wright, the more unease she felt about what might happen to her after Wright dispensed with Dedman.

Of all the assets she had dealt with over the years she had spent in Berlin, Dedman was the only one she had liked. Somehow, he differed from the others. Yes, he was a killer just like the rest, but he had always been well-mannered and amiable whenever circumstances had brought them together. Not friendly exactly. He seemed like a loner. But at least she hadn't found him threatening. Kara wished she had a way to get in touch with him, to warn him about what was awaiting him in Berlin. But she didn't.

The more she thought about what she had learned about the clinic and what she suspected about the assets, the more certain she became she would suffer a similar fate at Wright's hands unless she found some way to run and hide. He had had no reason to take her field box firearm away except to make sure she couldn't protect herself with it.

Eight a.m. finally came and the Langley analysts began filing into the room to start the workday. Kara shut down her computer, grabbed her purse and coat, and, without speaking to anyone, left the room. She went out the front door, down the stairs, and out of the safe house. She jogged out of the alley and across the street to her car, got in, and drove away in the Berlin morning traffic.

Chapter 29

Dedman and Drita boarded the nine-fifteen a.m. train to Rome separately and then met up in the second-class coach a few minutes later. They would arrive in Rome a little past one p.m. and then board the first fast train they could get to Berlin. Drita moved to the window seat when Dedman arrived beside her and he took the aisle seat. Drita reached out and grabbed his hand.

"What next, when we get to Rome?" she asked.

"We'll catch the first train available to Berlin. With luck, we should be in Berlin by three o'clock tomorrow afternoon."

"Will passports be a problem?" Drita asked, keeping her voice low.

"Maybe. Maybe not. A few years ago, it wouldn't have been a problem at all. But because of the mass migration crisis, I know many European countries have beefed up border security. Austrian border police could board at the second to last station before we leave Italy to check passports, and German border police might do the same before the train leaves Austria."

"Then you may get caught?"

"Hopefully not. The last few times I've traveled by train, I've only seen border police make detailed passport examinations when something made them suspicious. This train is almost full, and they always have limited time to check all passengers. I've seen passengers hold up their passports as the border police approached them and they have only nodded and continued on. With the migrant thing, they mostly are looking for people without passports. The migrants usually destroy any travel and identification documents they have before entering any European country to give them more flexibility to use alias identities."

"I hope we have no issues."

"You can say that again. I'm not eager to throw any border police off the train. If that happens, we will have to get off at the next station and find alternate, slower transportation."

"You're kidding, right? You wouldn't actually throw a policeman off a moving train."

But when Drita looked at Dedman, she realized immediately how wrong she was about that. He wasn't kidding at all.

"I wouldn't enjoy it, but I will do what I have to do to remove any obstacle that arises between us and getting to Berlin."

Dedman knew things could get that drastic if they had any problems with border police and passports. The agency had flagged his passport, and suspected that they had likely persuaded Interpol to flag Drita's passport by now with some bullshit charge on an international warrant. It had actually surprised him a little that she made it into Italy without getting detained, though he wasn't about to tell her that. Sending her across on the ferry had been risky, but it was the only reasonable option given the circumstances.

Throwing any border control officer who confronted him off a moving train in as discreet a manner as possible would be his only option. He had reluctantly tossed the pistol confiscated from the ground branch officer into a bathroom trash bin before boarding the train. That had been the smart move since under no circumstances would he have engaged in a gunfight inside a crowded train putting innocent passengers in a crossfire. Now his only weapon was the ground branch officer's folding tactical knife, which he had transferred from his pack to his pocket.

Noticing that Drita had fallen asleep with her head resting against the window, Dedman reclined his seat, closed his eyes, and tried to do the same. His years in the Army had drilled it into him. Sleep and eat when you can because you never knew when you would get another chance to do either.

* * *

When the taxi dropped them across from the alley behind the safe house, Wright saw four men getting out of a white unmarked cargo van parked down the side street. He and Buckley waited until the men reached them. Wright recognized one of them. Carlton Harrison had introduced them at the embassy the day he and Grossman arrived in Berlin. Harrison had tabbed the officer, Randy Wagner, as the team leader because, according to Harrison, Wagner was the most skilled. Besides his agency training, Wager had served several tours in Afghanistan with the U.S. Marines before joining the CIA.

"Good morning, Mr. Wright," Wagner said. "This is the rest of the team. Bowman, McKinney, and Estrada."

Wright nodded. They weren't ground branch, but the men looked confident and capable. "This is my associate, Mr. Buckley."

"Good to meet you, sir," Wager said to Buckley. Then he looked back at Wright. "Just tell us what you need us to do, sir."

"You're armed?"

"Yes, sir," Wagner said, patting the right side of his zipped leather coat. "All of us are good to go."

"Okay, keep your weapons concealed, just as they are now. We don't need some nervous civilian calling the Berlin cops. Until we locate the target in Berlin, I want two of you out of direct view in static positions at the front, and two of you in the alley there, where you can observe anyone approaching the safe house entrance. You've got my number. If anyone spots the target, call me immediately before confronting him."

"Got it, sir."

"If we get a location on the target, I'll call you."

"Yes, sir."

Buckley and Wright turned and walked across the street to the alley and the safe house entrance, while Wagner gave his team their assignments.

* * *

"We up on the woman's phone yet?" Wright asked Grossman.

"Not yet. Jansen is waiting for the cell phone carriers to get back to her. We don't even know which of the three the woman uses."

"Damn it, Andy, I need that phone. Where is Jansen? Her computer is dark. I want her to stay on top of nailing down the phone number."

"I don't know where she is," Grossman admitted. "We had the four to eight a.m. watch. When the rest of the team came in to start work, I gave them their assignments and then noticed Jansen was gone. I had someone check the bedrooms and bathroom, but she wasn't there."

"You're saying she left? Jansen left the safe house?"

"Looks that way, sir."

"Jesus, Andy! How could you let that happen?"

"Sorry, sir. She was here one minute and gone the next. Maybe she didn't know she couldn't leave and went home to shower and change."

"You have her address?"

"I'm sure it's in her file."

"Okay, well, you've cost yourself the chance to go back to the hotel to shower and rest for a few hours. Now you spend that time getting Jansen's address, going there, and bringing her back here to work."

"Yes, sir," Grossman said, suitably chastised. After finding the address, he went out the front door to collect Jansen.

"This Jansen, she's the caretaker?" Buckley asked.

"Yeah. She handled the comms and logistics.

"She going to be a problem? I assume she is read in on the program."

"She is," Wright acknowledged. "And she won't be a problem. I'll take care of it. Once Andy gets her back here, she won't leave again until it's over."

Buckley nodded, understanding that Wright had the Jansen woman on the list of loose ends he intended to tie up. "I've got some business to attend to here in Berlin," he said. "I'll be back later."

"Okay," Wright said, glad Buckley wouldn't be hanging around all day looking over his shoulder. He still didn't understand why Newton had sent him. He knew the man had no more respect for Herman Buckley than he did.

Chapter 30

Kara Jansen parked her Volkswagen Golf on the side street. After locking the car, she walked to the alley entrance and then swiped her key card and entered the safe house.

At her apartment, she had showered, changed, and packed a go bag, a day pack containing a change of clothes, five thousand dollars in cash, and her other passport. Jansen had a U.S. passport issued by the agency, but she had a second passport the CIA was unaware of. Her mother was an American, but her father was a naturalized American citizen born in the Netherlands, so she held dual citizenship and had a Dutch passport.

Kara had decided against running immediately after leaving the safe house earlier. That would be an irrevocable decision she only intended to make once she felt fully convinced Wright planned to kill her. At the top of stairs, she walked to the door, swiped her card and went in. There she found Wright sitting at her desk. He swiveled and looked at her.

"Where the hell have you been, Kara?" he demanded.

"I went home to shower and change. Was that not okay?"

"No, I don't want you leaving here unless I send you out for something. I just sent Grossman to your address to bring you back here."

"Sorry, I didn't know. You said nothing about not leaving, and you weren't here when my watch ended."

"Well, now you know. It isn't fair to the rest of the team. They are stuck here for the duration, and so are you."

"Fine. No problem."

Wright got up. "Get on the phone records. I need that woman's phone."

"Sure, I'm on it."

Kara sat down at her desk and switched on her computer. Wright stalked out of the room and into the back office. A few minutes later, Grossman came through the door breathing heavily like he had run up the stairs. He looked at Kara quizzically.

"Sorry, Wright just told me I'm not allowed to leave. I didn't know and went home to shower and change when our watch ended."

"Okay," Grossman said. "It's cool. Jerry just gets a little intense. Since you're back already, I guess you didn't get any rest."

"No, but I'm good."

"You working on the phone stuff?"

"Yes, I just got the number. I'm having Langley route any calls and texts through here. Nothing new. But the phone records show the last call she received was at eight seventeen a.m. this morning. No outgoing calls since she picked up Dedman in Greece."

Grossman nodded. "Any GPS data?"

"Yes, this morning the phone was pinging off a tower in Bari, Italy. I looked it up and there is a ferry that runs twice a day to and from Vlorë, Albania."

"The phone is still in Bari?"

"I don't know. It's no longer pinging. She must have pulled the battery or destroyed it."

"That would be Dedman," Grossman said. "Jerry in the back office?"

"Yes."

"Okay, I'll let him know what you found. Why don't you go claim a bed and get a few hours of sleep? We'll have the watch again tonight after we shut down for the day."

Kara nodded, got up, and headed to the bedrooms down the hall. She wasn't feeling great about Wright forbidding her from leaving the premises.

* * *

After Grossman had given him the phone information, Wright got up from the desk and walked back out to the operation center.

"New information people. The woman's phone shows she is now in Italy, last location Bari. We think she crossed over on the ferry. I want us up on all available CCTVs in Bari, Italy. I want the ferry terminal cameras, traffic cameras, ATMs, the airport, train and bus stations. Let's get to it."

As the analysts got to work, Wright turned to Grossman. "You can go to the hotel to shower and change. Be back here by two p.m. and then I want you keeping an eye on Jansen. Don't let her out of your sight and don't let her leave again."

"Yes, sir," Grossman said.

* * *

Herman Buckley got out of the taxi at a Hertz car rental in downtown Berlin and went inside. There, he rented a black Volkswagen Passat. Then he drove back to his hotel to call in an update to Maxwell Newton. He planned to have lunch at the hotel restaurant and rest in his room before heading back to the safe house later. He would then decide when to carry out his assignment from Newton.

* * *

Drita and Dedman arrived in Rome at one twenty-one p.m. and proceeded separately to the nearest departures and arrivals monitor. Drita pretended to study the monitor from one end while Dedman studied it from the opposite end and chose their train to Berlin, which departed at one fifty-five. He walked away a little distance and called Drita. He gave her the departure time, platform number, and told her to go there and wait just like she did in Bari.

Watching in the reflection of a retail store glass, he saw Drita walk away after they hung up. Then Dedman walked briskly to a kiosk and purchased their tickets, opting for first class reclining seats instead of a sleeper compartment. It was about a thirteen-hour trip, but Dedman didn't want to be trapped in a compartment if he had to deal with border police on the train. This, he knew, would be the riskiest leg of the journey with two border crossings.

Dedman arrived at the platform and at one-fifty he and Drita boarded the train from opposite ends. As planned, they met in the dining car after the train departed the station to have a late lunch.

"So far, so good," Drita said with a smile as they ate lunch together.

Assuming she referred to his passport problem, he replied, "That was a domestic trip from Bari. They don't have passport checks. If we have a problem, it will be on this train crossing two international borders."

"Hopefully, things will go smoothly."

"Yes, we can hope. But hope is never a plan. If something happens, I'll deal with it."

Drita frowned, already well aware of how Dedman dealt with problems.

"What will we do when we arrive in Berlin?" she asked, trying not to think about Dedman throwing border police officers from a speeding train.

"We will get a room and then I need to pick up a few things and buy some things I'll need tomorrow evening."

"Like what?"

"Things I'm picking up or things I need to buy?"

"Both."

"I need to pick up some belongings I want to take when we leave Berlin. And money. As far as the things I need to buy, the less you know about that, the better." Dedman smiled encouragingly.

"What happens after Berlin? After you end things, as you put it."

"We should talk about that," Dedman said. "You need to be sure staying together is what you want. We would still have to run until things settle some, so I can make certain it's over. We would have to fall off the grid for a while. For six months at least. Maybe longer. Are you sure that's something you want? It will mean no friends, no family, nothing familiar. And we will have to move from one place to the next frequently."

"Forever?"

"Not forever, but for a while. Six months, a year, maybe even longer."

"It doesn't matter. I know I want to be with you, Jake. And I'm up for whatever it takes to make that happen. I haven't much family. My father died when I was a child. My mom died three years ago from cancer. I have only a much older sister and we're not that close. My friends are more acquaintances than people I can't live without. And for a long while, I have felt Albania holds no future for me. Also, I would love to travel and I can imagine worse things than seeing the world with you." Drita smiled brightly.

"Okay, then maybe we will start with somewhere in Asia and then we will go from there."

"Awesome. I've never been to Asia. Actually, I've been nowhere except for Italy and Greece. This will be my first time in Berlin."

Dedman smiled. "Well, you will see a lot more of the world soon."

Drita smiled back. "I enjoy thinking about it, about seeing the world with you."

Chapter 31

The Following Day

Wright walked up the stairs of the safe house to begin his second full day in Berlin. He hadn't seen Buckley since the previous afternoon when he had stopped back by the safe house for a progress report. Buckley had seemed to understand that there wasn't anything else to do but wait for Dedman to show up in Berlin. He still wondered what Buckley was even doing in Berlin. He hadn't tried to assert any control over the operation. At least the man was staying out of his way, and he was grateful for that.

Wright was sure Dedman would arrive today or tomorrow at the latest. So far, they had had no luck getting any help from any of the local authorities along the route from Italy to Berlin. No one had come in contact with Dedman and the woman, assuming she was still with him. Tomorrow would be the end of the seventy-two hours, and he would lose Wagner and the rest of the team. Wright planned on splitting them up tomorrow, putting two of them on Dedman's apartment and two on the bank where Dedman had accounts. Those seemed the most likely places they might spot Dedman. That's all he knew to do with the clock running out.

Wright saw Jansen was at her desk and Grossman was leaning over the shoulder of Miranda Kemp, an analyst from Langley. Grossman looked up at him when he heard the door close and straightened up.

"Miranda's got something, boss."

Wright hurried over to stand behind Kemp.

"Back it up to the first video, Miranda," Grossman said.

The analyst rewound a video on her computer screen and then played it from the beginning.

"What am I looking at?" Wright asked.

"This is from a camera at the Bari ferry landing," Kemp said.

The video clip played for about two minutes before Kemp stopped it. There in the frame was an attractive brunette wearing a white puffer jacket and designer jeans.

"That's her?" Wright asked. The woman looked a little different from the photo he had seen of Drita Nikolli.

"That's her, boss," Grossman said. "No doubt about it. The photo from her Albanian license is a couple of years old. But that's definitely Drita Nikolli."

"Any sign of Dedman?"

"No, sir," Kemp said. "We have some other CCTV footage of her, but nothing on Dedman."

"Okay, let's see the rest," Wright said.

Kemp replaced the first video with another. "This is another angle from another CCTV camera."

Wright saw more footage of Nikolli from the back, walking away from the pier towards the customs and immigration checkpoint. Kemp opened another video.

"This is footage from the Italian customs agency CCTV."

Wright watched the woman walking towards the camera after passing through the checkpoint. The video quality was better, and he felt convinced he was looking at Nikolli.

Kemp switched to another video. "This is from a Bari municipal traffic CCTV camera."

This time, Wright saw a profile shot of Nikolli standing on a sidewalk at a pedestrian crosswalk. She was looking down at a cell phone. He searched the surrounding crowd, but saw no one resembling Dedman. Nikolli started across the street, and Kemp stopped the video and loaded another.

"This is another angle from a different camera."

Nikolli continued across the street to the opposite sidewalk and then turned right and walked along it. Kemp kept switching videos to track

Nikolli until she turned left onto the sidewalk along an intersecting street. Then other cameras picked her up and tracked her until she crossed that street at another intersection. She turned left and again and followed the sidewalk with a series of cameras tracking her until she stopped and then entered a retail mall. All along the way from the ferry landing to the mall, Wright saw Nikolli looking down at her phone frequently, as if she was expecting a call or text.

"Looks like she is expecting contact from someone," Kemp said.

"Maybe they split up," Grossman speculated. "She went to Italy alone. He's still back in Albania. She's waiting for him to call or text to see if she made it there, or she is texting him and waiting for a reply."

"Maybe," Wright said. "Or maybe he is on his way by some alternative form of transportation to Italy. It's obvious she breezed right through customs and immigration, so Interpol hadn't placed the flag on her passport yet. We already flagged Dedman's, so the ferry wasn't an option for him. I'm betting he crossed over too, but hadn't made it yet when these videos got recorded. You got anything else, Kemp? Her coming out of the mall?"

"No, sir. I've reviewed a lot more video from the camera showing her go in and from other cameras in the vicinity, but I found nothing showing her coming out."

"I'm sure she didn't just stay inside," Wright said. "It's a mall, not a hotel."

"I've reviewed videos up to when the mall closed for the evening," Kemp said. "I've looked at other videos that pick up all the alternative exits, but I didn't see her."

Unknown to Wright, Grossman, and the analyst, Drita Nikolli had got lucky. Yes, the new outfit she bought had helped a lot, even though she hadn't been trying intentionally to disguise her appearance. But where she got lucky was when she exited the mall out the same doors she had entered at the perfect moment. The angle of the sun was such that the glare from the sunlight hit the camera lens in such a way that it washed out her image from about her shoulders up. So, when the young woman wearing the gray tailored, knee length camel wool coat over a maroon turtleneck with black leggings and black trainers walked out of the mall, she was unrecognizable on the video, her face and even her hair color masked by the glare of the sun on the lens. That enabled Drita to escape the notice of the eagle-eyed analyst who gave no attention to the woman in the long gray coat.

"Any videos from the airport or the bus or train station?" Wright asked. "We already knew she was in Bari from the cell phone GPS data Kara found yesterday. What we need is where she went from there."

"The other analysts and I have been reviewing all the public transportation CCTVs," Kemp said. "We haven't spotted her on any of it and we're up on all those systems."

Again, the analysts had paid no attention to the woman in the camel wool coat who was also wearing a colorful scarf over her hair by that time, though several Bari central train station CCTV cameras had caught her from multiple angles lasting several minutes. And all the way up until she boarded the train to Rome. Had it not been for the lucky break at the mall, Kemp would have likely identified Drita and discovered which train she had taken to Rome.

"Okay, this is a bust," Wright said. "Forget Bari. She isn't there anymore. The next logical destination is Rome. Start focusing there. Same thing. Review all the CCTV footage we are up on and especially the trains and bus stations."

"Yes, sir," Kemp said,

Wright looked around at the other analysts. "That goes for everyone. It would help us to know how they are traveling to Berlin. I know that has to be their final destination."

The other analysts responded in unison, "Yes, sir."

"Kara!"

"Yes, sir?"

"Find out from Interpol the exact date and time they flagged her passport. It takes what, three hours to get from Bari to Rome by train? If Interpol placed the flag before she could have reasonably left Bari, then we can save time by assuming she wasn't able to travel by air out of Rome."

"Yes, sir, I'm on it," Kara replied.

"Doubtful she would fly, anyway," Grossman speculated. "It's not an option for Dedman. Why would he send her to Berlin ahead of him? I think they would stick together as long as they are still together."

"Probably right," Wright acknowledged. "And my gut tells me they are still together, so let's assume that unless we find a reason to believe otherwise."

Chapter 32

The train sped north across the Austrian border without the complications of border police boarding to check passports. Dedman's hopes that he and Drita would finally arrive in Berlin in the afternoon without getting detained or something worse happening soared. That is until the train slowed and stopped at the station in Matrei am Brenner, Austria to discharge and take on passengers before continuing north to Innsbruck and over the German border.

When Dedman scanned the station platform beyond the windows on the other side of the car, he tensed when he saw three people standing on the platform waiting to board the train, two males and one female, wearing the uniforms of the Bundespolizei, the German federal police. The Bundespolizei carried out a wide variety of law enforcement tasks, among them border protection and railway security.

Dedman knew the procedure. The German federal police officers would board and check passports during the approximately seventeen minutes it would take the train to travel from Matrei am Brenner to Innsbruck. That way, they could detain anyone without the proper travel documents to enter Germany, remove them from the train, and turn them over to Austrian authorities in Innsbruck before the train crossed the German border. Given the number of passengers on the train and the relatively short period the officers had to perform passport checks, Dedman could only hope they focused their attention on ferreting out illegal migrants. He glanced at Drita and saw she had also spotted the police officers.

Dedman leaned over and whispered to her as the doors of the train opened.

"Remember, when they approach us, just hold up your passport so they can see the cover. Hopefully, they will just continue past us. They don't have a lot of time to check the entire train before we get to Innsbruck."

"Okay," Drita whispered back, digging into her purse for her passport.

Dedman took his U.S. passport out of his backpack and held it in his hands. The three German police officers boarded the first car, two cars ahead of the one he and Drita occupied. Dedman couldn't see them once they boarded, but knew as the train left the station, they would begin working the length of the train from front to back.

Only a few minutes passed before the three police officers entered their car and began checking passports. Dedman and Drita sat in the third row on the left side.

The officer in the lead stopped and looked at the two passengers, a man and a woman, both flashing friendly smiles and holding their passports aloft before he had even said "passports, please." He noted the cover of the male's blue passport, and recognized the man was an American and then glanced at women's burgundy passport embossed with "Republic of Albania." Clearly these two weren't illegal migrants, the focus of the checks he and his colleagues were making. Probably partners on holiday. Nothing aroused his suspicions, so he didn't reach for the passports to give them further inspection. Instead, he nodded and continued to the passengers in the next row. "Passports, please."

Dedman heaved a sigh of relief and the tension he felt eased, although the shot of adrenalin still coursed through his bloodstream. He had already formed a plan of action if things had gone south. But to his relief, they had dodged a bullet.

"Are we safe now?" Drita whispered, looking over her shoulder and watching the German police officers reach the rear of the car and then pass through the enclosed vestibule into the next one.

"Should be," Dedman replied. "We will be in Innsbruck soon and then we'll be across the border in Germany. I don't expect any more passport checks before we get to Berlin this afternoon."

* * *

At two fifty-eight p.m., the train stopped at a lower-level platform of Hauptbahnhof, the Berlin central train station. Dedman had told Drita he would exit the train from the adjoining car while she exited from the car they had occupied. He told her to follow him, staying only close enough to not lose sight of him, up the escalators to the ground level and then to the main entrance on the south side of the station. They would then meet in the large, open paved plaza outside and walk to the taxi stand and get a cab.

Walking through the station, Dedman was on high alert, and trying to avoid security camera angles. He assumed Wright knew he would have to return to Berlin briefly before falling off the grid, and he had half expected at least a large Berlin police presence at the station. But he observed nothing unusual as he walked through the station with Drita trailing behind.

Dedman paused near the escalator to platforms thirteen and fourteen at the luggage lockers. He took a key from his pocket, inserted it, and unlocked the locker. Opening the locker, he removed a cardboard box and stuffed it quickly into his backpack. Then he continued to the exit, passed through the doors, and continued walking until he was halfway across the plaza to the street before he turned and waited for Drita to join him.

She looked around at all the unfamiliar sights as she approached him. Then, together, they continued to the street and toward the taxi rank. Drita was curious about what Dedman had taken out of the locker, but didn't ask.

Drita and Dedman slid into the back of a Mercedes E series and Dedman gave the driver an address on Silbersteinstraße. Ten minutes later, the taxi dropped them at the address in front of a nondescript three-story hotel. Dedman paid cash for a room for two nights, took the key from the clerk, and then the couple took the stairs to their room on the second floor. Dedman opened the door and followed Drita into a plain, small room.

Dedman dropped his backpack on the bed and went into the bathroom to wash his face. He dried with a hand towel and then walked back into the room. It was a spartan affair with a double bed, chest against one wall, and two wooden chairs. The carpet was threadbare. Drita stood looking out the window at the dingy alley below.

"Even the view is minimalist," she said without turning.

"It's only for a night or two at the most," Dedman said. "It's off the beaten path and serves our purpose."

Drita turned to look at him with the crooked grin on her face he loved. "Stayed here before, Jake?"

He smiled back at her as he sat down on the end on the bed. "Not really, I just sort of have a mental catalog of places I have checked out here in Berlin. Places I could go if I ever needed to disappear."

"I see."

"Listen, the people I worked for, they know I would have to return to Berlin to pick up the things I came here to get. The first places they would check after my apartment would be the nicer hotels, so we couldn't go near any of those where they require a credit card and passport."

"Jake, don't you think it's time to tell me a bit more about the man I've hooked up with? What work did you actually do before we met? You mentioned your government. Were you some sort of spy?"

"Drita, I can't tell you any of that. If I did, you would be more unsafe than you already are."

"I think I deserve to know, Jake. You've already involved me. What's wrong with me knowing exactly what we're up against?"

"I know," Dedman said. "I shouldn't have involved you." He took a deep breath. "I should have left you as soon as we crossed the border and were out of Greece. Then I should have left you with that police officer in Albania. I shouldn't have met you in Bari after putting you on the ferry."

"Then why didn't you leave me?" Drita asked, her bottom lip quivering.

"Because I'm selfish. I didn't want to leave you."

"I didn't want that either, Jake. I still don't. You keep talking about how much danger we're in, but then you won't tell me anything about what's going on. It would help me deal with it better."

"It's not too late, Drita. We can say goodbye and I can walk out that door and you can have your old life back. But I can't answer your questions right now. I may never answer all the questions you have."

"Jake, I care about you, and I believe you care about me. But if it's going to work, we can't keep secrets from each other."

Dedman stood up, his anger flaring.

"This is not some sort of game! These people will kill you if they have to! If something happens to me and they find you, no matter how much you believe you wouldn't tell them everything, you would. They would make you. That's what they do. Everyone talks when the pain gets bad enough. And if they found out that you knew things you shouldn't, they would kill you."

Drita looked at Dedman in utter astonishment, unable to speak.

"I'm sorry for frightening you, but I have to make you understand why I can't answer your questions. I'm the guy you agreed to drive to Albania a few days ago. That's who I am. That's where your knowledge about me starts and ends. I can't ever tell you anything about who I was before that day."

"What if that doesn't work for me?" Drita shouted.

Dedman strode across the room and grabbed her upper arms. "Keep your voice down," he hissed. "If it doesn't work for you, then we will go our separate ways. But not here and not now. I will get you somewhere safe and then you can do what you want. But for now, we have to stay together."

Drita leaned into him. Dedman relaxed his grip on her arms and put his arms lightly around her waist, and held her close.

"I'm sorry," Drita sniffed. "I'm just scared, but I want to be with you."

"I will not let anything happen to you," Dedman said softly. "As soon as I end things here, we'll go somewhere safe and things will get better. I promise."

"Okay, Jake," Drita said, pulling away and wiping her tears with her hand. "I trust you and I want to be with you. I've never felt so sure about anything in my life."

"And I want to be with you, Drita." Dedman leaned forward, and they kissed.

"I need to go out and get some things," he said. "Stay here and rest. When

I get back, there is a good restaurant up the street. We'll go there and get dinner."

"You promise you will come back? You won't leave me after my silly outburst?"

"I'll be back, Drita. I won't ever leave you unless you ask me to."

Chapter 33

Dedman left the hotel and walked two blocks down the street before entering a hardware store. After purchasing several hand tools, he left, walked another block, and entered an electronics shop. He bought items there and then left, heading back to the hotel. On the way, he stopped in at a pharmacy and purchased two more items. He hadn't identified the hotel previously while living in Berlin only for its out of the way location but also its proximity to shops in the area he thought he might need to visit, just as he had this afternoon.

Back in the room, he dropped off his purchases and then he and Drita left together for the restaurant a block up the street in the opposite direction from the shops he had just visited. After the meal, he would take Drita back to the hotel and would then begin the busy evening he had planned.

* * *

At the safe house, at five p.m., Wright called everyone together in the operations center. "Tomorrow will be a long day, people. If Dedman isn't in Berlin already, I feel sure he will be tomorrow. So, I want everyone rested. Andy will get a couple of taxis and take everyone to a hotel to get a good night's sleep."

The analysts murmured their surprise but approval. Wright had kept them sequestered at the safe house since arriving in Berlin and they looked forward to an evening away.

"Well, almost everyone," Wright corrected himself. "We're maintaining the overnight watches. Kara and I will stay here and cover the eight p.m. until midnight."

Inwardly, Kara Jansen groaned. She didn't want to be cooped up alone with Jerry Wright. In fact, the idea frightened her more than a little because she knew the operation was ending, one way or another. Without the station team of officers they had for only about fifteen more hours, Wright couldn't sustain the operation.

"Andy, I need you back here at midnight. Kara can get some sleep and you and I will cover the midnight to four a.m. watch. Pick two from the team to come back here to relieve us and to cover the four to eight a.m. shift."

Grossman nodded. He wondered why Wright would sacrifice his own chance for rest after saying they faced a long day tomorrow. It seemed odd. His boss had spent every night back at the hotel while Jansen and the analysts hadn't left the safe house. Wright had only allowed him to return to the hotel to shower and change after getting a few hours of sleep before returning once. And it looked like he was going to get the short end of the stick again tonight, covering the midnight to four a.m. shift with Wright.

"That's it," Wright said. "Get some rest, people, and be ready to hit it hard again tomorrow morning at eight."

Grossman and the analysts shuffled out through the door, heading for the stairs down to the ground floor. Kara looked at Wright. "What do you want me to do?" she asked. "I could go pick up takeaway for our dinner."

"You have a car downstairs?"

"Yes, parked on the side street a little way down from the alley entrance."

"Okay, but I'm not ready for dinner. You getting anything else on the woman's phone?"

"No, I'm sure she disabled it. It's not pinging towers anywhere."

"Then why don't you access the CCTV system at Hauptbahnhof? I feel sure they took the train from Rome. Start at eight a.m. this morning, go from there, and see if you can pick them up on any of the cameras inside the station."

"Miranda and Steven have been reviewing the Hauptbahnhof CCTV recordings all day," Kara said, not bothering to hide her opinion that looking at them again was a waste of her time.

"It's not a request, Kara," Wright said sternly. "I want you to review the video recordings again in case they missed something." Wright looked at his watch. "Stay on it until eight and then we can take your car and go somewhere for dinner. We can start the watch an hour late."

Kara nodded and swiveled her chair back to face her computer monitor. Wright headed to the back office. He sat down at the desk and called Wagner. The phone rang twice.

"Wagner."

"It's Wright. Listen, Wagner, we're working a little later this evening. I won't be leaving until around eight tonight and need you and the team to remain in position until then."

"Yes, sir."

Wright leaned back in the chair and put his feet on the desk, crossed at the ankles. He called Herman Buckley, who he had not seen or heard from in almost a day and a half. Mostly, he wanted to know if Buckley was even still in Berlin. When Buckley answered, Wright told him he intended to tie up the loose end at the safe house that evening by eight o'clock so he could concentrate on Dedman, assuring Buckley he would bag Dedman by the end of the following day and then they could all go home. It surprised Wright when Buckley just thanked him for the update, said he would be at the hotel if Wright needed him, and disconnected without his usual questions or complaints.

* * *

When Wright had disconnected, Wagner looked at his phone. *Shit.* He had plans for the evening and the Langley brasshole had screwed them up. He quickly called his team members one by one and broke the bad news. None of them sounded any happier about three hours of overtime than he did. Wagner was just glad tomorrow was the last day of this goat rope. He and his team hadn't seen a speck of evidence that the target was even in the city or that Wright's crew had any clue where the target was as far as he could tell. *Suck it up, buttercup*, he thought. Just one more day on this crap assignment and then his life would return to normal.

Chapter 34

Dedman had walked Drita back to the hotel room after dinner. He had then dumped the contents of his pack, pocketed the monocular, and then had put the items he needed inside the pack. After warning Drita not to leave the room until he returned or to open the door to anyone but him, he had left. The taxi he had called was waiting for him in front of the hotel when he had exited the building. He had given the driver the address on Wilmersdorfer Straße.

By protocol, Dedman shouldn't have known where the program's Berlin safe house was located. But he did. One day, when the custodian, Kara Jansen, had met him to hand off some documents for a mission, he had invited her to have coffee with him afterward. That was also against protocol. Jansen's job was providing logistical support to the Hydra assets, not socializing with them because protocol prohibited it. But Jansen had been eager enough to go to a coffee shop with him. She had followed his motorcycle in her car the short distance to the shop he had chosen. Then, after having coffee together, he let her leave first. He had then followed her clandestinely.

Jansen had parked on a side street off Wilmersdorfer Straße that ran beside a two-story building with a sign out front identifying it as a travel agency. From the corner, he had watched her walk to the entrance of the alley behind the building. After waiting several minutes, Dedman rode his bike down the side street, turned into the alley, and rode past the rear of the building. There, he had spotted a heavy steel door with a keypad affixed to the exterior wall beside the door. He had found the safe house. Dedman had done all of it out of an abundance of caution. He had figured if he ever needed the safe house, it would be easier if he already knew where it was instead of waiting for someone to give him directions.

* * *

The taxi driver dropped Dedman at the address he had given, a six-story building a block down from the travel agency, on the same side of the street. It was almost dark. He went inside the building, found a stairwell, and took it up to the sixth floor. Then he continued up another two flights of stairs that ended at a locked door that opened onto the roof. Using the lock picking tools he had bought at the hardware store, Dedman unlocked the door in less than thirty seconds and went through the door onto the roof.

He walked to the chest high parapet at the edge of the roof facing the travel agency building. Taking out the monocular, Dedman scanned the alley behind the building. Quickly, he located the two men in civilian clothing who thought they had concealed themselves. They looked like agency field officers to Dedman, but their tradecraft seemed lacking. It was obvious they were on static posts on opposite approaches to the rear entry door of the building.

Dedman left the roof and took the stairwell back down and exited the building. After crossing the street, he found a bench where he could sit and lean out past a metal trash bin and see the front of the travel agency across the street through the monocular. Again, it took him only minutes to find two more agency types standing in shadowed static positions on opposite ends of the building. That made four.

Getting to his feet, Dedman walked casually along the sidewalk until he was less than a half block from the travel agency building. He looked around and saw no foot traffic nearby. It was getting close to eight p.m. and all the day shifters had left work for home. There were cars parked at the curbs on both sides of the wide, darkened street.

The area was mostly a business district with no late-night coffee shops, restaurants, or bars on the block to attract people and foot traffic. But the parked cars suggested there were apartments nearby. Dedman selected a Volvo sedan simply because the fuel fill cover faced the sidewalk. He checked both directions again, and then knelt beside the rear quarter panel of the Volvo and pulled on a pair of latex gloves.

Dropping his pack, he took out a screwdriver with a wide tip and popped the fuel fill cover open. He returned the screwdriver to the pack and took out a cotton rag. He rolled it between his hands and then stuffed one end of the rag into the fuel fill neck opening. Once the rag was halfway down the fuel filler neck. Taking a bottle of nail polish remover from the pack, Dedman opened it and poured it on the rag, saturating it with the acetone-based solvent. Returning the empty, recapped bottle to the backpack, Dedman took out a disposable lighter. Lighting it with his thumb, he held the flame beneath the rag until it caught fire. Then Dedman grabbed the pack, stood, and walked casually back in the direction he had come from.

He crossed the street before reaching the intersection in a darkened area, and then following the sidewalk on the same side of the street as the travel agency. He was almost to the side street beside the building when the Volvo's fuel tank exploded.

Car alarms on both sides of the street blared, set off by the blast wave. He saw the two field officers out in the open, looking down the street at the burning Volvo, knowing the blaze had temporarily impaired their night vision.

Just as he reached the intersection, the two field officers Dedman had seen at the rear of the building ran towards Wilmersdorfer Straße on the sidewalk across the side street from him. Dedman veered right and crossed the side street on a diagonal course behind them. Once the men disappeared around the corner of the building, Dedman sprinted into the alley. He knew he probably only had a few minutes before the men realized their colleagues weren't under attack and returned to their static positions in the alley.

Dedman found two utility boxes attached to the rear wall of the building near one corner. He used the heavy-duty screwdriver to pry open both boxes. In the first he found several coaxial cables that delivered internet and television services to the building, and wiring for the alarm system. Using wire cutters, he cut all the cables first. Then he pushed the four wires to the alarm system in front to the side, knowing cutting any of those would activate the alarm. Instead, he cut the two wires behind them, one which provided electrical power to the security system and the other backup power from a battery.

In the second box, he found electrical wiring. Dedman located the main power breakers, two of them. He switched them both off, and then, using the screwdriver, he broke the plastic switches to make it impossible for anyone to turn the power back on without replacing the damaged breakers.

There had been lights illuminating the second-floor interior when he arrived, but looking up Dedman saw the building was now dark. Grabbing the pack, he raced around the corner of the building to continue his plan.

Shrugging on the backpack, he found a drain pipe, jumped up and grabbed it with both hands. With the toes of his shoe soles pressed against the brick exterior, he rapidly climbed up the pipe towards the roof. He already heard the sirens of emergency vehicles getting closer that were responding to the car explosion he had used for a diversion.

Chapter 35

When the explosion erupted, Kara thought it had come from out front of the building. There were no windows inside the safe house facing Wilmersdorfer Straße, but there was one at the end of the short hall at the head of the stairs that did. She walked to the door, intending to look out that window to see what happened. But when her hand touched the doorknob, Wright shouted at her.

"Where do you think you're going?"

Kara turned and saw Wright standing in the doorway of the back office. "I was going out in the corridor to look out the window to see what happened. Didn't you hear the explosion?"

"That has nothing to do with us," Wright growled, even though he feared it might. "Get back to work on those video recordings. It's five minutes until eight. We'll check it out when we leave for dinner." In truth, Wright wasn't letting her out of his sight. He turned and went back into the back office.

Kara sighed. She felt like a prisoner. But she returned to the computer and sat back down at her computer.

Wright sat back down behind the desk. He leaned over and pulled up his right pant leg and checked the knife in the sheath strapped to his calf. It had been a minute since he had done any fieldwork, but he was confident he still had the skills. Once they got in her car to go to dinner, he would put a neck hold on her and thrust the eight-inch blade between her ribs into her heart. He would leave her body in the locked car for someone to find the following morning, and then the late Kara Jansen would be someone else's problem.

When Kara sat down and looked at her monitor, she saw the computer had lost the internet connection. Then the alarm system chirped. Kara looked up at the alarm monitor on the wall beside her desk and it went dark. She heard Wright walk out of the back office and into the room. She turned her head to look at him.

"Something is wrong with the alarm system," she said.

Wright spoke, but stopped when all the lights went out, as did the computer monitors. There was one emergency, battery powered light in the room attached to the wall above the entry door, and it came on but only dimly lit the room.

"And now the power is out," Kara said. Wright just looked at her blankly and said nothing.

"It's Dedman, isn't it?" Kara asked, standing up.

"Be quiet," Wright demanded, turning back toward the back office. It was dark in there except for the dim moonlight coming through the windows. "I'm going to check the office."

When Wright turned toward the office door and walked toward it, he pulled the SIG Sauer pistol from Kara's field box from his waistband. More frightened by what had happened than she was by Wright at the moment, Kara followed him. She didn't want to stay out in the operations center alone.

* * *

When he had gained the roof, Dedman scrambled over to the edge above the fire escape outside a second-floor window. It had a retractable ladder to keep anyone on the ground from climbing it. But once he finished, he could unlock and lower the ladder and use the fire escape as his exit point.

Dedman squatted and opened the pack. He pulled out the small box he had retrieved from the locker at the train station. Opening it, he withdrew a Glock 23 and a full magazine. After inserting the magazine, he racked the slide and tucked the weapon into his waistband at the back. After stuffing the box back into the pack, he put the pack back on, grabbed the edge of the gutter, and swung his legs over the edge of the roof. He dangled by his arms for a moment before dropping almost soundlessly onto the fire escape platform.

He tried the window and found it locked. Flicking the blade of the tactical knife open, he pushed it into the gap between the two casement window frames and flipped up the lock. Then he pulled the windows open. Listening for a moment, he heard voices somewhere outside the room.

He pushed aside a curtain and scanned the room, but saw no one inside. Spreading the curtains apart, he climbed through the window into the room and closed the windows quietly behind him. He still heard the voices outside the open door and crept quietly to the darkest corner of the room, not reached by the moonlight.

Placing the pack on the floor, he stood with his back to the wall and listened. He heard a male voice approaching the open door, a voice he recognized instantly. "I'm going to check the office." Dedman pulled out the Glock and waited.

He watched the man enter the room with a pistol held out with both hands, sweeping the room with it side-to-side like a searchlight. He recognized the face behind the weapon. Jerry Wright. As Wright walked deeper into the room, checking potential hiding spots, a woman entered the office cautiously behind Wright. He recognized her, too. Kara Jansen.

"You want me to go downstairs and get the team?" Kara whispered.

Wright turned toward Kara, holding up a hand, either signaling her to stay or to stop talking. Maybe both. Dedman stepped out of the shadows with the Glock trained on the side of Wright's head.

"Put the weapon down or you die," Dedman said in a voice that brooked no argument.

Wright sighed and bowed his head to his outstretched arms. "Dedman?"

"Weapon down!"

Wright let the pistol drop from his hands to the floor.

Dedman motioned with the muzzle of the Glock for Wright to move towards the desk, away from Kara Jansen, who stood frozen just inside the doorway. Wright raised his hands to shoulder level and starting moving.

"Okay, what do you want…"

Before Wright finished the sentence, Dedman grabbed a handful of his jacket at the shoulder, turned him around, and slammed him face first into the wall beside the desk. Then he jerked the man back around to face him, grabbed him by the collar of his shirt, and pressed the muzzle of the pistol against Wright's forehead.

"I told you I quit. I told you to leave me alone."

Angrily, Wright slapped the muzzle away from his face and straightened his jacket. "What the hell are you talking about? You've lost it. Shit!"

Dedman said nothing in reply.

"You better start listening, soldier. I told you that was a decision you could not make. You are U.S. government property. You don't know what you're doing, do you, Jacob? No, you don't have a goddamn clue."

"Why did you burn me in Istanbul?" Dedman shouted back. "Why are you trying to kill me?"

"What happened with Sobeeh? What happened in Istanbul? How did you screw that up, Jacob? So help me, I'm going to make you tell me what went wrong if it kills me!"

"I did nothing wrong! I got blown! Turkish intelligence was waiting for me! I barely got away from them!"

"Bullshit!"

Stunned by Wright's anger and aggressive counter accusations, Dedman began doubting himself. Had he misunderstood everything? Was he the one in the wrong? He lowered the gun to his side, unsure of what to say.

Wright put a hand on his chest and shoved him back. "You told us when, you told us where, you picked the goddamn strike point. Then you failed. Then you disappeared. That's unacceptable, soldier! Do you hear me? You failed! And you're going to tell me why!"

"I did nothing wrong. Someone compromised me…"

Wright glared at Dedman. He looked back at Wright in confusion, not knowing what else to say to defend himself. But then, suddenly, he realized what was happening.

Wright was playing him, using the same tactics the instructors at The Point had used to break him down so they could rebuild him into what they wanted to make him become. They had made him feel like a failure so he would become pliable, dependent on them, crave their acceptance. His anger rekindled. But this time, he didn't raise his voice.

"I don't want to work for you anymore," he said coldly.

"You think you can just walk away? With everything you know about the program? It doesn't work that way, Jacob. You said you wanted to serve. You told us you would do anything to save American lives. Didn't you? You're not a liar, are you, Jacob?"

Dedman punched Wright in the solar plexus with the butt of the pistol, causing temporary paralysis of the diaphragm, knocking the wind out of him. Then, with a hand on Wright's chest, he slammed him into the wall again. Wright leaned against the wall, stooped over, clutching his chest and trying to catch his breath, but with his eyes locked on Dedman. Dedman had the Glock back up aimed at Wright's face.

"Jacob Dedman is dead. He died a week ago in Istanbul. You're going back to Langley and you're going to tell them Jacob Dedman is dead. You understand me?"

"Where the hell do you think you can go where we won't find you..."

Dedman punched Wright in the face with a right cross, causing the man's head to snap back against the wall. Dedman leaned in, his hand on Wright's throat and the muzzle of the Glock pressed against his chest.

"I swear to God if I so much as feel someone behind me, there is no measure of how fast I will start killing your people. I will kill them until you stop sending them. And then I will come and find you, and I'll kill you. I quit. Leave me the hell alone."

"Mr. Wright, you okay, sir?" a faint voice said. "Mr. Wright?"

Dedman looked down at Wright's waist, where his open jacket revealed the cell phone clipped to his belt. Wright must have had someone on speed dial and pressed the button. Now there was an open line.

"Who did you call?"

Wright stared at him defiantly, with a smirk on his lips. Dedman slammed the Glock into his face violently, using it as an impact weapon. Wright's head bounced against the wall and then he collapsed to the floor at Dedman's feet, unconscious.

Dedman turned and looked at Kara Jansen, gun down. She looked back at him, her eyes wide, looking petrified. Dedman walked quickly to the corner and retrieved his backpack, shrugged it on, and went to the window where he had entered the office. He pushed the windows open and put his left leg out on the fire escape, but quickly drew it back.

From the light of a street lamp, he saw a dark sedan parked in the alley that hadn't been there before. Exhaust curled from the back of the vehicle, showing the motor was running. He could tell from the glow of a burning cigarette that someone sat behind the wheel. Out on the fire escape, he would be in full view of whoever sat in the car and a sitting duck until he made it down the ladder. If he made it to the ground without getting shot off the ladder first. He altered his exit plan, although he expected getting out of the building was about to get a lot tougher. Brushing past Kara, he headed to the exit door.

Chapter 36

He had given up smoking ten years previously. But tonight, he was a bundle of nerves. After leaving the hotel, he had stopped off and bought a package of cigarettes, intending to smoke only one to calm his nerves. Cigarettes had always done that for him in the past. But after parking the car in the shadows of the alley where he could see the door, he couldn't stop himself. He smoked one cigarette after another, lighting the next with the previous one before tossing the butt out the window. He had done what he was about to do before, but not in a very long time. Still, he had to do it. He had no choice. And while he didn't like it, despite the nerves, he felt sure he could do it. But he would have to get close. And that's the part that bothered him most. He lit another cigarette off the last one and tossed the butt out the window, his eyes riveted on the door.

* * *

When Dedman opened the door, he heard running footsteps on the stairway headed up. A lot of footsteps. He left the door open and hurried to the corner beside the window just past the top of the stairs, tucking the Glock back into his waistband. He still didn't want to kill anyone unless they forced him to do it. Dedman waited in the shadows.

Four guys came up the stairs, one after the other, heading towards the open door to the safe house. The last in line was pointing a pistol slightly to the left, so he wasn't covering the men ahead of him. Dedman sprang out from his hiding place as the man topped the landing and chopped down on the man's wrists with his forearms, causing him to drop the weapon. He slammed the man in the chest with his left forearm, knocking him back against the wall across from the stairway landing, and then struck him in the throat with a right forearm, half collapsing his trachea. When the man grabbed his throat, Dedman grabbed his jacket, twisted the man's body left to right until he faced the wall, and then Dedman punched him right behind the right ear. The man sagged to the floor.

The guy who had been the third in line coming up the stairs whirled around when he heard the attack behind him. Dedman delivered a backward elbow strike to the man's face before spinning toward him. Already staggering, Dedman put both hands on the guy's chest and shoved him hard into the field officer behind him, who had also turned back toward Dedman. The temporarily incapacitated officer fell back into the man, trying to bypass him with his pistol thrust out, trying desperately to get the muzzle on target. While the guy he had elbowed continued falling, Dedman grabbed the wrist of the third guy's gun hand, pushed the muzzle to the right and spun the guy around by the arm before hurling him hard into the man behind him who had been first up the stairs. That fourth officer fell backwards, landing hard on his back, hitting his head on the floor.

Still gripping the wrist of the guy with the weapon with his right hand, Dedman first kicked the guy in the head he had elbowed in the face who was trying to get up, knocking him unconscious and then he slipped his left forearm beneath the gunman's arm and grabbed his jacket at the shoulder. Using an arm lever throw, he flipped the man, who landed hard on the floor on his back, banging the back of his head violently on the hardwood floor while Dedman simultaneously stripped his weapon from his hand.

Dropping the pistol on the floor, Dedman spun to face the man first up the stairs, who struggled to get back to his feet and back into the fight. He had just recovered his own dropped weapon. Dedman shoved the muzzle aside with a forearm against the gunman's wrist and then slammed an uppercut against the man's jaw, snapping his head back. With the guy reeling, Dedman grabbed the slide of the pistol with his left hand, chopped down on the man's wrist with his right hand and stripped the pistol out of the man's hand. Dedman used a hip throw to flip the man onto his back. The man's back hit the edge of the landing and the first step. He groaned loudly in pain, but raised his head and tried to rollover on his hands and knees to get up. But Dedman slammed the weapon against his head violently, knocking him out cold.

Catching the change in the light coming from the open door to the safe house, Dedman whirled toward the door in a shooting stance with the pistol gripped in both hands. But just as his finger tightened on the trigger, he recognized Kara Jansen outlined in the doorway by the dim lighting behind her.

"My car is parked outside if you need a ride," Kara said with uncertainty, her hands raised to her shoulders. "I'm not armed."

Dedman lowered the pistol and looked at her. "Why would you help me?"

"I'm leaving, anyway. I have to get away from here, too."

"Okay, then let's go downstairs before these guys come around. You first."

Kara nodded, dropped her hands, and started down the stairs with Dedman following. When they both got to the exit door, Dedman told her to stop and Kara turned back to look at him.

"Where is your car parked?"

"On the side street, just past the entrance to the alley."

"There is someone in a running car with the lights out parked in the alley facing that door. I don't know who it is. Once we go out the door, run diagonally toward your car and don't stop, no matter what happens. They may start shooting. I'll be right behind you and will cover you if they do."

"Okay, but I don't think it's anyone from the agency. I think you already got all of them. But I'll run and won't look back just the same."

"Good," Dedman said, grabbing the doorknob. Then he jerked it open. "Run!"

Kara took off at a sprint in the direction Dedman told her. He ran right behind her, looking over at the parked sedan with his pistol up and ready, but they passed beyond the view of anyone in the vehicle with no one shooting at them and he didn't hear a car door opening.

Kara pressed the key fob on the way, and the taillights flashed, and the alarm chirped. She opened the door and climbed quickly behind the wheel while Dedman slid into the front passenger seat. Before he got his door closed, Kara had already started the car, put it in gear, and the tires squealed as she pulled away from the curb. The car shot down the street and they were gone.

Chapter 37

Dedman lowered his window. Then he efficiently disassembled the weapon he had taken from the CIA officer and he tossed it piece by piece out the window. He raised the window back up.

"Where are we going?" Kara asked.

"I thought you knew."

"Well, if you have time, I need to run over to my apartment to grab my go bag. Then I can drop you wherever you need to go on my way to the airport."

"You're leaving Berlin?"

"Yes, if I can get to the airport before the last departure. I don't even care where it's going."

"You're running?"

"Hell yes, I'm running. I hope I'm out of Berlin before the word gets out about what happened back there."

"That wasn't on you."

"I know. But I think Wright planned on killing me tonight. He was giving off a seriously weird vibe, and he arranged for us to be alone at the safe house. He sent everyone else to a hotel."

"Kill you? Why would he do that?"

"He's shutting down the program and I guess he thinks I know too much."

"What? Hydra? Wright, is shutting it down?"

"Yes, him and Herman Buckley."

"Who is Herman Buckley?"

"Wright's boss. He's in Berlin too."

"Why are they shutting it down?"

"Because of the senate hearings."

"What are you talking about?"

"You don't know about the senate hearings? It's all over the news, even here in Berlin."

"I don't keep up with the news. It's nothing but propaganda. I don't waste my time on it."

"Okay, then you haven't heard about the leaks either?"

"Nope."

"Well, an NSA contractor, a systems analyst, stole a bunch of highly classified documents. Then he leaked the documents to the Washington Post and New York Times. Apparently, the documents implicated the agency, the NSA, and a bunch of other alphabet agencies in illegal activities. When it started coming out, the senate impaneled a select committee to investigate the allegations. I guess some documents mentioned Hydra and enough information about the program that the senate committee has some idea of what it is about."

"So, that's why Wright and his boss are shutting it down?"

"Right. To prevent the committee from finding any proof to substantiate what they think the program is all about. To save their own asses."

"But why would they want you dead? I don't get that part."

"They want us all dead, everyone who knows anything about that program who might go before the committee and testify. If there is no one to testify, then Wright and Buckley can spin it any way they want and cover it all up, covering their asses at the same time."

"Hang on. You mean that's why they are trying to kill me?"

"Yes. I'm sure they have already killed the other assets. You're the last one. I think Wright planned to take you out while you were on the job he was talking about back there, but somehow you escaped and his plan fell apart."

"You said he killed the other assets? How many of us are there?"

"You mean how many were there? I'm sure all the others are dead. There were five counting you when they started shutting down the program."

"Why do you believe Wright had them killed? That's insane."

"Because part of my job was tracking all of you. Your phones had locator beacons in them. I had to check your locations every day. The beacons were the electronic leashes. Anyway, the locator beacons of the other four assets all went dark on the same day, within minutes of each other. And when I reported it, based on past experience, I thought there would be a meltdown at Langley. But Grossman, Wright's assistant and the person I reported to, reacted like it was no big deal. It seemed like he already knew about it before I even called it in."

"Hard to believe, but I'm sure you know what you're talking about."

"That's not all. You know the clinic in Virginia you all had to go back to for annual medical evaluations?"

"Yes, I was supposed to go back next month."

"It's gone. There was a natural gas explosion that destroyed it and every member of the medical staff died in the blast or fire. And with all the other stuff that has happened, I don't believe it was an accident at all. I think Wright and Buckley sent someone to blow it up and make it look like an accident."

"That's fucked up."

"Tell me about it. When I started putting the pieces together, it terrified me. Maybe I was on the kill list, too. Now I'm sure of it. That's why I'm running."

"If they want you bad enough, they will track you with your passport and whatever other digital exhaust they can find."

"I have a plan for that," Kara said with a smile. "My father is Dutch. After the agency hired me, I applied for blood right citizenship and a Dutch passport. The agency doesn't know about my second passport. They will uncover it eventually and find out where I've gone from Berlin. But by the time they find out, I plan to be somewhere else. I'll get off and stay off the grid, destroy my credit cards, and pay cash for everything."

"It's difficult, but yes, it can be done," Dedman agreed. "I'm planning to do the same."

"What happened to the woman you were with? Are you still together?"

"Not your concern, Kara."

"Yes, that's fair. I was only curious. No offense intended."

"But speaking of her, do you know if they flagged her passport?"

"Yes, they submitted a bogus international warrant to Interpol and had them flag it."

"Shit, I was afraid of that."

"Actually, I submitted the warrant and had them flag her passport," Kara said cautiously. "Wright made me do it. So, if it matters to you, I could contact Interpol, cancel the warrant, and have them remove the flag."

"You can do that?"

"Yes, because I coordinated it through Interpol directly. But I'll have to do it fast. Once the agency realizes I'm gone, they will remove my access. But I have an agency laptop at the apartment I can log in to Langley's servers with. I'll do it as soon as we get there."

"I would appreciate it, Kara. Don't suppose you could remove the flag from mine?"

"Sorry, afraid not. I don't have the authority. I mean, I could remove it, but the system would flag it and probably in five minutes they would put it right back on."

Kara made a right turn and parked at the curb in front of a compact three-story apartment house. "I'll only be a few minutes, but you can come up."

"Sure, why not?" Dedman said, opening his door. He didn't mention he didn't want her out of his sight, since he didn't know how much he could trust her.

Kara used a key to enter the lobby and then led the way, with Dedman following her upstairs to her apartment. She unlocked the door and switched on the lights, and they went inside.

"Want something to drink?" she asked.

"Water would be good."

"There is bottled water in the refrigerator. Help yourself. I'm going to grab the laptop."

"Okay."

Dedman went into the small kitchen and got a bottle of water out of the refrigerator. Kara came out of the bedroom with a laptop, sat down at the kitchen bar, and booted it up. A minute later, she typed on the keyboard and the agency log on page popped onto the screen. Kara entered her credentials and a new page opened.

"I'm in. They haven't canceled my access yet."

After switching through several screens and a lot of typing, Kara logged out and closed the lid on the laptop.

"All done. Interpol will review it and hopefully, by tomorrow, they will lift the flag."

"Great. Thanks, Kara."

"No problem. Let me change and grab my go bag and we can get out of here before Wright or someone from Berlin station shows up."

Ten minutes later, they were back in the car.

"Where do you want me to drive you?" Kara asked.

"You sure you have time? I know you need to get to the airport."

"I've got a little time. I don't think the last departure is earlier than eleven p.m., so I can drop you somewhere."

"If you're sure, that would be great." Dedman gave her a cross streets address about six blocks from the hotel where he and Drita were staying. No, he didn't know how far he could trust Kara, but even if he trusted her implicitly, he didn't want her knowing which hotel they were staying in just on the off chance the agency caught up to her before she caught a plane out of Berlin. When the pain got bad enough, a person would give up everything they knew even if they didn't want to do it.

Chapter 38

Jerry Wright woke up on the floor of the safe house office. Slowly, it all came back. He remembered how he got there and why his entire body seemed to hurt.

Using the wall for support, he got to his feet unsteadily. Wright touched his face and his hand came away wet. He knew it was blood. He took a step and his foot kicked something. Trying to focus in the dim light, he saw it was the pistol Dedman made him drop. He groaned when he bent over to pick it up and glanced around the room. He was alone. At least in the office.

Holding the gun out, he went out into the operations center and scanned the room, illuminated by the emergency light. He found it empty. It seemed both Dedman and Kara Jansen were both gone.

Wright shook his head to clear the cobwebs from the blow to the face that had rendered him unconscious. He stepped out into the hallway through the open door with the pistol up and ready. There he found the four men, his borrowed security team, on the floor of the corridor. They were all down, but as far as he could tell, they were alive.

Gingerly, Wright made his way downstairs. He opened the exit door. Wright took a step out into the alley, looking left and right. He heard a car running nearby. Limping out to the side street, he looked down the street in the direction Jansen had said she had parked but saw no car. He didn't know how long he had been out, but he guessed long enough for Dedman to escape. Had he taken Jansen with him? Or had she got suspicious and left on her own?

Wright shoved the pistol back into his waistband and walked back towards the door. First, he needed to check on the unconscious officers upstairs. Then, he would call Grossman. Hearing a car door close, he stopped. Looking down the dark alley, he saw a parked sedan. He raised a hand to shade his eyes from the light of a nearby street lamp behind it.

* * *

He had tossed the cigarette out the open car window as soon as he saw the man limp out the door and toward the side street. It was Jerry Wright. Picking up the Beretta 92FS with the suppressor off the front passenger seat, he opened the door and got out, closing the door behind him, harder than intended. He had taken several steps toward him by the time Wright turned back from the side street and felt a knot in his stomach when he saw Wright holding a pistol.

He stopped dead in his tracks. Then, to his relief, Wright stuck the pistol into his waistband and limped back toward the door he had exited from. He continued walking toward Wright, who stopped when he seemed to notice the car. Jerry lifted a hand to shade his eyes as he continued walking toward him.

When they were no more than a dozen feet apart, he saw the recognition in Jerry's eyes when their eyes met. Leveling the Beretta, he shot Wright twice in the chest. Jerry collapsed to the ground.

He advanced to Wright's side and looked down at him. Then he aimed the pistol and put another bullet in Wright's forehead. It wasn't pleasant business, and not meant as a coup de grâce, something he thought vulgar. No, it was a dead check, something always best done in a circumstance like this one. Satisfied, Herman Buckley turned and walked back to his rental car, relieved it was over.

* * *

Neither spoke for several minutes as Jansen drove toward the address Dedman had given her when they left her apartment. Preoccupied with working out how he and Drita would get out of Berlin with his passport still flagged, Dedman was quiet. Kara seemed to sense he wasn't in the mood to talk.

Maybe he should send Drita somewhere alone once her Interpol passport flag got lifted. Then he could find some way to travel that didn't require a passport to the location they decided on and could meet her there. But what would it achieve? Dedman knew it was far from over. Wright would keep hunting him. Kara broke the silence.

"How did you know you could find Wright at the safe house to confront him? How did you even know he was in Berlin?"

"Educated guess that he was in Berlin," Dedman replied. "I know Wright. I know how he thinks. After his plan in Turkey failed and I escaped from the airport in Athens after they detained me because he flagged my passport, I knew he wouldn't just wait patiently at Langley for someone else to give him what he wanted. I knew he would come here, that he would come to Berlin because he would know I needed to come back here before I fell off the grid."

"And the safe house? Just a lucky guess?"

"Yes, in a way. It surprised me he was there so late. My objective had only been to verify he was using the safe house to coordinate his search for me. I couldn't imagine he would risk setting up at Berlin station when he was trying to find and terminate one of his assets. Too much of a chance something would leak and others in the agency would discover what he was doing. Then people would have asked questions. When I saw the guys outside, I breached the safe house just looking for someone who could tell me where Wright was and why he was trying to kill me."

"Well, you got lucky. Until this evening, all week Wright had always left the safe house by five p.m. and returned to his hotel. If you had come yesterday, he wouldn't have been there."

Kara was quiet for a moment. "I know how horrible it is to say it, but it's still the truth. I wish you had killed Wright instead of just knocking him senseless. It would have made both our lives easier if you had."

"Even after everything you've told me, Kara, I still couldn't have done that. I wouldn't have killed him. Right now, I'm innocent. I've done nothing wrong, and Wright has no justification for killing me. But if I had killed him, I would have gone from being innocent to being guilty in the eyes of the agency. That would have given them the justification for killing me."

"Yes, true. I guess I haven't thought the whole thing through. I just know Wright is still alive and able to hunt us both down, no matter where we go."

"You're smart, Kara. You will be fine. I know it will be hard knowing there will be people who love you thinking you're dead and you won't be able to do anything about it. But you must avoid family, friends, anything familiar. Get small, stay small, and fall off the grid. You can do it and they won't find you as long as you're careful and don't make stupid mistakes."

"Where will you go?"

Dedman looked at her, the greenish subdued lighting of the instrument panel illuminating her face. "You know I won't tell you that just as I wouldn't think of asking you to tell me where you plan to go. I wouldn't want to know."

"Yes, I get it. You're right."

"You said Wright's boss is also in Berlin?"

"Yes, Buckley. Why do you ask?"

"I don't believe I got through to Wright. I'm thinking maybe I should have a talk with Buckley too. If he has influence over Wright, maybe I can convince Buckley to tell him to stand down."

"I don't think that will work. I've seen how it is when Wright and Buckley are together. Wright shows him zero respect. He treats Buckley like he's the underling. I doubt Buckley tells him what to do."

"Still, I think it's worth trying," Dedman said. "Maybe it won't work, but since he is here in Berlin, I'm going to go see him. Do you know where he is staying?"

"Yes, the same hotel Wright is staying at. I overheard them talking about it. They are at the Grand Westin Berlin."

"Thanks."

Kara flipped the turn indicator, slowed, and pulled over at the curb. "This is your stop."

"Thanks for the ride, Kara," Dedman said, grabbing his backpack from the floorboard. He opened the passenger door to get out, but paused. "Good luck, Kara."

"Same to you, Jacob."

Dedman nodded, got out, and closed the car door. Then he walked away into the night. Kara Jansen watched him disappear into the darkness. She sighed and then pulled away from the curb, heading for the airport.

Chapter 39

It was after nine-thirty and his hotel was only about six blocks away. Dedman considered going there to check on Drita and to reassure her he was okay before heading to Buckley's hotel. But he didn't think he would be much longer and decided he would see Buckley first and then return to the hotel when he had finished.

What Kara had told him made sense. Maybe it would be a waste of effort. But since he didn't know Buckley, he couldn't be sure how the man would react. If he let Wright walk all over him the way Kara had described, maybe Buckley would be more susceptible to persuasion.

When he saw a taxi coming down the street ahead of him, he took it as an omen, and decided. He flagged the taxi. The driver stopped at the curb across the street, and Dedman jogged over and got in the back seat.

"*Grand Westin Berlin, bitte,*" Dedman told the driver.

"*Jawohl mein Herr.*"

As the Mercedes slipped away from the curb into traffic, Dedman looked at his watch. It was nine thirty-four p.m. and he hoped Buckley was in his hotel room.

* * *

The taxi driver delivered him to the front entrance of the hotel. Dedman walked to the front desk.

"May I help, sir?" the desk clerk asked.

"Yes, will you phone guest Herman Buckley, please? We're meeting in the bar, and I want to let him know I've arrived."

"Certainly, sir." The woman checked her computer and then picked up her desk phone as Dedman leaned over the counter and watched her punch the pound key and then the room number, 416. After several moments, she hung up the phone. "I'm sorry, sir, there is no answer. Is there a message?"

"No, thank you. He's probably already in the bar. Thanks very much."

"My pleasure, sir."

Dedman walked away thinking, then decided he would find a way in to Buckley's room and wait for him. He walked to the elevator bank and took an elevator up to the fourth floor. When he got off, he picked up the house phone on the table positioned between the two elevator doors and pushed the button for the front desk.

"Front desk, may I help?"

"Yes, this Herman Buckley, room 416. Housekeeping didn't leave me any clean towels when they cleaned the room today. Could you possibly send someone up with some bath towels, please?"

"Right away, Herr Buckley and I apologize for the inconvenience."

"I'm down the hall visiting with a friend in another room, but I'm heading back to my room in a few moments. But please, tell your staff member to go in and leave the towels if I don't answer the door when they knock."

"Yes, sir."

Dedman hung up. He walked to the alcove that contained vending machines and purchased a soda. Then we walked down the corridor, identified Buckley's room, and continued walking to the stairwell door at the end of the hall. He went through and let the door close, but held it open a crack in case it automatically locked. Standing behind the door, he peered through the small reinforced glass at the top.

Less than five minutes later, he saw the light above an elevator illuminate showing one had arrived. A young woman wearing a hotel uniform stepped out carrying an armload of towels. She walked up the corridor toward Dedman and then stopped at the door of Buckley's room and knocked. After several moments, she unclipped a key card from her uniform top, slipped it into the electronic door lock, and went in. The door closed behind her.

Dedman opened the door and hurried down the corridor, past the door of Buckley's room. Then he turned and watched the door. It opened and the young woman stepped out. Dedman took a quick step forward and put a hand on the door to stop it from closing.

"Oh, thank you so much for bringing the towels," he said with a big smile.

"My pleasure, sir."

Dedman held up the soda can. "I didn't expect you to bring them so quickly, and wanted to grab a soda. Guess I just missed you."

"I understand. Goodnight, sir."

"Goodnight and thanks again. I'll mention to the desk how pleased I am with the excellent service."

"Thank you, sir." The woman turned and walked back toward the elevators. Dedman pushed open the door, walked in, and let the door close behind him.

It was a suite with a seating area, separate bedroom, and en suite bathroom. Only a desk lamp in the seating area was on. After checking each room, Dedman dropped the unopened soda can into the bathroom wastebasket. Then he pulled the Glock out of his waistband, opened the closet door, and sat down on the floor with his back to the wall to wait. Satisfied the hotel employee hadn't seemed suspicious, he felt confident he could wait as long as necessary, but hoped that Buckley would return soon.

* * *

Herman Buckley parked the rental in the guest parking garage at the hotel and headed for the elevator. Finally, his stomach had settled after completing the assignment Maxwell Newton had given him. He had stopped at a bar on the way and had two drinks to relax. He now felt only relief that he had done the deed and it was all behind him.

Arriving on the fourth floor, he walked to his room. Buckley felt exhausted and wanted to sleep. But he couldn't go to bed for a while. Wright had told him when they spoke on the phone that he had sent everyone at the safe house except the Jansen woman to a hotel to get them out of the way. But Jerry had said he would resume the normal four-hour watches at midnight. Buckley knew there was no point in going to bed now before he received the inevitable call around midnight when someone discovered Wright's body in the alley.

He inserted the card, the lock clicked, and Buckley entered the room. He took off his jacket and draped it over the back of the sofa. Then he took the Beretta out of his waistband and laid it on the desk in the sitting room. He had forgotten the suppressor in his jacket pocket, but would remove it later. Right now, he felt like another drink.

Buckley walked to the minibar, selected two miniature bottles of Johnnie Walker Black, and picked up a crystal glass. He sat down behind the desk, cracked the seals on the bottles, and poured the scotch into the glass. Then he reclined in the chair, sipped the scotch, and thought about the stressful evening.

When Buckley had arrived and parked in the alley, it had been almost eight, the time Wright had told him he would take care of Kara Jansen. And Wright had told him how he intended to do it. Buckley had already decided he would eliminate them both when they exited the safe house.

It had alarmed him when he saw the four Berlin station security officers run into the entrance at just past eight. He had assumed they would have left the site by five as usual, but had assumed Wright must have kept them later, since he was there alone with Jansen. Buckley considered aborting, but he had waited to see what was going on.

Minutes later, the door opened. Buckley had reached for the door handle, thinking it was Wright and Jansen coming out. He didn't know where the security officers were, but they had never exited the safe house, and he was determined to finish the assignment. But to his surprise, Jansen and a man sprinted out the door toward the side road and disappeared. It hadn't been Wright.

Recovering from the shock. Buckley realized who the man must have been, and it chilled him to think about how close he had been to Jacob Dedman. He had waited, working up the nerve to enter the safe house to see what had happened inside, wondering if Dedman had killed everyone except Jansen. But while finishing a cigarette before getting out of the car, Wright had come out the door limping, heading for the side road. Buckley had decided he wouldn't miss his opportunity. He had tossed the cigarette out the window, and picked up the Beretta. But just as he got out and took a few steps, Wright had turned around with a pistol in his hand, heading back to the door.

Buckley's resolve had wilted. There was no way he was getting into a shootout with an armed Wright. But then Wright had shoved the pistol into his waistband as he limped toward the door. Buckley had realized Jerry had been hurt, and if he moved quickly, he could shoot Wright before he could get the weapon out again. So, he had continued walking towards Wright.

Wright hadn't recognized him immediately because it seemed the glare of the street lamp behind the car had interfered with his vision. Buckley had seen him shade his eyes with a hand. But after a few more steps, their eyes met, and Wright had recognized him. But it had been too late. He had put two bullets in Wright's chest and then walked closer for the dead check once Wright had fallen to the ground. There had still been no sign of the security officers. It had gone even smoother than he had hoped, and now it was all behind him.

Buckley lifted the glass, enjoying the feeling of warmth as the scotch slid down his throat.

Chapter 40

When Dedman heard the room door open and close, he pulled the closet door closed, stood, and continued waiting. He heard someone walking around in the sitting room, but then it got quiet again.

Dedman cracked the door open and peered out. He didn't see anyone or hear anything. Easing out of the closet, he walked silently to the bedroom door and did a quick peek. He saw Buckley sitting at the desk, his back to him, having a drink. Dedman crept across the carpeted floor until he was standing behind Buckley. Extending his arm, he pressed the muzzle of the Glock firmly against the base of Buckley's skull.

Startled, Buckley cried out, leaned forward in the chair, and reached for the Beretta on the desk. Dedman jammed the muzzle of the Glock harder against his head, and Buckley froze.

"That's a bad idea," Dedman growled.

"Dedman?"

Holding the Glock in his left hand and keeping the muzzle pressed against Buckley's head, Dedman reached out and grabbed the Beretta with his right hand. Then he shoved it into his waistband.

"Yes, Buckley, it's me," he said finally.

With a shaking hand, Bucket set the glass down, sloshing liquor on the desk.

"I knew it was you I saw running from the safe house with Jansen."

"Yes, it was, and that tells me you were the one in the sedan parked in the alley behind it."

Buckley, almost frozen by fear, said nothing. He felt sure Dedman must have killed the four security officers, but somehow Wright had escaped him and Dedman had fled with the woman. He expected Dedman was here now to kill him.

Dedman reached into his jacket pocket with his right hand and withdrew the micro recorder he had bought at the electronics store. He depressed the record button.

"Why are you and Wright trying to kill me?" Dedman asked in a tone that made Buckley's blood run cold.

"It was Wright, not me. We had to shut the program down, and Jerry said we had to eliminate everyone who knew about the program and what we were doing."

"But you went along with it, yeah?"

"I had no choice. I had let Wright run the program the way he wanted until things went too far. By then, he had pulled me into it as deep as he was. I couldn't stop him. If the truth came out, he and I were both going to federal prison."

"What about the brass upstairs at Langley? Didn't they authorize Hydra?"

"No! Why do you think we went to such extremes to shut it down? It's always been an off the books black on black assassination program."

"So, no one at Langley knows what you were doing?" Dedman pushed the muzzle a little harder.

"Max... Maxwell Newton, my superior, knows about it now. He knows about some of it. But I suppose you don't know how it works. Those upstairs want to keep their hands clean. They insist on plausible deniability where black programs are concerned."

"So, Newton, your boss, is okay with you and Wright murdering all the assets, blowing up the clinic, and killing the medical staff?"

Buckley gasped. Somehow Dedman knew everything. "That all happened before I told him about the program. Before he reviewed my budgets and asked direct questions. You were supposed to be the end of it and it would be clean. There would be no one alive who could tell the senate committee the truth and we could spin it however we wanted. The investigation would go away."

181

"But Newton knows you and Wright intended to kill me and Kara Jansen, and he has no problem with it."

"Dedman, you don't understand. None of it was personal. But the truth about Hydra cannot come out. No, we didn't want to go to prison, but it was far bigger than that. If the senate committee uncovered the truth about Hydra and the extrajudicial executions, it would not only embarrass the government, it would have far-reaching negative consequences for the agency."

"So, we all had to go."

"I'm sorry, but yes. I'm a patriot and have served my country. The country and the agency must come first."

"I think you and Wright are insane. But that's not why I'm here, Buckley. I've done everything asked of me. And now I want out. I don't want to do it anymore and now that you shut down the program, I'm out of a job, anyway. I'm telling you what I told Wright. Stop hunting me and leave me alone. I'm not telling anyone anything and you don't have to kill me to keep my mouth shut. You tell Wright that. You tell him to leave me the hell alone."

"I can't tell Wright that and I don't think he gives a damn, anyway."

"You're his boss, Buckley. You're going to tell him, and you better convince him."

"He's dead! Wright is dead!"

"The hell he is. I roughed him up, but he was still breathing when I left the safe house. Wright isn't dead."

Buckley sat trembling and said nothing.

"I get it now. You were in the car in the alley. And now I know why. If he's dead, you killed Wright, so he couldn't drag you and your boss down with him."

"No, that's not the reason! I only followed orders."

"Orders from who? Your boss, Newton?"

"Yes, things had gone too far, Dedman. Can't you understand that? Newton sanctioned it because it had to be done. Jerry wasn't getting the job done and had to go."

"I don't understand any of it, Buckley, because it's wrong. All of it."

"Don't moralize with me, Dedman. You're a killer. That's what we trained you to be, and that's all you will ever be. A killer. Now you're here to kill me, so just do it. Get on with it. Get it over with."

"I'm not here to kill you, Buckley. I have killed no one with the agency. You know why? Because I'm innocent and have done nothing wrong. Killing you, Wright, or anyone else in the agency would make me guilty and provide the justification for what you've been trying to do to me."

"You're not here to kill me?" The relief in Buckley's voice sounded palatable.

"No, you don't deserve the star they would put on the wall at Langley. You're a criminal, Buckley. I have killed the people Wright told me to kill because he said it saved American lives. I'm an executioner, but you, Buckley, are a murderer."

Dedman hit stop and rewound the recording. He held the recorder to Buckley's right ear and pushed play. Buckley listened in horror.

"He's dead! Wright is dead!"

"The hell he is. I roughed him up, but he was still breathing when I left the safe house. Wright isn't dead..."

"I get it now. You were in the car in the alley. And now I know why. If he's dead, you killed Wright, so he couldn't drag you and your boss down with him."

"No, that's not the reason! I only followed orders."

"Orders from who? Your boss, Newton?"

"Yes, things had gone too far, Dedman. Can't you understand that? Newton sanctioned it because it had to be done. Jerry wasn't getting the job done and had to go."

Dedman clicked the stop button and walked around the desk, facing Buckley. "I quit, Buckley. You tell them Jacob Dedman is dead. Stop looking for me." He held up the recorder. "Leave me alone, and no one ever needs to hear this. If you don't, I'll make sure everyone hears it." Then Dedman slammed the Beretta down on the desk before turning and backing to the door. Pocketing the recorder, he opened the door and slipped out.

* * *

Buckley sat numbly for a long while after Dedman had left the hotel room. His mind raced as he tried to find a solution. But the thing he kept coming back to was the damn recording. He tried to recall everything he had said. But it didn't matter. He knew he had said too much. He had revealed things about the program. The very things he and Wright had wanted to cover up. He had admitted to killing Wright and had even implicated his own boss in the conspiracy. And it was all on tape.

Herman Buckley saw no way out. He would live the rest of his life with that recording hanging over his head like the sword of Damocles. Just waiting for it to fall into the hands of some journalist at the Washington Post or New York Times. Buckley picked up the glass and drained the last swallow of scotch.

Buckley knew he was a patriot. He had served his country honorably for four years in the U.S. Army and almost thirty years with the agency where he had an impeccable record. His career couldn't end with disgrace. He wouldn't allow it and would not go to prison. He couldn't.

With a sigh and tears running down his cheeks, he reached out and picked up the Beretta. He pressed the muzzle beneath his chin, swallowed hard, and pulled the trigger.

Chapter 41

The driver of the taxi taking Andy Grossman from the hotel to the safe house apologized profusely when Grossman had to get out two blocks short of the address on Wilmersdorfer Straße, but it wasn't the driver's fault. The police had erected barricades blocking the street.

Grossman paid the driver, and he continued on foot past the barricades. In the distance down the street, they saw a fire truck with its emergency lights flashing, several Berlin police cars, and a wrecker loading a burned-out car.

That looks close to the safe house, Kemp thought. As he got closer, he thought maybe the activity was almost a block past the safe house, and hoped he was right.

It was a little past eleven-thirty p.m. and Grossman was heading to the safe house to take the midnight to four a.m. watch with Wright. He still felt confused about why Wright had insisted on taking the 8:00 p.m. to midnight shift with Kara Jansen.

As he got closer, he wondered if an act of terrorism had happened. He knew that the enormous influx of Middle Eastern immigrants into Germany and other European countries had sparked unrest. He easily imagined in the years to come, the streets of Berlin and lots of other cities in the West could become indistinguishable from the streets in Baghdad and Mosul. Grossman had been in Iraq as a soldier and had seen plenty of car bombings back then. From the looks of the burned-out hulk on the wrecker, an explosion had been involved.

He walked past the first-floor travel agency and saw workers up the street putting plywood over broken windows on the building fronts about a half block down. Grossman turned the corner and continued on the sidewalk along the side street, heading for the alley. He saw the ghostly reflection of more emergency lights emanating from the alley before arriving at the entrance. When he turned the corner, he saw an ambulance and more Berlin police cars.

"What the hell?" Grossman muttered, as he watched paramedics loading a gurney with a covered body strapped to it into the ambulance. What disturbed Grossman even more was when he glanced at the door to the safe house. There, he saw the four Berlin station CIA officers sitting on the curb with their hands behind their backs. No cops stood close to the men, so Grossman hurried over and saw the men all wore handcuffs.

"What happened?" Grossman asked the guy named Wagner.

He turned his head and looked up at Grossman, who saw dried blood covering the right side of Wagner's head and face.

"Grossman, right?" Wagner said.

Grossman nodded. Wagner jerked his head towards the ambulance and then winced.

"That's Mr. Wright in the ambulance. Someone shot him to death. The cops had me identify him and it looked like two to the chest and one to the head."

"Who did it?"

"Don't know," Wagner said. "Wasn't us. That's all I can tell you about it. But the cops arrested us, anyway. They let me make a call before they took our phones, and I called Berlin station. They are supposed to send someone over here to sort it out, but no one has arrived yet."

"Where were you guys when it happened?"

"We sort of ran into a buzz saw upstairs?"

"What?"

"Mr. Wright called me at about eight, right before we were supposed to call it a day. But he said nothing. It was an open line, and I heard him shouting at someone and someone shouting back. There was some other talking in the background I couldn't make out. I kept trying to get him to talk to me, but nothing. Then the line went dead. I called the guys out front and we all made entry and ran upstairs to see what was going on."

"Then what happened?"

"The buzz saw happened. Some dude came out of nowhere when we reached the landing and ambushed us. I never saw anything like it. He was like a machine, moved faster than anything I've ever seen. Long story short, he kicked our asses. All of us. I think two of the guys have concussions. Hell, I probably have one too, along with a busted head and maybe a skull fracture. We must have all been unconscious when Wright got it because he wasn't in the alley when we went inside."

"One guy did all that?"

"Yes, but he is no ordinary guy."

"Was he armed?"

"Sure, he had plenty of weapons. He took ours."

"Did he shoot anyone?"

"No. None of us, anyway."

"Did he kill Wright?"

"Maybe, I don't know. But that makes little sense."

"What do you mean?"

"As I said, Mr. Wright wasn't here in the alley when we made entry. I'm sure he was upstairs when he called. When I came to, I searched the upstairs and found blood on a wall and the floor. But no one was in any of the rooms. Once I got all the guys up, we came downstairs and ran right into the cops as soon as we came out the door. That's when I saw the body, Mr. Wright. I can't imagine that dude brought him down here to shoot him when he could have shot him upstairs."

"Maybe Wright escaped to down here, and the guy caught him?"

"I don't think so. He got shot in the front, not in the back. I don't think he was running away."

"Did the police find a weapon?"

"I don't know. They took our weapons, well, three of them. One is missing."

"I thought you said the guy who attacked you took your weapons?"

"Oh, he did. He took them from us. But we found all but one scattered on the surrounding floor when we woke up."

"Well, shit," Grossman said. "Dedman. It has to be." Then he looked back at Wagner. "Did the police go upstairs?"

"Yes, I tried to discourage them, but I couldn't really tell them anything without compromising the site. They have been up there and found the blood on the walls and floors, some of it ours, and now they say it's a crime scene. Guess you aren't working tonight."

"No, and I need to call this in," Grossman replied. "I have to call Jerry's boss, Buckley."

Wagner nodded.

"Well, good luck. I hope your guy gets here before they haul you and the others to jail."

Wagner nodded. "Well, if not, hopefully, the cops will take us to a hospital first. I can't see very well out of my right eye and the other guys are pretty messed up, too."

Chapter 42

Grossman had called for a taxi as soon as he was past the police barricades on Wilmersdorfer Straße and then returned to the hotel. Grossman had a room at the Grand Westin Berlin, the same hotel as Wright, when they first arrived in Berlin. But when Wright told him to take the team to a hotel, he had changed to the cheaper hotel he had booked for them.

Grossman knew Herman Buckley was also staying at the Grand Westin Berlin, but he didn't know the man's room number. He needed to call the front desk at the hotel to reach Buckley. As Wright's immediate supervisor, Grossman knew he needed to tell him about Wright's death and to find out if they would continue with the operation to take down Dedman. As soon as he got back to his room, he phoned the Grand Westin Berlin.

"Grand Westin Berlin. How may I direct your call?"

"Yes, I need to reach a guest there," Grossman said. "Herman Buckley. Can you ring his room, please?"

"Yes, sir. One moment, please."

The operator had put him on hold and recorded music filled the silence. Then suddenly, another voice, a male voice, came on the line.

"*Guten morgen. Hallo?*"

"Uh…Yes, hello?"

"You called about Herr Buckley? Herman Buckley?"

"Yes, is he there?"

"I am the hotel night manager here. You are a friend of Herr Buckley?"

"Uh… actually, a colleague. We work together and I have an important message for him."

"I have some very bad news for you, sir. I'm terribly sorry to tell you this, but Herr Buckley has passed away. An incident occurred in his room almost two hours ago…"

The news rocked Grossman. First, Wright and now Buckley. He had trouble getting his mind around it. He said nothing for several moments. The hotel manager waited patiently, assuming the unfortunate news had shocked the caller.

"Uh… sorry. I wasn't expecting that," Grossman said. "You said there was an incident? What happened?"

"I am sorry, sir. I am not at liberty to share details. The police are still here and they will have to answer your questions. I have sent a staff member to get the investigator to speak with you. Can you continue holding for a moment?"

"Yes, sure," Grossman said, his mind reeling as he tried to think of who he needed to call back at Langley. He decided he should contact Buckley's superior, Maxwell Newton, although he doubted Newton even knew they were all in Berlin. Still, he didn't think he should involve the Berlin station until he talked to Newton. *What a mess!*

"I am terribly sorry to be the one to tell you this," the manager said. "This is very bad. Terribly sad. Another guest phoned about hearing a suspicious noise and when hotel security went to check Herr Buckley's welfare, the incident became known to us."

"I understand," Grossman said, even though he didn't know what the hell the manager was talking about.

"Ah, the inspector is here, sir," the manager said. "I will give him the phone."

Another male came on the line.

"*Hallo.* You were a colleague of Herr Buckley? Herman Buckley?"

"Uh… yes. That's right."

"I'm with the Berlin criminal police and responded here to the hotel. You were his co-worker?"

"Well, Herman Buckley was the supervisor of my immediate superior, but yes, we all worked together."

"Your name, please?"

"Uh… Grossman. Andrew Grossman."

"Herr Grossman, is it possible for you to come here to the Grand Westin Berlin to make the official identification and to answer a few of our questions?"

"Can you tell me what happened, inspector?"

"When you arrive, yes."

"All right, I will have to get a taxi."

"Unnecessary. Tell me where you are and I will send a car."

"Um… fine." Grossman gave the detective the name of his hotel.

"Very well. A uniformed officer will arrive in ten minutes to fetch you."

"Okay… I'll meet him in the lobby."

"Thank you for your cooperation." The detective hung up.

Grossman ran a hand through his close-cropped hair. *What a mess.* He had to call Maxwell Newton before the cop arrived to pick him up. He needed to know how much to tell the detective when he got to Buckley's hotel.

* * *

Maxwell Newton had left his office at Langley at four-thirty that afternoon. Now, just after nine in the evening, he was sitting in the den sipping a Bushmills on the rocks and watching the Washington Commanders and the Chicago Bears playing on Thursday Night Football. His wife was in Connecticut visiting their daughter and the grandchildren. Both of their sons had families of their own and Newton had the house to himself until Gretchen returned from Hartford.

The Chicago kicker booted a twenty-two-yard field goal after an eleven-play drive stalled and the Bears were already ahead ten to zip in the first quarter. It looked like Washington was already flirting with another loss and against a team who hadn't even won a game so far. Newton's cell phone vibrated on the table beside his chair. He picked it up, saw it was Langley, and answered.

"Newton."

"Sir, this is the duty officer. Sorry to bother you at home, but I've got an officer on the line, Andrew Grossman, calling from Berlin. He says it is urgent."

"All right. Put him through."

"This is Max Newton."

"Yes... uh... Chief Newton, this is Andrew Grossman. I'm Gerald Wright's assistant in SAC..."

"Yes, I know Grossman. My question is why are you calling me, or is there something you don't understand about the chain of command? Why aren't you talking with Wright's supervisor, Herman Buckley if you have a situation your boss can't take care of?" Newton was a stickler for rules and procedures and work calls after he was at home for the evening always irritated him under any circumstances.

Grossman just blurted it out. "Someone shot Gerald Wright to death in Berlin this evening. I didn't have Mr. Buckley's cell phone number and tried to call him at his hotel. They informed me some incident had occurred there and Buckley is dead."

Now energized rather than irritated, Newton set his cocktail on the table and stood up. "You've got to clean that up, Grossman."

"I can't clean it up. This is Berlin. The Berlin police were already all over it when I found out about Gerald Wright. And when I called Herman Buckley's hotel, a police inspector came on the line so they are all over that situation too. They are going to question me and I need direction on what to say."

"Good lord! Jacob Dedman? He killed them? I know you were all in Berlin on that matter."

It surprised him that Newton even knew about Dedman. He had thought nothing about the program went any higher than Buckley. "I don't know. Maybe. But the lead on the team Berlin station loaned us for the op doesn't think so."

"So, what the hell happened, Grossman?"

"I don't know any of the details, sir. I only know they are both dead. I'm unsure how much to tell the cops."

"All right, Grossman. Calm down. Of course, you don't tell them a damn thing involving the agency. Let me see... all right, do this. You tell them you and Buckley work for the U.S. Department of Agriculture and were in Berlin for a meeting with German counterparts. Don't say a word about the Dedman matter. You have the number for the Berlin station?"

"Yes, sir."

"Okay, if the police want to verify your USDA story, give them that number. As soon as I hang up, I'll call Berlin station and they will back stop your story."

"Yes, sir. What about the op? How do I proceed?"

"You don't, Grossman. Answer whatever routine questions the cops ask, then, as quickly as you can, shut it all down. Get everyone you have from Langley over there on a plane and get back here. That includes you."

"Yes, sir."

"Before you hang up, what is the current status of the operation?"

"Dedman is definitely in Berlin, but I don't know where specifically. And there is one other thing."

"What's that?"

"We have a safe house here, the program I worked on with Gerald Wright. The caretaker is missing. I don't know what her status is."

"All right. We won't worry about that now. Just get everyone the hell out of Berlin and on the way back here as soon as possible. Understood?"

"Yes, sir."

Newton ended the call. *Jesus Christ.* Now he had to go to his boss, the deputy director. And knowing that ass-covering asshole, he would probably take it all the way up the chain to Director Cooper. And as everyone in the agency understood, shit rolled downhill and Newton didn't like his chances of not getting buried in it. *Fucking Buckley.*

Chapter 43

Dedman woke up with sunlight lancing through the hotel room window. Turning his head, he looked over at Drita. She was still asleep, lying on her left side facing him, with her cheek resting on folded hands on the pillow. He watched her chest rising and falling with each rhythmic breath. A lock of her brown hair had fallen over her right eye. Gently, Dedman touched the hair with his index finger and brushed it back behind her ear. She stirred, but didn't wake.

Dedman lay on his back. He looked up at the ceiling, thinking about all he had to accomplish today. It would be the most difficult day in Berlin. He needed to go to his apartment to pick up some things, but before that, he needed to go to the bank to retrieve money from the safe deposit box. The agency could watch both places, which was what made two simple tasks difficult.

He thought about the night before. Getting to Wright and then fighting his way out of the safe house had been tough enough. Buckley had been less of a problem. Unlike Wright, Buckley was a weak man. He couldn't imagine Buckley working up the courage to kill Wright, but even weak men could accomplish desperate things in desperate times.

He thought about Wright and wondered whether the man's death would be advantageous or disadvantageous for him. Or maybe it would be no factor at all. He felt sure that Wright would never have given up and left him alone, but maybe with the recorded confession in play, along with the man's inherent weakness, Buckley might be a different story. Maybe he would quit and go back to Langley.

From the little he knew about the inner workings of the program, he speculated that no one above Buckley knew much, if anything, about Hydra. He felt sure no one knew what the program actually was and the type of missions the assets like him had performed. No, Dedman felt certain that had all been down to Wright and his former boss had then pulled Buckley in deep enough to make sure the man wouldn't interfere.

Dedman's thoughts turned to Drita. When he had returned to the hotel, he had seen the relief wash over her, but he had also seen the fury in her eyes. She had been angry he had been gone longer than promised and hadn't even called to let her know he would be out longer than planned. But by the time they went to bed, most of her anger had dissipated. He hoped she would have moved past it all when she woke up this morning.

Carefully, he got out of bed, trying not to wake Drita. Then he went to the bathroom and got in the shower, letting the warm water cascade over his skin and relax his aching muscles. He thought about Kara Jansen, hoping she had made to the airport in time for a flight out. But then he wondered if she would have gone at all had she known Wright was off the table. Maybe Buckley wouldn't have concerned her enough to run.

Dedman turned off the water and dried with the thin bath towel. Then he wrapped it around his waist and stepped out of the bathroom. He found Drita sitting on the edge of the bed in her T-shirt and panties, rubbing the sleep from her eyes.

"Sorry I woke you," he said, digging a pair of clean underwear out of his backpack.

She smiled at him. "It's okay. Time to get up, anyway."

"I shouldn't be gone as long this morning," Dedman said, slipping on the underwear. "When I get back, we'll have lunch and this afternoon I'll find us transportation out of Berlin."

Drita shook her head. "I'm going with you this time. I'm not sitting here all day again worrying if something happened to you."

"Drita, it wouldn't be safe," he said, pulling on a pair of jeans. "They will probably have watchers on the bank and my apartment. Today may be more dangerous than last night."

"I don't care," Drita said, getting up. "I'm going. If you leave me here, I won't be here when you get back." Then she walked into the bathroom and closed the door. A minute later, Dedman heard the water in the shower.

Dedman sighed. He didn't believe she would make good on her threat. But the last thing he wanted was Drita moving around Berlin on her own. That would be even more dangerous. Well, he wouldn't call her bluff out of an abundance of caution. He would let her go with him. He would just have to make sure she stayed in a safe place during the tough parts he would have to deal with.

He had dressed and was tying his shoes when she came out of the bathroom, her hair wrapped in a towel and another wrapped around her body.

"Just give me a few minutes to dress and I'll be ready to go."

"It's okay," Dedman said, revealing his acquiescence to her demands. "The bank doesn't open until nine and I want to go there before going to the apartment. We have plenty of time."

Drita smiled, realizing she had won the argument. "Time for breakfast and coffee, too? I'm starving."

"Yes, we'll get something on the way to the bank."

* * *

At about the same time as Dedman was getting out of the shower in Berlin, Kara Jansen was waking up in a hotel off the A2 motorway in Wolfsburg, Germany. The city, best known as the headquarters of Volkswagen, lay about two hundred twenty-five kilometers west of the German capital.

While Jansen had believed she would take a flight anywhere the previous evening, when she arrived at the Berlin Brandenburg Airport, she had discovered the only remaining departure was bound for Istanbul. For many reasons, she hadn't felt enthusiastic about going to Turkey and changed her mind about fleeing Berlin by air. She had retrieved her car from airport parking, got on the motorway, and driven west. She had stopped in Wolfsburg only because she had been so exhausted that she feared she might fall asleep at the wheel. So, she had exited the motorway and got a hotel room.

Not that Jansen felt any less frightened about Wright coming after her. She had just convinced herself traveling from Berlin to Amsterdam, the capital of the Netherlands, made sense. For one thing, instead of abandoning her fully paid for auto at the Berlin airport and taking the loss, she believed she could probably sell it in the Netherlands and better her financial circumstances. With her Dutch passport, she wouldn't have any problem entering Germany's western neighbor. And if the agency looked for clues at the airport to determine her destination, they wouldn't find any. Jansen felt she had made a wise decision.

Jansen had no intention of remaining in Amsterdam because she wanted to put a lot more distance between her and Berlin. While she didn't wish Dedman any ill will, she thought it almost a sure thing that Wright would focus his efforts more on finding Dedman than her. She intended to leverage that by getting as far away from Berlin as possible before Wright and the agency found Dedman, if they ever did. Once she converted her car into extra cash, she would choose a destination and fly out of Amsterdam. The agency might never even consider that possibility. She might get away clean, leaving no trail.

Jansen rolled out of bed, heading to the bathroom for a shower. Then she planned to get breakfast and fill her fuel tank before getting back on the road to Amsterdam. She should make it there with about five more hours of driving.

Chapter 44

Three people sat at the table in the seventh floor conference room at the CIA Headquarters at Langley, for a hastily called meeting. CIA Director Will Cooper, Deputy Director of Operations Angela Alexander, and Chief of Special Operations Group Maxwell Newton.

Newton had just briefed Cooper and Alexander on the situation in Berlin. He had pulled no punches and shared everything he knew about the operation, although when he discussed Operation Hydra, he had minimized his role in it and his prior knowledge about it. Instead, he threw his two dead subordinates under the bus. He claimed Herman Buckley and Gerald Wright had gone live with a black program they had presented to him as only a training program.

Director Cooper, who had spent three consecutive days on Capitol Hill getting raked over the coals by Senator James Glover and other members of his U.S. Senate select committee, was not a happy man. He had gone on the record, categorically denying that the Central Intelligence Agency conducted assassinations, much less employed assassins. But he had just learned that throughout his tenure, Buckley and Wright had run a rather robust extrajudicial execution program without his consent and right under his nose.

If the Glover Commission uncovered the facts behind Operation Hydra, getting removed as the head of the CIA by the president was the least of his concerns. Cooper was a retired United States Navy admiral, but he had no intention of going down with this ship. And to prevent that eventuality, he had to do some major damage control.

Cooper glared at Maxwell Newton. He sensed the man had not been completely forthcoming about what he had known and when he had known it, before catastrophe had struck. Regardless, he no longer had faith in the man, but he would deal with that at a later date. At the moment, his priority was to right the CIA ship by stopping the bleeding.

"Two rogue CIA officials establish and operate an off the books black assassination program staffed with a genetically enhanced super assassin. Then this assassin goes off the reservation, shoots one of them dead and the other commits suicide for reasons yet unclear. You couldn't even make this stuff up if you tried." Cooper shook his head in disgust. "So, what does he do now? This Jacob Dedman?"

"I'm not sure, sir," Newton said. "The last time I spoke with Herman Buckley, he mentioned something about Dedman believing the agency was trying to kill him. Sounded like he suffers from paranoia. Maybe he snapped. The medical technology they were using is experimental and there may be undetected side effects."

"Well, I would think if it's experimental, they surely had him medically evaluated periodically. Anything in his medical records showing paranoia?"

"We have found no medical records or any other documentation at all. My staff has searched Buckley's office and Wright's office. They found nothing. The only document that exists is the white paper Buckley submitted to me requesting approval for a training program he claimed looked promising."

"For a program like this, I expect there is no paper trail," Alexander interjected. "They wouldn't risk it. I'm certain there are program files, including medical files, but I'm willing to bet it is all digital and stored on a dedicated server somewhere off-site."

Cooper looked at Alexander and nodded. "That makes perfect sense. Angie, what I need to know is, what kind of threat to us is he?"

"It's obvious he's an enormous threat!" Newton exclaimed. "He murdered Gerald Wright. Besides that, he knows all about the program. For all we know, he may already be talking to the Washington Post or CNN about everything. We must stop him."

"Do we have witnesses who saw him shoot Wright?" Alexander asked

Newton. "I haven't seen the report yet."

"Do we have anyone who watched him pull the trigger? No. But it's the only reasonable conclusion. We have four Berlin station field officers who confirmed Dedman was inside the safe house. When they confronted him, he neutralized them by rendering them unconscious. Later, when the Berlin police showed up, they found Wright's body in the alley behind the safe house."

"He took out four armed field officers?" Alexander asked. "Without using a weapon?"

"Yes, but it's hardly surprising given the training he received and the genetic enhancements."

"If he shot Wright, why didn't he just shoot the four field officers? Especially since they had weapons. That would seem much simpler and safer for him, to me."

"I don't know, Angela. Like I said, maybe he snapped. Who knows why a mentally impaired man trained to kill does anything? How could anyone predict it? Maybe he had a grudge to settle with Wright."

"Okay, enough," Cooper said. "I asked Angie for her opinion. Stop interrupting, Newton."

"Yes, sir."

"If he wanted to hurt us, he could have already gone to the media," Alexander said. "It doesn't look like he has. And Max is only speculating that Dedman killed Wright. We don't know that he did for a fact. I want to reserve judgement on that until I talk with the Berlin police investigators. The paranoia is also only speculation. We have nothing to substantiate it. I see no basis to support he is a threat to us of any kind at the moment."

"While all that may be true, my motto is always hope for the best, but expect the worst and you will never get disappointed," Cooper said. "As far as I'm concerned, I consider Dedman a threat to this agency until proven otherwise, and that is how we will proceed."

Both Newton and Alexander nodded.

"We have a CIA-trained super assassin running around Europe with no restraint of any kind who may have already murdered a CIA officer," Cooper said. "That's beyond the pale and completely unacceptable. Angie, I brought you in to take charge of this. Clean this up by any means necessary. I will provide any resources you feel you need and then go to Berlin. I want Dedman in custody as soon as humanly possible. That's your primary mission. Investigating what happened with Buckley and Wright is your secondary mission. I want this to all go away."

"Yes, sir."

"Newton, go to Berlin with her and provide any help Angie needs. And I also want you to make certain there is not one shred of anything about Hydra left at the safe house. I want it clean."

"Yes, sir."

Cooper dismissed them, reminding Alexander to get him a list of needed resources. After they left the director's office, Newton said, "A word, Angela?"

"Sure, let's go to my office."

* * *

They took the elevator down and went to Alexander's office, which Newton noticed was much nicer than his. He wasn't happy that the old man had brought Alexander on board, much less put her in charge. He had expected the director to let him resolve the problem.

Newton believed he was better positioned to do the job because he already understood the necessary spin it would require. Unless he was careful, Alexander could prove a problem. It shocked him when she had told Cooper she was unconvinced Dedman even posed a threat.

"What's on your mind, Max?" Alexander asked after they had sat down.

"Andrew Grossman, Wright's assistant, is on a flight back here from Berlin and should arrive in a couple of hours. If you have no objection, I'd like to take him along as my assistant. Once this is behind us, I may promote him to fill Wright's position."

"Sure, I have no problem with it if you want him."

201

"Thank you. Next, I know you will have a full plate coordinating the search. Grossman and I can liaison with the Berlin police. That's besides, whatever else you need me to do."

"That sounds like a good idea. As far as an operations center, we won't be taking a staff with us. I plan to run the intelligence gathering and targeting right here at Langley through my assistant, Danny Garza. We'll coordinate that."

"Are we using Berlin station personnel for a grab or kill team once we find Dedman?"

"No, other than logistical support, given the delicate nature of this situation, I have no intention of using Berlin station. There is a ground branch team that just returned from Albania. We will take them this with us."

"You think using paramilitary operators in Berlin is a good idea?"

"Well, Wright and Buckley used Berlin station field officers. How did that work out? I want professionals trained specifically for the task."

"Yes, okay, I see your point," Newton said, resenting what he considered her condescending attitude.

"Anything else, Max?"

"One thing I forgot to mention in the meeting with the director you should know about."

"What's that?"

"Grossman told me the special projects officer, Kara Jansen, who served as caretaker at the safe house and provided logistical support, is missing. That could be another problem we need to address."

"What do you mean, missing?"

"She was at the safe house when Dedman showed up there and afterward she disappeared. We don't know under what circumstances."

"Do we think she is dead, too?"

"Honestly, I suspect she may have conspired with Dedman and has also gone rogue. I've seen nothing to show she is dead. I expect she is very much alive."

"You have evidence she conspired with Dedman?"

"Not at the moment. I just think it bears looking into."

"Okay, add it to your list. As you heard the director say, my priority is Dedman. That's what I will focus on."

"Understandable. And that's all I have. I suppose I should go home and pack."

"Yes, as soon as I complete the resource request memo for the director to sign, and make a few phone calls, I'll do the same." Alexander looked at her watch. "You said Grossman lands in two hours?"

"Yes, a little less than that now."

"Okay, it's two-forty now. He will need some time to repack. Plan on wheels up from Dulles at eight this evening. I'll call the air branch and set up the transportation."

"Fine, Grossman and I will meet you at the airport."

Alexander watched Newton walk out of her office. She had never cared for the man. His failure to mention the missing Berlin safe house caretaker to the director seemed like more than an oversight. Was there more to it than that? She would have to keep an eye on Newton. She had detected he wasn't happy to be working for her on this. Maybe it was just male ego issues, or maybe there was more to it than that.

Chapter 45

Dedman told the taxi driver to drop them at the Hotel Bristol Berlin, one block from Suisse One Deutsch Bank on Kurfürstendamm, one of the most famous avenues in Berlin, known primarily as a shopping mile. After getting out of the taxi, he and Drita crossed the street and walked west past the many upscale shops of international brands and famous names.

Dedman had left the Beretta with Buckley the previous evening for one reason. He hoped the man would use it to kill himself, knowing that if Dedman released the recorded confession, his CIA career would end in disgrace. But Dedman had already fled down the stairwell before Buckley had done exactly that.

Not only did he not know with certainty Buckley was dead or that the deaths of both Buckley and Wright had temporarily roiled the search for him. He also didn't know the CIA director had assigned Buckley's supervisor and a deputy director to take up the chase.

So, Dedman logically assumed Berlin station operatives would be surveilling Suisse One Deutsch Bank, the financial institution where he had received his monthly government direct deposits and did his banking. But he needn't have worried because it wasn't the case.

Operatives had been staking out the bank and Dedman's apartment, but the Berlin chief of station had called them off as soon as someone at Langley informed him about the deaths of Wright and Buckley and told him to take no further action in the Jason Dedman matter.

Dedman steered Drita into a café, the German equivalent of a coffee shop, behind the bus stop across the street from the bank. They had already had breakfast before taking the taxi ride across town, but Dedman ordered coffee for both of them so that they could linger inside the shop at a table against the front windows.

"Stay here while I go in the bank," Dedman said, pulling the monocular from his jacket pocket. "The people I worked with are probably watching the bank and if they try to take me, I don't want you getting caught up in it."

Dedman scanned the sidewalks around the bank, looking for anyone who seemed out of place. But he saw no one who looked suspicious. Of course, if there were operatives with solid tradecraft watching the bank, they wouldn't stand out from the many pedestrians he saw walking up and down the crowded sidewalks. Still, he noticed no one who seemed in static observation posts.

That offered little comfort since there could easily be people watching from behind the glass of the upper floors of the many buildings on this side of the street, ready to vector field officers to the bank as soon as they observed him entering it.

"You don't think talking to those men last evening convinced them to leave us alone?" Drita asked.

"I don't know if that accomplished anything. We will have to wait and see. In the meantime, we can't take any chances. To stay safe, we have to expect the worst."

"But you're taking a chance if you go to the bank, right? If they are watching it, they will try to grab you."

"Yes, it's a risk, but we need money to run. I only have a little over three hundred euros left, but I have plenty of money in a safe deposit box in that bank."

"But what if you get caught?"

"I won't get caught, but I might have to fight my way out. Getting in will be the simple part."

"But what if you do, Jake?"

"Then you will have to do the best you can on your own. You've got the two thousand euros and the woman I told you about that I used to work with removed the flag they put on your passport. Get to the airport and get out of Berlin."

"But what about you?"

"If they catch me, you can't do anything to help. You need to take care of yourself. But I promise. They will not catch me. I'll find a way out."

"I'm frightened for you, Jacob."

"Don't be. If things go sideways, keep a clear head and get yourself out of Berlin. Then stay off the grid."

"All right. Just be careful."

"I will," Dedman said, standing up. He had done all he could to locate any watchers. Now it was time to get it over with. "I'll be back in ten or fifteen minutes."

"Okay."

Dedman pushed out the door onto the sidewalk. Then, negotiating a couple of bike racks, he crossed straight across the street, avoiding traffic, instead of walking to the corner to use the crosswalk. The sooner he completed his business here, the better.

* * *

The lobby of the bank was ornate but techie and formidable at the same time, with the presence of the two uniformed armed guards. Dedman walked briskly to the desk to the right of the counter with the tellers, as he had done many times in the past. The young woman seated behind the desk looked up at him when he stopped before her.

"May I help?" the woman asked in German.

"I'm here to retrieve something from my safe deposit box."

The woman nodded and slid a card and a pen across the desk. Then she switched to English, since Dedman hadn't replied in German.

"If you will fill in your information, I will have someone assist you."

Dedman entered his name and safe deposit box number on the card and handed it back to her. She examined the card and then picked up her phone, dialed, and spoke to someone for a moment before replacing the receiver.

"It will be only a moment, Herr Dedman."

"Thank you."

A young man wearing silver wire-rim glasses and a dark gray suit appeared from the corridor behind the desk and took the card from the woman. After looking at it, he looked at Dedman and smiled.

"This way, please, Herr Dedman."

Dedman nodded and followed him up the corridor. They stopped when they got to two more serious looking uniformed armed guards standing beside an electronic device which Dedman knew was a bio-metric scanner he had encountered during past visits to the bank.

"Place your right hand on the scanner, please," a guard instructed.

Dedman stepped forward and placed his open hand on the screen. The guard pressed a button on the device. After a few moments, he told Dedman to remove his hand. When he did, a perfect and detailed image of his hand print appeared. Blinking pinpoints of red lights traced over the fingerprints of all five fingers. A few moments later, a square green light flashed above the screen. The guard turned and nodded to Dedman's escort.

"Thank you, Herr Dedman," the man said, and then turned and lead him to an elevator. They got in and the elevator descended to the basement level. The doors opened, and they walked down a short corridor, passing a counter manned by two other men in conservative suits. Dedman saw the open enormous steel vault door at the end of the corridor. His escort stopped and pushed back a maroon, floor-length drapery, revealing an alcove with a counter mounted to the wall.

"You may wait here while I retrieve the box," the man said. Then he turned and walked toward the vault.

Dedman stepped inside the alcove and leaned his back against the counter facing the corridor. Two minutes later, the banker returned with a large, shiny steel box. After placing the box on the counter, he removed a ring of keys from his pocket and selected one. Then he inserted it into a lock on the box, turned the key, and withdrew it. He pointed to a rack at one side filled with a stack of flat green drawstring bags.

"The bank bags are complimentary should you need one," the man said.

Then he turned and left the alcove.

Dedman turned, grabbed the drapery, pulled it closed, and turned his attention to the box. Lifting the hinged lid, he removed the empty, shallow tray on top and set it aside. Inside were stacks of banded currency, U.S. dollars and euros. Picking up one of the green bank bags, stenciled with the name of the bank, he quickly removed the stacks of currency and transferred them to the bag. He didn't count it as he already knew it amounted to about five-hundred-thousand dollars depending on the current euro to dollar exchange rate.

After emptying the box of the currency, Dedman picked up the four clean, crisp passports from the bottom of the box—passports with four different names from four different countries, but all with his photo inside. He put them in the bank bag with the money.

There was also a stack of credit cards inside the box bearing his name and the other names on the four passports, but he left them in the box. If the agency hadn't already canceled them, using the cards would allow them to track him.

The last items he removed and transferred to the bag included six prepaid cell phones, a micro-chip phone tap disguised as a GSM Plugin SIM Adapter card with a corresponding adapter and plug, a lock pick set, and a Bluetooth phone headset.

Dedman pulled the drawstrings to close the bag, replaced the top tray inside the box and closed it. Then he slung the bag over his left shoulder. He scooped up the safe deposit box with his right hand and tucked it under his arm. After slipping through the drapery, he headed back up the corridor. After placing the box on the counter in front of the two men, he walked back to the elevator, where his escort stood waiting. They got on the elevator and returned to the ground floor.

"*Guten morgen*, Herr Dedman," the banker said as they exited the corridor into the lobby.

Dedman nodded. "Thanks." Then he crossed the lobby and went out the front entrance, scanning to his left and right. He saw a Berlin police officer to the left and instead of jaywalking as he had done, he turned, walked the opposite direction and crossed the street at the crosswalk with a crowd of other pedestrians still scanning left and right. To his relief, no one shouting and waving a weapon appeared.

Back on the opposite side of Kurfürstendamm, he hastened along the sidewalk back to the coffee shop. There he found Drita standing outside looking at a newspaper.

"We're done here, and I didn't have any problems," he said, approaching her. She glanced up at him, stricken with fear.

"What's wrong?" he asked.

"Look at this," she said, holding out the newspaper.

Dedman glanced at it. "Oh, shit." Above the fold was a photo of him and Kara Jansen below the headline in German that he quickly translated. "Pair sought in connection with the murder of an American citizen."

"What does it say? My German sucks."

"Not now," Dedman said. "We have to move." Then he hailed a taxi.

Chapter 46

Angela Alexander sat in the back seat of the black Tahoe Berlin station had left for them at the Berlin Schönefeld Airport. Andrew Grossman drove and Maxwell Newton sat in the front passenger seat.

Before boarding the plane in Washington, D.C., Alexander had called Berlin and spoken to a police inspector investigating the murder of Gerald Wright. While she had clarified that she had no proof either of them was the shooter, she told the inspector witnesses placed Jason Dedman and Kara Jansen at the scene at the time of the murder and suggested they should interview them if they could find them in Berlin. She also suggested they might want to seek the help of the local media to locate the pair.

Alexander remained unconvinced Dedman or Jansen had killed Wright, but the sooner they were located, the better. So, she wanted to use the local police and media as force multipliers hoping to get quicker results. While he had said nothing of the sort, she expected the director had her on a short leash, and showing fast progress was the best way to maintain his confidence in her.

Despite Newton's disagreement with the idea. Alexander had decided to use the Berlin safe house as the base of the operation. She didn't want to use either the embassy or Berlin station facilities and didn't want to waste time securing another safe house. Newton didn't want to use the existing safe house because Dedman knew its location. But Alexander thought it unlikely he would return there. And they had the ground branch with them for security who were following the Tahoe in the passenger van Berlin station had also provided.

As soon as they got in the taxi, Dedman read the newspaper article after giving the driver the address of their hotel. The Berlin police spokesperson the reporter had interviewed hadn't named him and Jansen as suspects, but as persons of interest connected with the murder of Gerald Wright that the police wished to speak with.

Having his photo plastered on the front page of the Berlin papers and probably on the television media would make things even more difficult. Drita had again asked what the article said after he finished reading it, but he whispered to her he would tell her after they got back to the hotel.

When they arrived, Dedman paid the driver, and they went to their room. Drita was already pestering him to tell her more about Kara and what the news article said before they got inside.

"Kara Jansen is my former colleague who fixed the problem with your passport. The article says the Berlin police consider us persons of interest in the murder of one man I went to talk with last night."

"But you didn't kill him? Did you?"

"No, neither of us did. But I know who did."

"Then you could speak to the police and tell them."

"No, I can't. The people I worked for are behind this. They are just using the cops and now the public to find me faster."

"And they want to find your former colleague as well?"

"Yes, they want her dead, too. But she's gone. She took a flight out of Berlin last evening."

"What are we going to do?"

"First, we're going to grab our stuff and leave this room. Then we're going to my apartment, so I can get what I need there. After that, we're getting out of Berlin."

"And going where?"

"Warsaw. Poland is the closest country, and Warsaw has an international airport. We need to get out of Germany now that the police and media are involved. Then we can get a plane out of Warsaw."

"But your passport is no good."

"I've got some other clean passports now that were in my safe deposit box."

"Other passports?"

"The people I worked for provided me with alias passports. They have never been on the grid, but I can't risk using any of them more than once because when I do, they will pop up and get flagged."

Drita knew better than to ask why he needed alias passports. She didn't want another argument. He wouldn't tell her anyway. "Okay, I have everything, Jake."

"Good, let's go."

"Taxi?"

"No, there is a Deutsche Bahn stop three blocks from here. We will take the tram. Taxis are too risky now."

* * *

A half hour later, Dedman and Drita got off the tram at a stop a block from his Berlin apartment and started walking.

"Since you had no problem at the bank, do you still think they are watching your apartment?"

"Maybe not. But we can't let our guard down."

"So, I have to wait somewhere again while you go in?"

"No, you can go up with me. There isn't really a place nearby you could wait. We won't be there long. The longer we stay in Germany, the more dangerous it will be."

"How are we getting to Warsaw?"

"I've got a bike at the apartment. We'll take that."

"Motorbike?"

"Yes, sort of like the one we borrowed in Albania."

"Yeah, okay. That works."

Dedman led Drita directly to his apartment house. He saw no one suspicious on the streets and if the agency had operators staking it out from inside nearby buildings, there was no chance that he would see them anyway.

When they arrived, they climbed the steps outside to the lobby entrance. Drita pointed to the buttons on the panel beside the door.

"That's you. J. Dedman."

"Yes, that's me."

"Well, at least now I know for sure that's your real name, even if I know little else about you."

Dedman grinned. "Yes, I'm sure you feel so much better now."

He used a key to unlock the lobby entrance door. Then they took the stairs up to his third-floor apartment. He used another key to unlock the door, and they went inside.

Drita looked around. It was a huge, rambling flat with a large entry hallway, tall doors and ceilings, and a big living room. She saw it was obviously expensive. But it seemed cold, completely impersonal. She saw no photographs, no mementos, no human history of any kind.

Dedman picked up the pile of mail from the floor, shoved through the mail flap when Deutsche Post delivered it. He carried it over and dropped the pile on a large wooden desk with a chair, phone, wastebasket, and bookshelves along the wall.

"This is your office?"

"Yes."

"It's big. This is an amazing apartment. This is really yours?"

"Yes. Well, the people I worked for provided it."

Dedman checked the phone for messages while Drita roamed around taking everything in. She found a well-appointed kitchen with an industrial size stove, large refrigerator, and cooking pots, pans, and utensils neatly hanging from brackets attached to the wall.

Leaving the kitchen, she found an enormous bedroom. She walked in, stopped at a closet that took up an entire wall and slid back the door. Inside, neatly arranged were suits, crisply pressed dress shirts, casual pants and shirts. On a rack inside were dozens of pairs of shoes. And she saw nothing but men's clothes. It was a bachelor pad, and she liked that. After looking into the spacious bathroom, she returned to the living room. Dedman was putting a manila folder inside his backpack and closing the desk drawer.

"I love this apartment. I wish we could stay here."

"Well, we can't. We've been lucky so far and we shouldn't press it. I've got most of what I wanted to pick up. I just need to grab some clothes and we can go."

"You mind if I use the bathroom first?"

"Sure, go ahead. It's no problem."

When Drita came out of the bathroom, Dedman had changed clothes and had another set of clothes, underwear, and socks on the bed next to his backpack. He dumped the contents of the pack on the bed to repack it. Then he dumped the green bag he had brought back from the bank. Her eyes popped out at the sight of all the banded stacks of currency. He began neatly stacking the money inside the backpack.

"You think you have room in your backpack for some of this?" he asked. "I don't have room in mine for all of it and it's better to split it up, anyway."

"Sure. Where did you get all this? Waste management must pay very well."

Dedman laughed. "You might be surprised."

Drita emptied her backpack so she could put the money at the bottom. She started stacking it inside while Dedman finished packing his.

"How much is there?"

"Around a half million, I guess. Enough, so we won't have to worry about money for a while."

Once they had finished packing, Dedman removed the Glock tucked in his waistband. He had left it under the bed mattress at the hotel while they had gone to the bank. He hated to leave it behind, but it was risky carrying it around, and he hoped he wouldn't need it any longer. So, he shoved it beneath the mattress of his bed.

"Okay, let's go," he said.

They both shrugged on their packs and left the apartment.

Chapter 47

At the Berlin safe house, Alexander took the back office and left the large open room for Newton and Grossman. Grossman was on his cell phone, getting the power and security system back online. Alexander was on her phone talking to Garza back at Langley, organizing the analysts and targeting analysts there to get them started working on locating Dedman.

The ground branch team, led by Carter Johnson, had stowed their gear inside the two bedrooms and his team was out in the large open room, sitting on the floor with their backs against the wall, cleaning their weapons.

Johnson had his full team together again. Besides a few remaining bruises, Garcia and Rollins had recovered from the injuries sustained in their first encounter with Jacob Dedman in Albania. He and Jones hadn't got the chance to engage and hadn't suffered injuries. Chris Perkins, his assistant team leader, was back from emergency leave, and Ronnie Hill had recovered from his minor wound without complications. All his guys were good to go.

Johnson was still pissed at Angela Alexander. She was the one who had allowed the chief of station in Tirana to task his team without asking any questions. The chief of station hadn't asked enough questions of the asshole who had asked him for a team to snatch up Dedman. As a result, he and three of his team members had gone in blind and two of them got seriously injured.

Johnson figured the asshole who requested his team, Gerald Wright, was who he owed the ass kicking to. But he had learned someone, probably Dedman, had triple tapped Wright, so that ship had sailed. Maybe Dedman wasn't such a bad dude after all. But that didn't make Johnson any less eager to tangle with Dedman again to get a little payback. And it wouldn't stop him from putting a hollow point in Dedman's forehead if the opportunity presented itself.

* * *

Kara Jansen stopped in Diemen, a town and municipality with a population of about thirty thousand in the province of North Holland, Netherlands, just after crossing the border. Diemen was only about six kilometers southeast of Amsterdam's city centre. After topping off with petrol, she checked into a hotel, and then walked to a nearby restaurant for a late lunch. Since she was alone, she took a seat in the bar section and watched a television there showing news with volume muted. The channel covered news in both the Netherlands and Germany, probably because of its proximity to the border.

Kara had just taken a bite of her sandwich and almost choked on it when she glanced up at the television screen. There she saw in full color a photo of Jacob Dedman next to a photo of her. She found the Chyron at the bottom of the screen even more disturbing. "Pair sought by Berlin police in slaying of American citizen."

Fortunately, there were only a few other customers in the bar area and none seemed to pay any attention to the television. Jansen left the money to pay for her meal on the table and quickly left the restaurant, heading back to her hotel. She got in her car and went in search of a pharmacy. Once she found one, she went inside and bought hair dye and a pair of scissors. Then she continued to her hotel.

* * *

Back at the hotel, she flipped through the complimentary newspapers in the lobby and found a copy of the Berliner Morgenpost. The same photos appeared on the front page above the fold. But more importantly, it had a news story to go with it and she took the paper with her to her room.

Sitting at the table in her room, Kara read the story and discovered to her surprise that not only was Gerald Wright dead, someone had shot him to death. The article only gave the approximate address on Wilmersdorfer Straße, but mentioned an alley and Kara just knew someone killed Wright behind the safe house.

The Berlin police spokesperson had named her and Dedman as persons of interest they wanted to talk to. Kara knew neither she nor Dedman had killed Wright. He had been lying on the floor unconscious when they fled the safe house. *So, who killed him?* Suddenly, she remembered the car parked in the alley Dedman had mentioned before they had made a run for it to her car, but she hadn't even glanced at it. *Had the car belonged to the killer?*

Kara removed her shirt and took the black hair dye and scissors to the bathroom. After putting on the disposable gloves, she separated her hair into sections as she applied the dye, starting with the roots. Once she finished with the dye, she applied the included conditioner to seal her hair and rinsed it under the tap.

Finished with the dye job, she combed her wet hair and cut her shoulder-length hair short. After blow drying it, she brushed her hair and looked at herself in the mirror. Going from blonde with dark highlights to black drastically changed her appearance, and she felt confident unless someone examined her closely, they wouldn't recognize her as the woman in the papers and on television. Especially if she used more makeup than she usually did.

Finished with her hair, Kara lay down on the bed and considered what Wright's death might mean for her situation. *Did it mean she was out of danger? Could she return to her job in Berlin?* Of course, they had shut down the program so she wouldn't remain in Berlin as the caretaker of the safe house, providing logistical support. But with Wright out of the picture, maybe the agency would simply transfer her to another duty station.

Going back would certainly be simpler and less stressful than going on the run. Provided her life was no longer at risk. Not only would returning be better for her, it might be the only way she could keep them from framing Dedman for a murder he didn't commit.

She tried to think of someone at Langley she knew and could call to get more information. Then she thought of someone. An analyst she had dated for a while before they picked her for Hydra and Berlin. He wasn't part of the program, but he was always tuned in on all the gossip. He might know who was leading the search for Dedman now that Wright was dead. Kara got up and picked up her phone.

Chapter 48

Halfway down the stairs, Dedman stopped.

"What is it?" Drita asked.

"I forgot something I meant to get," Dedman said. "Wait here. I need to go back up to the apartment. It won't take me over two minutes. I'll be right back."

Dedman turned and ran back up the steps. He unlocked the door and went in. The more he thought about his and Kara's photo in the paper and the article he had read, the more certain he was the agency was behind it. They were leveraging the cops and the media to find him. It was Buckley or Langley had sent someone else. They wouldn't stop. Not ever. Not unless he made them stop. He and Drita would never be safe. They could never have a life. He would always look over his shoulder, waiting for a bullet. No, that was unacceptable. He was already tired of running and had barely started. No, he would make them stop. He would go on offense and end it now. The gloves were coming off.

Racing to the bedroom, Dedman dropped the pack on the bed. He reached under the mattress and pulled out the Glock and stuck back in his waistband at the back under his jacket. Opening the closet, he took down a box from the back of the shelf. Placing it on the bed and removing the lid, he took out three full magazines for the Glock and two boxes of ammunition and crammed them inside his pack. He also transferred a four-pack of Tile Pro Bluetooth GPS trackers and another electronic gadget from the box to his pack.

Shouldering the backpack, he went out, locked the front door, and went back down the stairs where Drita was waiting.

"Are you sure you got everything this time?" she said with a grin.

"Yes, let's go."

Dedman led her out the back exit where there was a covered car park and over to a BMW M 1000 XR motorcycle. He unlocked the chain securing the bike to a support beam and handed Drita the helmet hanging by the chin strap from a hand grip.

"So, we're riding this all the way to Poland?" she asked, putting on the helmet.

He smiled. "That was the plan."

Drita found the wording of his reply strange and thought he had given her the saddest smile she had ever seen. But she dismissed it. She knew she was prone to worry about everything.

"Where do you think we should go?" Dedman asked.

"You mean after Warsaw, somewhere to go off the grid?"

"Yes, that."

"Well, you suggested Asia when we talked about it before. That works for me. Do you have a specific place in mind?"

"I was thinking about Bangkok, maybe. At least for a while," Dedman said, straddling the bike and starting the engine.

"Yes. Yes, Bangkok. Why not?" Drita said, climbing on behind him. Dedman had shifted his pack to the front, and she wrapped her arms around his waist. Dedman shifted the bike into gear and they roared out of the car park.

* * *

Dedman took the exit off the motorway for Berlin Brandenburg Airport. Riding behind him, Drita noticed the sign. *Had he changed his mind? Were they flying instead of riding this motorbike to Poland?* She didn't ask. He couldn't hear her for the wind. She would just have to wait until he stopped.

Dedman drove into the airport and didn't stop until they arrived in front of the terminal for international departures. He switched off the engine. Drita climbed off with a confused look.

"We're flying instead?"

Dedman climbed off.

"You are."

"What? Me? Alone? What are you talking about, Jake?"

"I need you to go now. Get on a plane. You've got enough money in your backpack to make a life. Any life. Just get out now while you can, while your passport is clean."

Drita didn't move. She didn't speak. She just stared at him, confused.

"The newspaper. That was them. The people I worked for. They won't stop, Drita. We would never be safe. We could never have a life. Moving every week or two, trying to stay a step ahead. That's no life for you. I want you to be safe."

Drita stared at him, her bottom lip quivering. But she refused to cry.

"What was I thinking, right?" she said, taking off the motorcycle helmet.

"I can't protect you anymore."

"What about you?"

"I'm going to end this."

"You already tried, Jake! What more can you do? Let's just go. Let's go together. You have the passports now. We'll get on a plane and go to Bangkok like you said."

Dedman shook his head. "I'm going to end it. I'll do what I should have done in the first place instead of trying to reason with them."

"So, this is it, huh?"

"I can't protect you. Go, Drita. Go now."

Drita took one last look. Then she dropped the helmet, turned, and ran into the terminal.

Dedman stood there for a long moment. Watching her go. He almost went after her. Then he saw an airport police officer heading toward him. He picked up the helmet, put it on and climbed astride the bike. He started the engine and sped away.

* * *

Kara Jansen had reached her contact at Langley, Troy Cohen. After some small talk, she told him she had read an article in a Berlin paper about Gerald Wright getting killed. True to form, Troy had already heard the gossip. He told her it seemed one of Wright's field officers had murdered him. Then he shocked her, telling her according to the grapevine, Wright's boss Herman Buckley had committed suicide the same night Wright died.

When Kara asked him if he had heard anything else about what was happening in Berlin, Troy lowered his voice and continued in a conspiratorial tone. After swearing her to secrecy, he told her he had a friend in ground branch whose team was going to Berlin on an op, but of course his friend couldn't talk about it. But he said the rumors were that they were going to Berlin with Angela Alexander after Wright's killer.

Kara didn't recognize the name and asked who Angela Alexander was. Troy told her she was the DDO, and he had heard that the director sent her to Berlin to quarterback the hunt for Wright's killer. Kara chatted with him a little longer so he wouldn't get suspicious about why she had called and then said goodbye, promising Troy that she would call him the next time she was in the area.

Troy's information had made Kara's decision. She checked out of the hotel, got back in the car, and headed back to Berlin. She expected she would get back to Berlin late that evening. There she would get a hotel room instead of going to her apartment out of an abundance of caution. The following morning, she would reach out to Angela Alexander.

Chapter 49

When he left the airport, Dedman rode directly to an industrial area and then stopped at the gate of a storage facility. He punched in a code and the chain-link fencing gate slid open along the steel tracks. Dedman rode through the open gate and down the paved road between the rows of storage units.

Near the back of the complex, he turned right onto another road and continued between more rows of storage units before stopping about halfway down. He shut off the engine, dropped the kickstand, and climbed off. Taking off the visored helmet, he left it on the seat and walked to the door of the unit he had parked in front of. He glanced left and right and then took out a key and inserted it into the Master Lock Magnum heavy-duty stainless-steel discus padlock.

After removing the lock, he lifted the cover of the box attached to the wall beside the door and punched in a code. The red light above the keypad turned green, and he opened the door, went inside, turned on the overhead florescent lights, and closed the door behind him.

Crossing the concrete floor, he stood in front of the gate of the welded steel bars barrier that protected access the rest of the unit's interior. He inserted the same key in a lock identical to the one on the exterior door and opened it. He removed the lock and opened the steel barred gate.

Inside was a workbench stocked with hand and power tools, shelves holding bottles and cans of various chemicals, several locked steel lockers, and an upright gun metal gray gun safe against an interior concrete wall that was bolted to the cement floor. The cage, secure as a cell inside a super max prison, was Dedman's clandestine cache, where he stored the tools of his trade that the agency had furnished through Gerald Wright.

After keying in another code on the keypad at the top center of the steel gun safe door, a green light flashed and Dedman spun the five-spoke vault handle to release the eight one-inch steel looking bolts. He pulled open the door, revealing the interior of the safe.

The rack on the left held two rifles and a tactical shotgun. On the opposite side were open bins taking up half the width and height of the safe, containing multiple boxes of ammunition of various calibers. The flat shelf above the bins held a black polymer Pelican case. Rubber coated steel brackets mounted to the interior side of the safe door secured seven handguns of various calibers. An eighth empty bracket was where the Glock in Dedman's waistband had come from.

Dedman removed the Pelican case and set it on the workbench. Then he unslung his backpack, laid it on the workbench surface, and opened it. He removed the stacks of banded currency and put them on the shelf he had taken the Pelican case from. He ripped off the paper band from a stack of euros, took a thin stack of notes from it, and, after folding them, stuffed the money inside his pocket before returning the rest of the stack to the vault. Then he turned to the workbench and opened the polymer case.

Taking a narrow padded, black nylon, custom tactical rifle pack from a hook next to the workbench, Dedman carefully transferred the components of the Nemesis Arms Valkyrie modular takedown sniper rifle from the Pelican case to the tactical pack including the 4-16X 44 mm scope. Retrieving a box of 6.5mm Creedmoor cartridges from the safe, he loaded the ten-round box magazine before adding it to the pack. Then he returned the ammunition box to the safe, closed the door, and spun the vault handle.

After shrugging into the straps of the backpack, he slung the tactical rifle pack carrying strap over his left shoulder. He exited the cage and locked it. Then he went out the unit's entry door, locked it, and punched in the code on the box beside the door to rearm the security system.

Dedman got back on the motorcycle after donning the helmet, started the engine, and drove back to the storage facility entrance. After exiting the gate, he set a course for the safe house on Wilmersdorfer Straße.

He figured if the agency was still hunting him, they would still use the safe house facility. Hydra, the program they were shutting down, had been a black-on-black hit squad program, and they were cleaning it up by terminating everyone who knew anything about it.

Dedman seriously doubted they would use the embassy or Berlin station to operate from. Too much chance someone might find out what they were doing in Berlin and he still didn't believe anyone on the seventh floor at Langley had a clue that Hydra had even existed or would have sanctioned what had already happened or was now happening in Berlin. And he also doubted those at the safe house would ever imagine him returning there again.

* * *

Dedman found a place to park the bike and returned to the same building he had used before. He went back up to the roof. He wanted to accomplish two things. Dedman wanted to confirm the people trying to kill him were still using the safe house and wanted to find out if it was Herman Buckley or someone else running the cleanup op now after removing Wright. He would wait as long as it took. If there was one thing Dedman had learned at The Point, it was patience.

Dedman selected a platform beneath an elevated HVAC unit for his nest. There he would not be in view of anyone who might come through the door accessing the roof and shielded from the view of any low-flying helicopters that might pass over the building.

Dedman expertly and quickly assembled the rifle, deployed the tripod, and positioned himself prone behind it. He removed the covers from the lenses of the scope and adjusted it until he had a perfectly clear view of the alley behind the safe house and the entrance door. He would see anyone going in or coming out the door, which was only a block away, well within the eight-hundred-yard effective range of the rifle and ammunition. Satisfied, he inserted the magazine and manipulated the bolt to send a cartridge into the chamber.

If he saw Herman Buckley, Dedman already intended to kill him and would then make any necessary adjustments to his plan going forward. Attempting to use reason and minimal force hadn't gained their compliance, so now Dedman intended to go lethal.

* * *

Angela Alexander was sitting in the back office working on a list for the analysts back at Langley when Andrew Grossman knocked on the frame of the open door.

"Yes, Andy?" she said, looking up at him.

Grossman stepped into the room, looking anxious.

"Can I talk to you?"

"Sure, what's on your mind?"

"In private."

"Okay," Alexander said. *What's this about?* "Close the door."

Grossman shook his head. "Not here. I mean, *private.*"

That piqued Alexander's interest even more. She had planned to pull Grossman aside at some point so that she could get a reading on where his loyalties lay.

"Actually, I was about to go down the street to get coffee. We could talk there at the café if you would feel more comfortable."

"That works."

"Okay, let's go."

"Give me a minute to get downstairs," Grossman said. "I don't want Newton to see us leaving together. I'll tell him I'm going out to buy a pack of smokes."

"Sure, that's fine."

Alexander watched him walk out, overheard him speaking to Newton, and then heard the door open and close. She was really interested in what

Grossman had to say now, given the cloak and dagger vibe. She waited a few minutes and then grabbed her wallet and walked out of the office.

"I'm going down the street to get coffee, Max. Bring you some back?"

"That would be great if you don't mind, Angie. Let me give you some money."

"I've got it. I'll be back soon," Alexander said, walking out the door.

Chapter 50

After descending the stairs, Alexander exited the building and found Grossman waiting for her at the corner of the building, out of sight of the security camera. They crossed the street and walked side by side down the block to the coffee shop she had already scoped out after arriving at the safe house. They both got coffee and then sat down at a table towards the back.

"So, what's on your mind, Andy?"

"I'm very uncomfortable with what's going on. I'm requesting that you send me back to Langley?"

"That's not my call, Andy. Max wants you here as his assistant. I assume because you were on the ground here at the start and know what's going on."

"Of course, I know what's going on. I'm just not sure you do."

"What do mean by that?" Alexander asked defensively.

"How much to do you know about the program?"

"I received a briefing at Langley before we left for Berlin. Beyond that, I admit I don't know a lot because no one can find any program files."

"That's because none exists. Not on paper anyway."

"And you know what went on before and what is going on now?" Alexander asked.

"Yes," Grossman said, looking around to make sure no one was close enough to overhear. "Hydra was a black-on-black kill squad. Dedman wasn't the only one. There were nine when we started. Four died on missions and there were five left, including Dedman, when the treasonous NSA clown stole the highly classified documents and leaked them and compromised the program."

Grossman gave her a minute to let it all sink in. "Wright and Buckley had to shut the program down, and Wright had the other four assets terminated. He also ordered the medical facility in Manassas that did the genetic enhancement shit blown up to kill everyone there. You want to know why Dedman went off the reservation? Because Wright was trying to kill him and he figured it out."

"That's why he killed Wright?"

"Newton didn't show you the reports we picked up from the Berlin cops this morning, did he?"

"What reports?"

"Ballistics reports and autopsy reports. The same weapon used to kill Wright was the weapon Buckley shot himself with. I don't think Dedman killed Jerry. Buckley did. Then something happened that spooked him, so he did himself."

"I can't believe this."

"I'm telling you the truth. Look, I was in the army for fourteen years, the last six at JSOC, before joining the agency. I don't question orders. Never have. I carry them out, trusting that the people giving them know what they are doing. But the longer I worked for Jerry, the more uneasy I felt with what he was doing. And I also don't trust Newton."

"Why is that?"

"Because Newton knows a lot more about the program than I'm sure he lets on. He and Jerry frequently met and discussed things behind Buckley's back because Jerry always said Buckley didn't have the stomach for what needed to get done. But he said Newton did. Jerry wanted to eliminate everyone that knew anything about the program to save the medical research and his own ass, and I believe Newton has the same motivation."

"Andy, not that I don't believe you. You are in the position to know what you're talking about. But now that you have told me all this, I need you to stay more than ever so you can keep me up to speed on what Newton is doing."

Grossman looked forlorn. "You can make me stay, but I will not help you kill Dedman."

"I don't want to kill him," Alexander said, lowering her voice. "I want to bring him in alive."

"I guarantee you that will not happen for two reasons. Dedman doesn't trust us anymore, and I can't fault him for that. And I guarantee Newton won't let that happen. Let me tell you something, Ms. Alexander. You should pray you never see Jacob Dedman. Because if you do, it means he is tired of getting hunted and he is hunting us. Jacob Dedman is a genetically enhanced apex predator. He is your worst nightmare."

Alexander felt a chill at Grossman's words.

"That's all I wanted to say," Grossman said. "I've got to get back before Newton gets suspicious." He stood, turned, and walked out, dropping his untouched coffee in the trash on his way out.

* * *

From his nest, Dedman peered through the scope and saw the door to the safe house open and a man step out. After looking furtively up and down the alley, the man hastened to the corner of the building near the side street and stopped. Then he turned back and watched the door as if he was waiting for someone. Dedman recognized him, Andy Grossman, Gerald Wright's assistant. Dedman had spoken to him on the phone many times and met him several times. Grossman had been the one who drove him to the medical clinic in Manassas after he had recovered from the operations at Walter Reed after the helicopter crash that had almost left him paralyzed.

Yes, they were still hunting him and it didn't surprise him Grossman was part of it. Putting the crosshairs on the back of Grossman's head, he moved his finger to the trigger. But before squeezing it, the door opened again, and a woman dressed smartly in a cream-colored blouse under a navy jacket and wearing matching slacks stepped out. She looked mid-fifties to Dedman, but tall and fit like a long-distance runner, blonde with darker roots just starting to show and an attractive, strong face. She had the agency look about her and through the scope Dedman saw the bulge on the right side of her jacket, the imprint of a holstered handgun.

Dedman moved his trigger finger back to the index position and let it play when he saw the woman stop and exchange words with Grossman. Then they turned the corner and walked together toward Wilmersdorfer Straße. He watched them cross the street and turn left when they reached the sidewalk.

Leaving the rifle in place, Dedman left the nest and jogged to the front of the building, where the roof faced Wilmersdorfer Straße. He pulled the monocular out of his pocket and picked them up again on the sidewalk across the street. They walked side by side until they were almost directly across from him and then turned into a café. Dedman was interested in finding out who the woman was. From his demeanor, Dedman had observed that Grossman showed deference to her, as if she was his superior.

He ran back to the nest, disassembled the rifle, and put it back into the tactical pack. Looking around, he saw an air intake cover on the side of the HVAC unit. Using his knife, he removed the screws at all four corners, and removed the cover. He stuffed the rifle pack inside. Then, after removing a ball cap from his backpack, he stuffed the pack inside with the rifle and reinstalled the vent cover.

Pulling the cap down low over his eyes, Dedman jogged back to the door and took the stairwell down to the ground floor. After exiting the building, he headed up the sidewalk, staying on the opposite side of the street from the café. He walked into an empty bus stop shelter and sat down on a bench where an advertising panel on the front glass partially concealed him from the view of the front windows of the café.

Looking through the front windows of the café with the monocular, he found Grossman and the woman at a table near the back, next to a hallway that Dedman assumed led to the restrooms or to the entrance behind the front counters. Grossman was standing holding a coffee cup, but the woman sat at the table.

He watched as Grossman turned and walked away. He lost sight of him for a moment and then saw Grossman exit the café, heading back toward the safe house alone. Once Grossman was halfway down the block, Dedman got up and jogged straight across the street, dodging traffic.

Chapter 51

Arriving at the café, Dedman sneaked a peek through a front window and saw the woman was still at the table, looking down at her phone. He entered the café and strode straight to the back, where the woman sat, still looking at her phone. He quickly pulled the Glock from his back waistband while walking and shifted it to the front, holding it out of view inside his jacket. Striding toward the woman from an angle, she didn't notice him until he snatched the phone from her hand and pocketed it.

"Hey! What the hell do you…"

Dedman already had her by the upper arm, pulling her to her feet and spinning her to face the hallway. Through his jacket, he jammed the muzzle of the Glock into her ribs, leaning in to whisper.

"You scream, you die."

Keeping the pistol in his right hand pressed into her ribs, he put his left arm around her shoulders, feigning affection like a meeting of old friends or lovers, and then directed her towards the hallway, glancing around and seeing no one looking at them.

Dedman escorted her down to the end of the short hallway to the door of a unisex toilet. Keeping her between him and the door, he reached around with his left hand, turned the knob, and then pushed her with his body into the bathroom. With the Glock out and pressed against the back of her head, Dedman reached back and locked the door. Then he put his left palm between her shoulder blades, he shoved her roughly across the small room.

Wearing three-inch heels, the woman lost her balance, slammed into the wall, and only avoided falling but putting her hands out on the wall. Dedman was on her immediately. With the Glock in his left hand pressed against her head and his shoulder pressed against her back, he reached his right hand under her jacket, unsnapped the retention trap on the leather holster, and yanked out a Walther PPK. He tossed the weapon into a trash bin.

"Dedman?" the woman asked in a clearly frightened voice.

Instead of answering, Dedman shifted the Glock back to his right and pressed his left palm between her shoulder blades to keep her pinned against the wall off balance.

"I'm going to ask you some questions and you're going to answer them honestly or I swear to God I'm going to kill you. I could have killed you five minutes ago when you walked out the door of the safe house."

"Okay, just take it easy. You don't have to do this."

"Lady, if you only knew how many people have said that to me an instant before I pulled the trigger, you would piss yourself right now. Is Herman Buckley still running Hydra?"

"What? No... Buckley is dead. He killed himself."

"I wasn't sure he had the balls, but I hoped that had happened. Who are you? Are you running Hydra now?"

"No, Hydra has been shut down. I'm Angela Alexander, a deputy director from Langley."

"If you aren't running Hydra, why are you here in Berlin? What do you people want with me? Why are you trying to frame me?"

"I'm not trying to frame you. I only want you to come in. We thought you killed Wright, and the director sent me."

"I didn't kill Wright. Buckley did. I only confronted him at the safe house and tried to reason with him using minimal force. But he wouldn't listen. I knocked him out so he wouldn't follow me and left. End of story. Wright was alive when I left him, and Buckley killed him afterward. Here, listen to this..."

Dedman took the micro recorder out of his pocket, pushed play, and held it up near Alexander's ear. She listened to the entire recording from Buckley's hotel room the night he had shot himself. When the recording ended, Dedman hit the stop button and stuck the recorder into a pocket of

Alexander's jacket.

"Now, you have the proof. You can go back to Langley and tell them I didn't kill Wright and they need to leave me alone."

"They can't do that, Dedman. They won't do that. Come in and we can talk about it. I know what Wright was doing, and it was wrong. That's not us. But until you come in and talk and satisfy them that you're not a threat to us, they won't stop. If you kill me, they will only send someone else."

"Who else is here with you?"

Alexander swallowed her fear. "I won't talk about that. I'm willing to answer questions you have concerning your personal situation, but I'm not telling you anything about anyone else. It's none of your business."

Dedman foot swept her, pressing down on her shoulder, and Alexander went down hard on her knees, striking her head on the wall. Dedman pressed the muzzle of the Glock harder against her temple.

"You better get a grasp on what's happening here, Angela! You better stop poking the bear because that's a big mistake! The last mistake you will ever make!"

"Okay, okay," Alexander sobbed, humiliated by her weakness. "Just don't... don't kill me." Her pathetic plea sickened her, but he terrified her. A dangerous killer had a gun pressed to her temple and he would kill her right here, right now. Angela didn't want to die on a dirty restroom floor thousands of miles away from home and her husband and daughter.

"Max... Maxwell Newton, Buckley's boss, is here. Andy Grossman, Wright's assistant. And a ground branch team."

"You better listen, Angela. I was never a threat to my country or the agency. I did everything they told me to do to save American lives. And for that, you people have been hunting me like an animal. After I told Wright, I told Buckley, and now I'm telling you. Leave me alone. I quit and I'm not doing it anymore. I want you people to forget I ever existed and to leave me alone. You go back and tell them Jacob Dedman is dead."

"I told you they won't listen..."

"You better make them listen because I'm not running anymore. You people keep sowing the wind and you're going to reap a whirlwind. I've only used minimal force to protect myself. But no more. Starting now, I will kill anyone who comes after me and I will keep killing until the reason for it is gone. You tell them back at Langley, I will burn the whole damn thing down if they keep hunting me. You tell them I will come for them and will bring hell with me."

Suddenly, the door slammed, and he was gone. Alexander raised her head to look and then collapsed back on the floor, sobbing uncontrollably. Her pathetic behavior disgusted her, but she had never been so terrified in her entire life. But at least she was alive.

Chapter 52

Alexander regained control of her emotions and got up from the floor. *Thank God, no one walked in and saw me.* To add to the shame she already felt, urine had soaked her pants. She tried to dry them as best she could with paper towels. Then she dug to the bottom of the trash bin through wet paper towels and who knew what else until she found her weapon. She put it back in the holster and washed her face at the sink. What a mess. She couldn't go back to the safe house in her present condition.

Steeling herself, she walked out of the restroom and glanced around. Dedman had gone, thankfully. Then she saw her phone on the table next to her unfinished coffee. She had forgotten he had taken it, and he must have dropped it on the table on his way out. She left the coffee cup but picked up the phone and left the coffee shop before people started looking at her. Outside, she saw a taxi approaching and flagged it down. The Mercedes pulled to the curb, and she got in.

"Berlin Marriott, please," Alexander told the driver. Then she dialed a number and put the phone to her ear.

"Hello?"

"Andy, it's Angela. Let me talk to Max."

Maxwell Newton came on the line.

"Angie, where are you? I expected you back fifteen minutes ago."

"I saw Dedman."

"You saw Dedman? Where?"

"He ambushed me at the coffee shop."

"Oh, my God! Are you okay?"

"I'm okay, just a little shaken. But I'm not hurt. He just left. Anyway, I spilled coffee all over my clothes and I have to go to the hotel and change. I'll be back there in about an hour."

"You want me to send Andy to you?"

"No, it is unnecessary. I'm fine now."

"What did he say? Did you see which direction he went?"

No, I didn't see where he went. He disappeared. I'll be back there in about an hour and I'll tell you all about it then. Alexander ended the call before Newton could ask more questions. She couldn't deal with that. She had to get a grip first and regain control of the operation.

* * *

Dedman was back in the nest with the rifle before Alexander had left the coffee shop. He had dropped a Tile GPS tag in her other jacket pocket while they were in the restroom. The tag was light and barely noticeable, so she might not find it right away.

He had also copied the SIM card and used a CHIP DRIVE device and the GSM plug in adapter to pair her phone to one of the encrypted burners he had retrieved from his safe deposit box. An app on his phone would now record every call or text Alexander made or received using her cell phone. Now he could tap into her communications anytime he wished.

The app would alert him whenever she used the phone. His burner was now a clone of her phone and he could simply listen in on her phone conversations, but that might alert her to the compromise. Dedman would play the safe bet by listening to the recordings with the app once she disconnected.

Dedman felt only a little guilt for treating Alexander the way he had. His argument wasn't with her. Not yet, anyway. She was only following orders and hadn't appeared especially hostile to him. But he needed to put the fear of God in her by making her understand his willingness to visit violence on her and anyone else with the agency if they persisted in hunting him.

He hoped Alexander was more reasonable than Wright and Buckley had been. He bore her no malice personally. Yet, if she continued down the path she was on, he would kill her without hesitation.

* * *

"Johnson!" Newton shouted.

"Yes, sir?" Johnson replied as he hurried up the hall from the shared bedroom at the safe house.

"Dedman attacked Angela Alexander five minutes ago down the street. Get your team out in the area searching for him. He's close."

Johnson turned and shouted for the rest of his team to saddle up, then turned back to Newton. "Is she okay?"

"She said she was fine. Just shaken up."

"Did she say which way he went?"

"No, she didn't see. Angela was probably not thinking too clearly after the encounter with him. Just get out on the streets and try to find him."

"You're wasting your time looking for him," Grossman said in disgust. "If you don't see Dedman, if he isn't right in front of you, he's gone. You guys won't find him."

"Knock it off, Andy," Newton chided. "They might find him."

"Go ahead. No skin off my ass, but it's a waste of time. I'll tell you this, though. If you see Dedman, it's only because he wants you to see him and that will probably be a split second before he puts a bullet in your head."

"That's enough, Andy," Newton said. "Go downstairs and have a smoke."

"Happy to," Grossman said, getting up and walking out the door.

The rest of the Echo team had gathered around their team leader. They didn't gear up fully and had only their pistols and light body armor beneath their civilian jackets. They couldn't run around downtown Berlin in broad daylight in full battle rattle.

"Just do the best you can, Johnson," Newton said. "Maybe you won't find him, but doing something is better than doing nothing when he is this close."

"ROE?" Johnson asked.

"The rules of engagement? I authorize you to go lethal. If you see that son of a bitch, I'm giving you a shoot on sight directive."

"Roger that," Johnson said, and then he led his team out the door.

* * *

"Lot of ground to cover, boss," Perkins said when they exited the safe house. "You want us to split up?"

Johnson shook his head. "No singles. We've already seen what this dude can do. Three teams. Rollins on me. We're team one and will take this block. Chris, you and Hill take the block with the coffeehouse on the other side of the street. You're team two. Garcia and Jones are team three. Take the next block over. Check the shops, vehicles, and alleyways. Everyone stays in comms and after you clear your block, we'll go from there."

"Roger that," the team said in unison and Echo team split up, heading for their assigned areas. Andrew Grossman exhaled and took another drag while he looked on in disgust. Door kickers were useless against someone like Dedman unless they had a fixed location to breach and assault. They were only wasting their time. Dedman was gone.

* * *

Dedman watched the paramilitary officers boil out the door of the safe house. They all wore ball caps, sunglasses, and civilian clothes. He could tell they all wore light body armor under their shirts that would stop pistol rounds, but 6.5mm Creedmoor would punch right through and out the other side. He could probably shoot three of them before the rest realized what had happened.

But not here in the middle of Berlin. He could probably get away with one shot, but multiple shots would have the Berlin cops, including choppers, swarming into the area, making it difficult, if not impossible, to exfil. No, he would patiently wait until they tired themselves out and returned to the safe house empty-handed. He hadn't even the slightest concern about them finding him. They would search the area at street level until they gave up, not look for him on a building roof.

Ground branch was the wrong tool for this kind of job. They needed a fixed target to breach and then to go in hard and shoot the bad guy or guys. The agency had trained him as a paramilitary officer at The Point and he had great respect for ground branch teams when they ran the operations that they were suited for. They were as good as the SEALs and any JSOC team. Most of them had served in one or other before getting into the agency and ground branch. But you didn't use a sword for a job that called for a scalpel.

Dedman had listened to the recording of Alexander's brief call to Newton at the safe house. It was obvious she wasn't ready to quit. Even with the quiver in her voice on the phone that betrayed her fear, he had to respect her for not folding like a cheap tent. Still, he hoped she would re-think the situation once she had time to process their impromptu meeting.

Dedman had no problem with killing her, but it wasn't something he was eager to do. He had believed he could reason with her and hoped he had judged her correctly. For her sake.

Chapter 53

She had thought about calling first, but Kara Jansen settled for just showing up at the safe house entrance and pushing the buzzer. Andrew Grossman had come downstairs to meet her instead of just buzzing her in. He opened the door, and she stepped inside.

"Where have you been, Kara?" Grossman asked. "I thought Dedman either kidnapped or killed you."

"I just ran after he showed up here and confronted Wright. But I wasn't afraid of Dedman. I was afraid of Wright. So, I hid until I read in the paper someone killed him."

"You haven't talked to the cops?"

"No, the article in the paper was insane. Why would anyone think I had anything to do with Wright's death? I'm a special projects officer. I don't shoot people."

"I don't think Dedman killed him either," Grossman admitted.

"I know he didn't," Jansen said, without offering the details about fleeing the safe house with Dedman. "He knocked Wright unconscious. He was still down but alive when Dedman left."

"Well, Newton is here, Buckley's boss, and he's pushing the theory that Dedman killed Jerry. You better watch your back, Kara, coming back here. Newton is the same as Wright was. He has the same motivations."

"So, he wants to kill Dedman, too."

"That's my guess. Anyway, we better go up. He knows you're here and wants to talk to you."

"Is he running the op now?"

242

"No, the director sent Angela Alexander over as the lead. You could say Newton works for her, but just like Jerry was with Buckley, I think he will try to go around her and handle things his way."

"Wonderful. Who is Angela Alexander?" Kara already knew thanks to her Langley contact, but she didn't want to appear to know too much.

"The DDO."

"They read her in on Hydra?"

"Some of it. Newton briefed her and the director. But my guess is he left a lot out. Like Wright and Buckley, he just wants to make it all go away, so he gets protected."

"So, they pushed Buckley out of it? It was another question Kara asked to disguise how much she already knew."

"Oh, shit. You wouldn't know about that. Buckley is also dead. He killed himself the same night Jerry got shot to death. Just between you and me, I think Buckley killed Jerry."

"Seriously?"

Grossman nodded.

"Okay, well, we better go upstairs so I can face the music and find out what my future looks like."

"My advice is to play things close to the vest with Newton. He is the only one here now, but Alexander should be back soon. You can probably trust her more, but Newton is a snake."

Kara nodded her understanding, and they climbed the stairs to the second floor.

* * *

"So, you're Kara Jansen?" Newton said, after introducing himself. "Where have you been, Kara?"

"Honestly, hiding. I was here when Dedman showed up and went at it with Gerald Wright. I didn't know what to do, so I ran and I've been keeping my head down until I could find out what was going on. Then when I read

243

in the paper someone killed Gerald Wright, and that the police wanted to talk to me, I came back in."

"What's your relationship with Jacob Dedman?"

"I have no relationship with Dedman. I've only spent time with him twice and in my official capacity as logistical support. Well, three times counting the other night when he showed up here. I hardly know him."

"Then you're not sympathetic to his point of view on all this?"

"I don't even know what his point of view is. I only know he is an asset who apparently left the reservation."

"Okay, fine. Well, the director has the DDO, Angela Alexander, quarterbacking the search for Dedman. She is not here now, but is probably on her way back. Angela has the back office. You can wait for her in there. When she gets here, she can decide what we're going to do with you. The program the agency sent you to Berlin for is all but shut down, so I guess you're out of a job. She may send you back to Langley for reassignment, but that's her call."

"Yes, sir." Kara turned away, heading for the back office, hoping she hadn't made a mistake by coming back. But before she reached the door, she overheard Newton's comment to Grossman.

"Despite your opinion earlier, Andy, we'll get Dedman soon. He made a mistake going after Angela. Now we know he is still in Berlin when I had worried he might be on another continent by now."

Kara turned back. "It wasn't a mistake. They don't make mistakes. They don't do random. They always have an objective. Dedman only let you know he is still in Berlin because he has a reason for wanting you to know. You should be worried, but not about Dedman being somewhere else. You should be worried he is still in Berlin, because that means we are the objective. We are his target. Dedman is coming after us." Then she turned and went into the back office, smiling at the abject fear she had seen in Newton's eyes.

Chapter 54

Dedman had left the nest as soon as the ground branch team returned to the safe house. They had searched the area for over forty-five minutes, which he knew was stupid. They only had six guys, not nearly enough to do an effective search. Even if he had been at street level with them, they wouldn't have found him. And in forty-five minutes, he could have been fifty kilometers away. He figured they had stayed at it that long just to make a showing for the benefit of whoever was running them.

After leaving the area on his bike, Dedman returned the rifle to the cache and found a room at another low-rent hotel in central Berlin where they didn't insist on passports and accepted cash. The room offered excellent sight lines and alternative exits. If a deputy director was running the show now, he assumed the full power and resources of the agency back in Langley were now engaged in hunting him. He would have to exercise more care to avoid CCTV cameras and in Berlin, like most European cities, cameras were ubiquitous.

Dedman felt safe enough from traffic cameras while riding the bike because the tinted visor on the helmet obscured his face and the agency didn't know about the motorcycle. He had purchased it second hand from an individual after arriving in Berlin and had never changed the registration. He just paid the annual registration fees when due in the name of the previous owner.

With the agency's first-rate facial recognition software, walking around was when he would be most vulnerable. He could get blown even by passing an ATM camera. The agency could tap into any CCTV system in the world and often did when it suited their purposes.

With his photo on the front page of Berlin's major newspapers and television news, Dedman knew he would have to spend the daylight hours in his hotel room and he would have to avoid restaurants and bars. He also couldn't risk staying in the same place for more than one or two days. Not a problem in a city the size of Berlin, offering thousands of lodging options.

Dedman ate his dinner cold from a can and washed it down with bottled water. It hadn't been tasty but was filling and served his purposes. He lay on the lumpy bed staring up at the ceiling, thinking of Drita and wondering where she was.

Forcing her to leave alone had proved much harder than he had ever expected. He couldn't forget the look of hurt and betrayal in her eyes. But while he felt tremendous guilt over it, he felt happy knowing she was safe.

No matter what Drita might have believed, he knew she had no clue what life with him would have been like on the run, moving from city to city and country to country every week or two or more often whenever he felt someone on their tail. It wouldn't have been any life at all. Now that they had separated, he felt confident the agency would forget about her. And he intended to do whatever he could to force them to put all their focus on him.

Dedman admitted he missed her, and it hurt. He couldn't recall ever missing anyone so much. He had been with plenty of women, but never in a relationship. Given his occupation, a relationship not only made no sense, it would have been a liability.

Drita was better off away from him and she would no longer slow him down or prevent him from doing what he now understood he must do. The only way he could see to end it now was to make the agency's campaign against him more costly than those on the seventh floor at Langley were willing to pay, since they would pay in flesh and blood. He believed their will to continue would break before they could get him.

Unable to sleep, Dedman went to the desk and sat down. He chose another encrypted burner from his pack and picked up the tourist guide he had found in the hotel lobby. He turned to the recommended lodging section.

Strangely, the section didn't include his hotel. He laughed.

Dedman doubted even deputy directors got cleared for five-star hotels, so he focused on four-star properties closest to the U.S. Embassy. He knew those were popular choices among the federal employee's community when traveling to Berlin on official business. He dialed the first property.

When the operator answered, Dedman asked for Angela Alexander. When the operator checked and said they had no guest by that name, he hung up and crossed it off his list. On the fifth try, he struck pay dirt, and the operator transferred his call to Alexander's room. He hung up on the first ring. He only wanted to know where she was staying. Next, he would locate her room number, but he would have to wait until dark because he would have to visit the property for that.

* * *

Angela Alexander had felt human again after showering and putting on fresh clothes. She had bagged the suit soiled earlier, intending to send it to the cleaners later. Then she had left the hotel and taken a taxi back to the safe house.

It surprised her when she arrived at the safe house and Newton told her Kara Jansen was sitting in the office waiting for her. Alexander chided herself for not even thinking about Jansen sooner since she should have wondered what had become of the safe house caretaker when she first arrived.

Chapter 55

Alexander sat behind the desk and Jansen sat in a chair across from her. Alexander examined her as they talked, thinking Jansen looked a little worse for wear. For one thing, the haircut looked amateurish and with her light complexion, Jansen's decision to dye her hair jet black didn't suit the young woman well. It was too goth.

After Alexander had asked Kara the same questions Grossman and Newton had asked regarding her recent whereabouts, the deputy director went deeper to get a feel for Jansen and her loyalties.

"So, what has your cover been here in Berlin?"

"I'm a student at American University. I actually attend classes there majoring in German culture and language."

"What exactly was your job with Hydra?"

"I had three primary responsibilities besides caretaker of the safe house. I coordinated logistical support as needed for missions. Another was monitoring the health of the assets and making sure they stayed up to date with their annual medical evaluations at the clinic in Virginia. Finally, I kept track of all their locations 24/7, seven days a week."

"How did you do that?"

"The locator beacons installed in their agency-issued phones. I had software on my computer here and on my phone. The beacons showed up as icons on a map whenever I checked the app. Technically, I kept track of where their phones were, but protocol required them to have the phones with them or close by at all times and Wright strictly enforced it."

"What were the annual medical evaluations about?"

"Their mental health, mostly. Because of what the doctors did to them at the beginning and because of what they went through, they were prone to a variety of problems. Some the doctors treated with medications."

"What kind of problems?"

"Anger, depression, compulsive behavior. Things like that."

"How often did they go off the reservation?"

"Before Dedman? Never."

Alexander sensed the last question had made Jansen uncomfortable. She changed tack.

"Were you familiar with the genetic engineering treatments and their training?"

"The details? No. I mean, Wright mentioned the treatments enhanced their physical abilities. They had faster reflexes, they were stronger than someone of similar physical size. They ran faster, processed information and stimuli faster than normal. Wright also told me it was all strictly voluntary, the medical part and joining the program." Kara shrugged. "I'm not sure if that was true or not."

"Why do you say that? You aren't sure if it was true or not."

"Because I don't think anyone explained to them exactly what the doctors did to them, or what the potential side effects were. I mean, you take some serious genetic changes mixed with behavioral modification and pharmacology, and I guess you might get something dangerous and hard to control."

"I have to ask you some hard questions now. I have to decide whether you can stay with us until it's over or to send you back to Langley for reassignment. Did you ever feel sorry for Dedman? Sorry for what he went through?"

"You're making it sound like we were friends or something. I only met him alone twice to hand off things he needed for jobs."

"You felt nothing for him? No spark? Two young people working together for the same agency, on the same program, alone in Berlin together far from home? It wouldn't be unusual for a romance to blossom under those circumstances. I know of cases where it has happened before."

"You mean, did I ever date him?"

"Did you?"

"Dedman is a killer by occupation. It's his job. Wright made them into apex predators and kept them wound up tight. You think I would date a great white shark or a Doberman?"

"Some women like sharks and Dobermans."

"What do you want from me?" Jansen asked, feeling defensive. "I did everything anyone told me to do since coming to Berlin. I received positive annual reviews. It feels like you're giving me some kind of test."

"See, here is my problem, Kara. I need to know where your loyalties lie or whether Dedman has fooled you in some way. Whatever he is doing, we must end it. This is the kind of mess you can't just walk away from. The director wants to know if Dedman is a threat to us. If I let you stay with us, I need full confidence you don't feel competing loyalties to Dedman."

"I am loyal to the agency and always have been. But if I can speak frankly, I'm not sure you understand exactly what you're up against here. Ever had the urge to take a swim with saltwater crocodiles or take a selfie with a grizzly bear in the wild? That's what you're doing essentially by chasing Dedman. He knows Wright was trying to kill him. I heard him tell Wright that and that he had quit and just wanted to be left alone. He probably doesn't trust anyone in the agency now."

"I'm curious about your opinion of Dedman. I know you aren't trained to diagnose psychiatric conditions. But do you think he may have suffered some traumatic breakdown? Do you believe he is a threat to us?"

"First, I believe Dedman is as sane as any of us. But look, I know all about the NSA contractor who leaked highly classified information to the media. I know about the senate committee investigating some things that have come out of it. If you mean, do I think Dedman is a threat to the agency in the sense he might reveal things about Hydra to the media to embarrass the government or make things difficult for the agency, then no. I don't believe Dedman is that type of threat to us."

"You were his contact here for years and you were with him the night Wright died. You don't believe he is a threat at all?"

"I didn't say that. I am pretty sure I know what I would expect from someone like Dedman if I kept provoking him. He has hurt a few people, including Wright, but he has killed no one. Yet. If you people don't leave him alone, that will change. Unless you have a death wish, my advice is stop provoking him. Let him quit and stop chasing him. The program is over anyway. Just let him go."

"Thank you for your candor, Kara. I will consider what you've shared. Why don't you go home now and get some rest? Come to work in the morning at your usual time, and I will give you my decision. Then we'll go from there."

"Okay. Thank you," Kara said. Then she got up and left the office.

Chapter 56

Maxwell Newton entered the office without knocking as soon as Kara Jansen left.

"What do you think, Angie?"

"About Kara?"

"Yes, I didn't buy her story when I talked to her. I think she is up to her neck in this with Dedman. Maybe she was sleeping with him. I don't think we can trust her and she needs to go."

"Back to Langley?"

"Hell, no. I mean, terminate her. And I don't mean hand her a pink slip."

"On what basis? You have no authority for lethal action."

"Oh yes, I do, Angela. The director told us to clean this mess up, to use any means necessary to neutralize the threat. After we finish with Dedman, I'm sending someone from Johnson's team to terminate her. And it's all legal."

"This is about Dedman, not Kara. And you have no authority to kill her. She is one of us. You are misconstruing the director's instructions. That isn't what he meant. He didn't even give us authority for lethal action against Dedman. He told us to take him into custody as soon as possible."

"Dedman thinks we tried to kill him. He wants revenge, Angela. The only realistic way to deal with this is to eliminate the threat. And that includes Jansen. She betrayed us."

"You don't know that, Max."

"When I wake up in the morning and the ground is wet, it rained, Angela. I don't have to see it rain to know that."

"You still don't have the authority to kill her or Dedman!"

"For Christ's sake, Angela, they know everything about the program. Names, dates, locations. You want that out there in the world?"

"I think the entire world, including the senate, is well aware we have rendition and lethal action capability at this point, Maxwell. And I have seen nothing showing Dedman, much less Kara Jansen has any intention of telling anyone anything about Hydra."

"I can't understand why you don't see terminating Dedman, and Kara is the only rational way to make certain they can't compromise the agency by leaking what they know."

"Probably I don't see it that way because you're the one making the argument for using lethal force and I suspect your motives."

"What the hell is that supposed to mean, Angela? Let's cut the crap!"

Alexander thought about the recording Dedman had given her. She had already thought about what she would do with it.

"I want to know what happened with Wright."

"What happened? Dedman happened. It went wrong. Wright screwed up and he couldn't fix it, couldn't find Dedman. He couldn't make it clean. It all went sideways. Finally, only one option remained."

"So. you had Buckley kill Wright. I mean, as long as we're cutting the crap."

Newton felt blindsided. "What are you after, Angela? You want to burn me? Is that it? I have given nearly thirty years of my life to the agency and have shoveled shit on three continents and in twelve countries. I'm planning to retire next year, and I need my pension. If you think you are going to burn me with this, you can go to hell. It had to be done. I don't know what happened with Buckley, but it was unavoidable collateral damage."

"Here is my take, Maxwell. Wright needed to shut down Hydra quickly. He thought the best way to do it and cover his ass was to eliminate everyone, every single person who knew about the program and might be a threat to him. Buckley went along with it because he wanted his ass protected. I think you are in just as deep and willing to kill to save your ass. I think there has been enough killing. As far as Dedman goes, I think the only way this has a happy ending is him deciding to come in voluntarily."

"He isn't ever doing that, Angela. Don't you see that?"

"Look at it from his perspective, Maxwell. Wright tried to kill him. Now we show up and you want to kill him. You think he has any warm, fuzzy feelings for the agency right now? He's pissed and doesn't trust us. I have a hard time blaming him for that. I'm calling the director when I get back to the hotel and I am recommending we shut this down and all go home."

"If you don't have the stomach for what needs to be done, Angela, why don't *you* go home and leave it to someone who does?"

"Fuck you, Maxwell. You don't have a clue what you're doing. If we keep provoking Dedman, things really will go sideways. He is going to go loud and start killing us and breaking things. I'm pretty sure that isn't what the director wants. Now get out of my office. After I talk to the director, I'll tell you what he decides. But my advice is to go back to the hotel and start packing, because as far as I'm concerned, you're going home no matter what else the director decides."

Chapter 57

Alexander called for a taxi and left the office. She felt sure Newton's eyes tried to burn a hole through her as she walked out, but she didn't even glance in his direction. She could have told Grossman to drive her in the borrowed Tahoe, but she wanted the time alone to compose her thoughts. Then she would call the director as soon as she was back inside her hotel room. Regardless of his decision about Dedman, she intended to press him to recall Newton.

* * *

Inside her room, Alexander kicked off her shoes. She went to the closet and dug the micro recorder out of the pocket of the jacket she had worn earlier. Then she sat down at the table in front of the window with her phone and called Director Cooper's office at Langley. His secretary asked her to hold. A minute later, Cooper came on the line.

"Good news, Angie?" Cooper asked hopefully.

"It's a mixed bag, director," she replied. "But I have something to discuss with you. I need your guidance."

"Fine. What's on your mind?"

"I think Dedman is done, sir."

"Define done."

"Director, I do not believe Jacob Dedman is any threat to us."

"Explain your grounds for that belief."

"I first suspected it when I learned I was here chasing him for something he didn't do. Jacob Dedman did not kill Gerald Wright."

"You have proof of that, Angie?"

"Yes, sir. I have a brief recording I want to play for you if you have the time to listen to it. I believe you should hear it. The subjects you will hear are Jacob Dedman and Herman Buckley. I think you can tell who is who if you want to hear the recording."

"All right. Play it, please."

Alexander held the micro recorder next to her phone and pushed play. Then she pushed the stop button when the recording ended.

"Did you hear it okay, sir?"

"Yes. Unfortunate, isn't it?"

"We could say it that way."

"You're certain the recording is authentic?"

"I believe it is. Of course, when I get back to Langley, I'll have the lab check it to confirm no one tampered with it. But I have the both the recorder and the original tape. I believe it is authentic."

"So, you believe Dedman isn't a threat to us based on the recording?"

"That's only part of it. Dedman isn't suffering from paranoia. Wright was trying to kill him. He figured it out, and that's why he left the reservation."

"You can prove that?"

"I have a witness, someone intimately involved in the program, who can substantiate Wright was trying to kill Dedman, had four other assets in the program killed, and had twenty-nine innocent U.S. citizens killed, the entire medical staff involved in the program's genetic enhancement activities, by directing someone to blow up the medical facility and make it look like an accident."

"This just keeps getting better."

"Finally, I talked to Dedman and know what he wants. It isn't to damage the agency or to embarrass the government."

"You talked to him face to face?"

"Yes, sir."

"If you found him and talked to him, any reason why he isn't now in our custody?"

"I didn't find him, exactly. He found me when I was alone and expressed no interest in coming in voluntarily. Seems reasonable when you look at it from his perspective. He has good reason to believe we want to kill him."

"In fairness, whatever Wright did, he did not represent us."

"No, sir, but Dedman knows Wright is dead and knows who killed him, yet the agency has sent others to pick up where Wright left off. Can't say I fault him for his lack of trust."

"All right. I'm certain you will include in your report the details surrounding your meeting with Dedman. We will table that for now. But you said you know what he wants. Enlighten me."

"He doesn't trust us and doesn't want to work for us anymore. He wants us to leave him alone. Not unreasonable, given the totality of the circumstances. I recommend we let him quit and leave him alone."

"Well, by the very nature of his assignment, Dedman certainly possesses information that might severely damage our ability to perform our critical role and that would embarrass the government. I'm not sure I concur he isn't any threat."

"Director, I stake my reputation on it. Dedman has no interest in revealing anything he knows. Even if we brought him in and talked to him, I don't think that would provide us with any greater assurance."

"Anything else you wish me to consider before deciding how we will proceed?"

"Just this. No doubt if we bring the full weight and resources of the agency, including lethal action, down on Dedman, ultimately, we will prevail. However, he impressed upon me he will not go quietly. He will kill a lot of good people before it's over. Fighting that war here holds the potential for innocent German civilians to get caught in the crossfire. That would be problematic."

"True enough."

"The chances any serious journalist would believe Dedman with no corroborating evidence is unlikely even if he tried to leak something. Weighing that against the chances of an almost certain blood bath and the chance of a serious international incident suggests the juice might not be worth the squeeze if we persist in pursuing Dedman."

"Very well, Angie, shut it down and bring everyone home. We'll do it your way, but let me be clear. I will defer to your judgment on this since you're on the ground there. But should your assessments turn out to be wrong, you will not only be risking your reputation. It will imperil your career with the agency."

"Yes, sir, I would expect nothing less."

Cooper ended the call, and Alexander sighed in relief. She had full faith in her assessments and appreciated the director expressing his faith in her, despite the obvious threat at the end of the conversation.

Maybe Dedman would never come in voluntarily, but she felt certain it was time to cut their losses for now before things spiraled completely out of control. Yes, she was still angry with Dedman for terrifying her. The humiliation she had suffered because of it still felt raw. But Alexander strongly embraced fairness, and Gerald Wright and Buckley hadn't treated the man fairly. Far from it. Dedman had every right to be angry, to distrust the agency, and to demand they stop hounding him even though his heavy-handed treatment of her hadn't been fair either.

The crisis had passed for now. Alexander undressed and got in the shower. She would change, have an early dinner, and call Newton later to tell him and Grossman to pack for the trip back to Langley. The Dedman matter was over.

Chapter 58

The moment night fell and the street lamps came on, Dedman climbed on his motorcycle and headed for the Berlin Marriott near Potsdamer Platz. He found a place to park the bike a block away and made the rest of the way to the hotel entrance on foot. Dedman wore casual clothes in keeping with the styles of the business people and other travelers in and around the hotel, so he would blend in with the crowd. He had the ball cap on, pulled low over his eyes to shield full views of his face from the many CCTV cameras he knew he would encounter inside one of Berlin's most popular and stylish hotels.

As soon as he entered the lobby within the impressive ten-story atrium, Dedman kept his head down as though immersed in looking at his phone screen to avoid the security cameras from capturing images of his face.

A frequent traveler, Dedman knew how upscale hotels worked. Many guests wanted a high floor accommodation for a variety of reasons, such as wanting a more peaceful environment, or believing a higher level provided better views. While top-floor rooms could be quieter and have nicer views, the price paid for them was greater than for the rooms on lower floors with identical facilities. The price difference probably didn't matter to many tourists, but the U.S. government didn't reimburse federal employees engaged in official travel for frivolous and unnecessary lodging expenses. Not even for agency executives like Angela Alexander.

Alexander's room wouldn't be on any of the top three floors of the ten-story hotel. He also knew spooks avoided the first-floor like a plague because it made it too easy for opposition forces to pull a black bag operation or affect an abduction if that was the objective. Many avoided second-floor rooms for the same reasons. No, he felt sure Alexander's room would be somewhere between the third and seventh floors. He would start his search on the third floor and then work his way up floor by floor until he located her room, provided she hadn't discovered the Tile tag already.

Dedman eschewed the elevators, knowing some had cameras and even microphones inside and made for the stairwell. Yes, he expected CCTV cameras there also, but he felt wearing the hat and looking down while making his way upstairs would do the trick and prevent the agency from finding any useful video recordings. Entering the first-floor stairwell, he climbed the stairs to the third floor.

Walking the corridors with his eyes down, glued to his phone screen, Dedman struck out on the third, fourth, and fifth floors. Alexander could have found and disabled the GPS tag he had slipped into her jacket pocket back at the coffee shop, but he would still have to check all the remaining floors to confirm she had done so. He would even check the three top floors in case Alexander had been willing to make up the difference between the price of a more expensive and the government lodging allowance out of her own pocket. But that didn't become necessary.

Two-thirds of the way through the sixth floor, the app on his phone chimed through his Bluetooth earpiece. He kept walking until he zeroed in on the exact room. He glanced at the door without stopping and saw Alexander had room 619. Arriving at the stairwell at the opposite end of the floor from the one he had taken up, Dedman entered and took the stairs back down. It was time for the second phase of his evening operation.

From the interior location inside the hotel, Dedman had worked out that the windows of Alexander's room faced Ebertstraße. After leaving the lobby from the front entrance, Dedman crossed the street and walked to the nearby Ottobock Science Center Berlin with its conspicuous white aluminum facade across from the Berlin Marriott.

He had visited the center many times before and knew it housed a large range of very interesting exhibits and interactive features that made the in-depth presentations of the science of human development fascinating but easy to understand for non-scientific types. But this evening, enjoying the exhibits and interactive features wasn't on the agenda. He took the elevator up to the sixth and top floor of the science center, where there was an outdoor balcony where visitors could enjoy the marvelous views of the Berlin city centre.

He found an out of the way spot on the balcony and scanned the sixth floor of the Marriott, looking through the monocular and searching for the room. After a few moments, he paused and adjusted the magnification. There, through the window with the drapes open, he saw Alexander sitting at a desk in front of the window.

Through the monocular, she appeared so close that he could reach out and touch the woman. She had her phone to ear. He had heard the alert on his phone earlier after entering the Ottobock Center, indicating Alexander was using her phone, but knew he could listen to the recorded call later. She looked a little careworn to Dedman.

Alexander put the phone down on the table and stood up, wearing a T-shirt and flannel pants. She looked as if she was about to go to bed. While stretching, she ran the fingers of both hands through her hair. Then she disappeared from view but reappeared moments later with a wineglass in her hand and sat back down at the table, staring out at the cityscape.

* * *

After having dinner at the restaurant grill inside the atrium, Angela had returned to her room. Thanks to the jet lag, the stressful encounter with Dedman earlier, and the conversation with the director, she felt exhausted by the time she had returned to her hotel room. She undressed and put on a T-shirt and pajama bottoms to prepare for bed, but she had to make two phone calls before retiring.

She had made the unpleasant call first, the call to Newton. He had sounded livid when she told him the Dedman operation was over. He argued and threatened to call the director himself. Angela had told him to knock himself out, but it would be a waste of time. The director had accepted her assessment and told her to shut it down and to return to Langley. She told Newton to call Grossman, and that she expected them both at the airport by ten the following morning for the flight back on the agency Gulfstream. Newton snarled back at her they would be there, but under protest.

After ending the call with Newton, she had called Kara Jansen. Alexander told Kara that she and the others were returning to Langley and that the Dedman operation was over. She then instructed Jansen to show up at the safe house the following morning at her usual time to finish closing it down. She told the young officer that after she had transferred the remaining agency property to the storage facility, to wait in Berlin until she called her back from Langley in a day or two, letting Jansen know she would call her as soon as they had decided where to reassign her. Kara had sounded happy and relieved, and the second call had been far more pleasant than the first.

After standing and stretching, instead of shutting off the lights and getting straight into bed, Angela wanted a glass of red wine from the minibar to quiet her mind before trying to sleep. She had selected a mini bottle of red from the bar in her room and had poured it into a wineglass. Then she had returned to the table with it and had sat down.

After taking the first sip, her cell phone rang. *What now?* She picked it up and answered without looking at the screen, expecting Newton was calling back to continue his bitching and she was ready to tell him off properly this time.

Chapter 59

Using a second burner with an encryption app installed, Dedman called Alexander's cell phone number. He had her number on the other burner paired with hers and had programmed it into the second phone earlier in case he wanted to call her. She answered after the second ring.

"This is Angela Alexander."

"This is Jacob Dedman." Still watching her through the monocular, he saw her reel in surprise. She had almost dropped the wineglass. But she quickly recovered.

"Hello, Jacob. How did you get my number?"

Dedman ignored the question and said nothing.

"Have you decided to come in?" Alexander asked, feigning cheerfulness, realizing he wasn't telling her how he got her cell phone number. "If you're calling, you must want to talk to me. Why don't we arrange another more cordial face to face and talk about it?"

"Sorry to burst your bubble, but I'm giving that one a hard pass. You must forgive me for my lack of trust in people who are trying to kill me when I've done nothing wrong."

"Fair enough. So, what's on your mind, Jacob?"

"It's a little out of character for me, but I want to apologize for the rough treatment earlier. But I needed to make sure you understood my position." Dedman wasn't sorry for any of it. Not really. But he wanted to keep the woman talking to see if he could learn anything useful.

"Oh, don't worry. I got the message loud and clear. I'm a little sore, and candidly a lot pissed at you for that. But I'll live and I'm a big enough person to accept your apology."

"Thanks."

"And, by the way, thank you for the recording. It's been helpful."

"You believe I didn't kill Wright?"

"Yes, I'm satisfied Buckley killed Wright on orders from Newton. Newton didn't feel Wright was cleaning up the mess he had made fast enough to suit him. So, I guess I owe you an apology, too."

"Is that official?"

Alexander chuckled. "No, just personal. You know how it is."

"Sure."

"Look, Jacob. We've shut down Hydra and I've shut down the op here. I've closed the Jacob Dedman case."

Now it was Dedman's turn to feel surprise. He sure hadn't seen that one coming.

"The agency won't continue pursuing you. I'm clearing the flag on your passport and I will pull the warrant Wright sent to Interpol. Tomorrow morning, before I leave on the flight back to Langley, I will meet with the Berlin police and clean that up. They won't keep looking for you."

"Why the change of heart?" Dedman asked with suspicion. It all seemed too good to be true.

"It isn't because you intimidated me earlier, if that's what you think," Alexander said bitterly. Her tone softened. "It's just the right thing to do. I realized that as soon as I discovered I was after you for something you didn't do."

"Just like that? I'm off the hook and don't have to keep looking over my shoulder."

"Let me put it this way. We're offering a truce. But, Jacob, if you get any ideas about leaking anything about the program to harm the agency or embarrass the government, all bets are off. We will come after you. I believe you're smart enough to know we would get you eventually wherever you go. That's your part of the bargain, and we will hold you to it."

"You don't have to worry about that. I have no intention of telling anyone anything. And the agency is safe from me as long as I feel safe from the agency."

"Sorry, but I have to say it one more time. The best option is you coming in voluntarily. That would be the best way to convince the director that you're not a threat to us."

"I won't do that. I'm not coming back to the agency. The trust is broken. But you can believe me. I will keep my part of the bargain."

"I understand. I only want you to know the door is open if you ever change your mind."

"Okay, goodbye."

"Jacob, wait…"

When he didn't hang up, Alexander continued quickly. An idea had popped into her head.

"You've served your country well, Jacob. There is another way you could continue serving your country that doesn't involve you rejoining the agency. If you're interested."

"I'm listening."

"We often use deniable contract assets for delicate matters that we can't afford to get connected back to the agency. You would be paid by the job whenever we had something for you. You've got a lot of skills the agency could still use."

"I don't think so. I'm not really interested in going back to my old job as a contractor."

"Just think about it. It wouldn't be just like what you've done before. There are other mission types. Renditions, intel gathering. And as a contractor, you would always have the right of refusal. If we offered you a mission and you decided it wasn't for you, you could just turn it down with no hard feelings on our part."

Dedman admitted to himself he didn't hate the idea. He would need some way to support himself now that he was off the agency's payroll.

"I'll think about it," he said. "I'm not giving you an answer right now."

"Fine. How do I contact you?"

"That's easy. You don't. I'll contact you if I decide I'm interested."

"Fair enough. Just think about it. It could be a good deal for both of us."

"I will."

"Then I guess it's goodbye for now," Alexander said.

"Goodbye, Angela. And get some sleep. You look exhausted." Dedman smiled and ended the call.

* * *

Alexander sprang to her feet and stood at the window, looking out, trying desperately to spot him. Dedman had been looking at her the entire time.

Giving up, she drew the drapes closed with a shiver. He might have been out there in the darkness with a sniper rifle, looking at her through a scope. Her mind raced. Then she ran to the closet, picked up the bag of soiled clothing from the floor, and dumped it. Quickly she checked the pockets and then she found it. She pulled out the Tile GPS tag. He must have slipped it into the other pocket of the jacket back at the coffee shop earlier.

"Damn you, Dedman," she growled. Then, as she snapped the tag into pieces heading to the bathroom to flush them down the toilet, she burst into laughter. Angela Alexander had to admit he was good. Damn good. She found herself hoping even more fervently that Jacob Dedman would take her up on the offer she had just made to him.

Chapter 60

Drita had quickly fallen in love with Bang Krachao, an artificial island in the middle of the Chao Phraya River that was a green oasis in the heart of Bangkok. The locals called it the "Green Lung of Bangkok" because of its abundant green space. While there were no white sand beaches and coconut trees and the island was nothing like the tropical paradise of Koh Lipe or Koh Kood, Drita found it unique and amazing in its own way. She found the tranquil island with its cleaner air much preferable to living in the congested city.

The best way to get around Bang Krachao was by bicycle, and rentals were popular with locals and tourists alike. The problem, Drita soon realized, was that there was only one small bike rental shop at Bang Krachao Pier with a limited number of bicycles to rent. Most days, especially heavy tourist days, well before eleven in the morning, there were no bikes left available to rent the rest of the day. People tended to rent them by the day, not by the hour.

Drita had solved the problem for herself by buying her own mountain bike. But she had worked out that the demand for rental bikes on Bang Krachao far outstripped the supply.

She had come to Bangkok with plenty of money, especially since the cost of living in Thailand was a fraction of what it had been back in Europe. But she had been thinking about starting some kind of small business, if only to pass the time.

Drita had spent her first months in Bangkok traveling around and seeing all the sites touted by the tourist guides, but that had grown old. Drita had wanted something to do to stave off boredom, and staying busy would mean less time spent dwelling on painful memories. And then, she had discovered Bang Krachao and the pent-up demand for rental bikes. *A bike rental shop*, she had thought. *Why not?*

She found a retailer in the city and invested in a good selection of hard tail mountain bikes to rent that featured twenty-four to twenty-seven gears and solid front suspensions. She charged fifty baht an hour, three-hundred baht a day, and eighteen baht a week.

Drita spent hours watching YouTube videos to learn how to keep the bikes well maintained to avoid any safety issues. Then she organized a well-stocked bicycle maintenance and repair area at the back of her little shop near the Bang Krachao Floating Market. She understood comfortable and well-working bikes enhanced the ride. That turned locals into repeat customers and earned her top reviews on social media from tourists. Soon she was earning enough to support herself without dipping into the funds she had brought to Bangkok with her.

Drita hadn't really expected to stay in Bangkok permanently when she first arrived. In the state she was in when she left Berlin, she had only bought the ticket to Bangkok because they had talked about it and she couldn't think of anywhere else to go. But after arriving, she had found the people friendly and hospitable and with the discovery of Bang Krachao and establishment of her successful business venture, she couldn't really imagine moving somewhere else.

Drita had adjusted to the weather, which was pretty much always hot, and had formed a few friendships. One friend, Chailai, who owned a shop at the floating market making handcrafted goods to sell to tourists looking for authentic Bangkok souvenirs, was helping Drita improve with her Thai speaking. All in all, Drita felt pretty happy with her life in Thailand.

* * *

After Angela Alexander had closed his case and the agency stopped hunting him, Jacob Dedman had moved to Amsterdam. No longer a fugitive, he had gone to Zurich to establish a bank account. He moved his remaining bank balances and investments there from the bank in Berlin and had deposited the bulk of the funds from his safe deposit box. Dedman knew if he ever agreed to accept Alexander's offer, he would need a secure account to receive payments and one he could access from anywhere in the world. Then he had spent six months in Amsterdam working out to maintain his high fitness level in case he decided to work for Alexander, that and working on writing a spy novel, something he felt suited to do given his past.

Jacob had entertained the idea of reclaiming his true name, Ethan Ross. But since the CIA had falsified the records declaring him dead, he knew that would probably open a can of worms he didn't want to deal with. And when he thought of his life as Ethan Ross before the agency, it now seemed more like someone else's life, so he remained Jacob Dedman.

As the months passed, he continually battled the strong desire to see her again. But he had told himself that wherever she was and whatever she was doing, Drita Nikolli was better off without a man like him in her life and was probably happy now. He had almost ruined her life once, and that had been one time too many. But images of the pain and betrayal he had seen in her eyes that day at the Berlin airport when he had put her on a plane alone filled his dreams.

Dedman had often wondered where she had gone. They had talked about going to Bangkok together, but she might have gone anywhere. Drita might have just gone back to her former life in Albania. After all, that had been her home before he had barged into her life.

Once the first year had passed, he began believing the CIA had actually forgotten him, and the dreams had continued to plague him. Dedman began losing the battle with his own will. Finally, the last of his resolve crumbled, and he called Angela Alexander. He told her he would accept her offer if she still wanted him as a deniable contract asset, but he had one thing he had to do before he could accept any assignments and needed a favor.

Alexander had still been interested in getting him on board and agreed to the favor. She had called him back an hour later with the information he had requested. Angela told him it had been over a year since Drita

Nikolli's passport had last popped up on the grid when she had passed through customs and immigration at Suvarnabhumi International Airport in Bangkok, Thailand. Drita had gone to Bangkok after all and apparently had never left.

Dedman had moved his belongings to storage, gave up his apartment in Amsterdam, and bought a ticket on a flight to Bangkok.

Epilogue

Finding one person in a city of over fifteen hundred square kilometers and over ten million inhabitants seemed daunting. But in his past life, Dedman had learned how to find targets under similar circumstances when intelligence had been spotty and all the agency had given him was the name of the city where the target lived.

Starting at the city's center and working outward, he must have spoken to over a thousand different people, locals on the streets, police officers, and tourists, before he got a solid lead. One day, three weeks after arriving in the city, he met an Australian digital nomad type in a bar who claimed he had been everywhere in Bangkok worth seeing, along with most of Thailand. So Dedman had asked him if he had ever come across an eastern European woman, about thirty, named Drita Nikolli in Bangkok.

The man scratched his head and said not that he recalled, but then said he had remembered something. While he said he couldn't say for certain, he believed he had met a woman of that description on the island of Bang Krachao. He said the woman ran a bicycle hire shop near the Bang Krachao Floating Market and he had hired a bloody good mountain bike from her. He had also said her name might have been Drita, Brita or Rita, but he couldn't recall for sure. But he had remembered the woman spoke English with a European accent as though she hadn't been a native English speaker.

***

After a short ferry ride across the Chao Phraya River from Bang Na Pier, Dedman arrived on the island of Bang Krachao. He found a motorbike taxi and asked the driver to take him to the floating market. As they arrived, he saw a modest building with bicycles out front and a painted sign saying Cycle Fit Rentals. Dedman told the driver to stop, got out, and paid the fare.

The shop was more an awning with a thatched roof and three rusted tin walls than an actual building. The modest front of the shop was two open, expanded metal gates that could be closed and padlocked when the business day ended.

Dedman entered the shop, weaving through some mountain bikes. Behind the counter, in the back of the shop, he saw a woman with light brown hair pulled into a ponytail. She was bent over an upended bicycle on a low work bench. She wore a light gray tank top and a pair of cargo shorts. Drita had very fair skin, but the woman was very tanned. Dedman swallowed his disappointment. The woman was the right size and age, but the hair color was lighter and the skin tone was wrong. It wasn't her. He turned to leave.

Drita had been trying for fifteen minutes to remove a stubborn rusted nut from one of the rusted bolts that secured the hanger that attached the rear derailleur to the frame. A customer had either crashed into something or dropped the bike down on the right side and had bent the hanger. Once bent, the derailleurs and pulleys didn't align with the sprockets, making it impossible to shift the gears.

If she ever got the damn nut off, she would replace the hanger with a new one and align it with a derailleur hanger alignment tool to return the bike to service. She used her fingers on the middle of the wrench to hold tension and struck the opposite end with a rubber mallet, hoping to loosen the stubborn nut. The box end slipped off the nut, and she smashed her knuckles against the frame.

"*Mut! Mut! Mut!*" After cursing, Drita brought her injured knuckles to her mouth and sucked on them.

Dedman smiled and turned back. He knew little Albanian, but he had heard that Albanian swear word before. It was her! He felt incredibly nervous now.

"Think I could rent a bike for an hour?" Dedman called, purposely speaking with an affected Dutch accent.

Drita was cross because of her injured knuckles and the rusted nut. She didn't turn to look at the man behind her, who had spoken with what she thought sounded like a German accent. She had met heaps of Germans vacationing in Bangkok, so it wasn't unusual.

"Yes. Yes. If you've got ID and fifty baht. Give me a moment, please."

"Sure. I'm in no hurry."

Drita threw down the wrench in disgust, held out her hand to the side, and shook it. The knuckles felt slightly better. She stood, turned, and looked at the man.

Dedman looked at Drita. Her eyes grew as big as silver dollars and her mouth gaped open. She looked to Dedman like she was seeing a ghost. Then she took a breath and flashed the crooked grin Dedman remembered so well.

"It's cheaper if you rent by the day or the week. How long are you here for?"

Dedman smiled back. "I'm not sure. I'm here to visit an old friend. It depends on whether she is glad to see me."

"I see," Drita said, circumspectly, as she made her way around the counter toward him. Stopping in front of him, her smile grew larger, then suddenly, she threw her arms around him and hugged him tightly. She let go for a moment, stepped back, and let her hands drop to his waist. She looked up at him, still smiling, but with tears filling her eyes. Then she grabbed him and hugged him tightly again with her cheek pressed against his shoulder while he nuzzled her hair.

About the Author

Larry Darter is an American author best known for his crime fiction novels written about the fictional private detective Malone. He is a former U.S. Army infantry officer, and a retired law enforcement officer. He lives with his family in Oklahoma.

You can connect with me on:
🌐 https://www.larrydarter.com

Also by Larry Darter

COMING IN FALL 2024

The Dedman Ascendancy

After three happy years immersed in the vibrant tapestry of Thailand alongside his beloved Drita, Jacob Dedman believes he has finally found solace and sanctuary from his tumultuous past. However, just when he's let his guard down, an unexpected shadow threatens to shatter their idyllic existence, tearing him from the safety of his newfound paradise. In an instant, the dormant embers of his past ignite, pulling Jacob back into a labyrinth of spies, secrets, and treacherous intrigue.

www.ingramcontent.com/pod-product-compliance
Lightning Source LLC
Chambersburg PA
CBHW021512240626
47154CB00002B/594